SKIN DEEP

MICHAEL CRANNOC

Printed in Australia

Published by Hidden Door Books

Cover and internal design by Coven Press

www.covenpress.com.au

First printing: October 2025

Paperback ISBN 978-1-7641-4764-4

eBook ISBN 978-1-7641-4763-7

Hardback ISBN 978-1-7641-4765-1

A catalogue record for this work is available from the National Library of Australia

Distributed by Lightning Source Global

For Thomas.
The best son a father could ever want.

CHAPTER 1

Seb's hand flew to the Beretta on the bedside table, sweeping the pistol up fast. Eyes straining, peering into the dark recesses of the bedroom, he swung his head about, certain that someone was there. Within moments, the hammering in his chest slowed, and he flopped back onto the mattress. Sweat clinging to his body, he kicked out tangled legs and heard his cell phone slip down to clatter onto the floorboards.

His dreams had become plagued by *the cliff house* – a darkened room, the still form of a creature standing utterly still, its hairless body melting into patterned, antique wallpaper, the turn of its noseless head, and the dreadful snake-like eyes that always met his in a stare that held both intelligence and utter malice.

The nightmare involving his parents' car-accident was almost forgotten and perhaps would never return. And lately, he rarely dreamt of the tours in Afghanistan. These old familiar nightscapes were fading away, only to be replaced by new nightmares that were less predictable, and less mundane.

On other nights, Krystal came to visit in the wolfing hours between midnight and dawn. The psycho-killer bitch would suddenly appear, taking *centre stage* when least expected. The short blond always wore her trademark skin-tight, black leather catsuit.

She brought with her both lust and terror, in rapid, fragmented dream-sequences, leaving him confused and exhausted. Alternately aggressive or submissive, she tried to either seduce or kill him. Some nights, they fought, and others they made love. And some nights - he had murdered her. On these occasions, the guilt he experienced seemed very real, until he fully awoke.

Krystal was dead, he always reminded himself - would definitely stay that way too - except in his dreams, where she seemed destined to haunt him forever. And the *cliff house* had been utterly destroyed – burnt to the ground, taking with it the secrets it held.

Through the window, the San Francisco city lights faded as the glow of the sun emerged from behind silhouetted warehouses. Aware sleep was no longer an option, Seb rubbed his eyes and swung his legs over the side of the bed. He bent, collected his phone, and returned it to its charging dock.

An hour later, the sun bright, he ran, sweat trailing through slick hair, between shoulder-blades and down his back. He followed a dirt track across sparse hills, now and then afforded a view of San Francisco harbour. There was a slight haze in the air, which held the promise of a day that would be too warm. Knowing the carpark was a mile away, he glanced at his watch, setting himself a new time to beat. Pushing harder, breath ragged, a familiar ache having already formed above the right knee, he gritted his teeth and lengthened each stride, running shoes kicking up a trail of dust with each loping stride.

Entering the parking lot, he collapsed onto a bench and began massaging his right leg. He felt his throat's pulse, then closed his eyes, concentrating on lowering his heart rate using a steady breathing technique he had learnt in the army.

Sensing that he was being observed, he glanced up as two people approached. Their grey suits, crisp white business shirts, polished black leather boots, and dark sunglasses all shouted 'FBI'. So, when they opened their wallets and flashed shiny gold badges, Seb barely glanced at their credentials. The female agent handed over a bottle of water, which Seb gratefully accepted and twisted open.

'Mr Straeker.'

'What do you people want now?' asked Seb, not even bothering to make eye contact with the pair.

'Come with us,' said the male agent.

'What about my car?'

'Maybe you'll get lucky, and someone will steal it,' said the female agent without a hint of humour.

'Hilarious.' Seb gazed with fondness at his car. 'You know that this particular Camaro is considered a *classic*.'

'Get in – we don't have all day, Mr Straeker,' said the male agent.

Seb followed them to their SUV, making a point of taking his time, then slid into the back seat, a trail of salty sweat smearing the black leather. He had wondered how long it would be before he was brought in for more questions, and now he knew. The drive back into the heart of San Francisco was in awkward silence, with Seb staring out the window expressionless, and the two agents occasionally turning to gaze at him blankly through dark lensed sunglasses.

Twenty-seven minutes later, the trio stepped from a service elevator designed for cargo or heavy equipment, and Seb followed the agents onto the fifth level of a brick warehouse, which he guessed had once been a factory office. The hardwood floor had been recently swept but was marked by years of heavy use. There were tall windows, without coverings, and the ceiling was high, criss-crossed by a maze of water pipes and electrical conduits covered by a thick layer of grey dust.

On the other side of an oak desk waited Jaz Freeman, the mysterious, striking FBI agent who six months prior had helped him locate his missing sister *Angel*, held captive by a gang of bikers and their lunatic boss. That gang – the *Dagons Riders* were involved in kidnapping and murders, the former activity supporting human experiments that ended in the victims being fed to a creature living in a laboratory cell. Even as he considered this memory, he wondered how he could ever discuss those events with anyone without them thinking he'd gone complete *nuts*. No - easier if he said nothing… easier if he pretended none of it happened at all. Normal, *real* life could only continue if he buried all that shit in some dark hole and never let any of it out to see the light of day again. Meetings like this would not help him move forward, would not help him forget what needed forgetting.

Feeling the edge of cold anger looming, he forced himself to switch focus to Jaz, aware now of how she had changed in subtle ways. Her hair was longer, and tied back, it accentuated her high-cheekbones and slender neck. There was something feline in the shape of her eyes, and he was reminded of how they could regard him with unwavering scrutiny. The FBI agent's attire was more professional than he remembered too. Maybe she had moved up in the world and was herself now a boss.

Beside Jaz sat a clean-cut guy in a pressed suit, who to Seb, could not have looked more like a bureau guy if he tried. A mature version of the goons who brought him in, he met Seb's face with a searching gaze.

They waited as Seb took his sweet time, eventually settling into his seat opposite Jaz. The pair watched him, Jaz with an amused half-smile, the *suit* with a look of slight annoyance. One of the agents who had collected him stood nearby, her back turned, staring out the window, seemingly disinterested in the meet.

'Thanks for coming in, Seb,' Jaz said brightly.

'Did I have a choice?'

Jaz smiled, ignoring the question. 'You know, I was just telling my colleague where we met. Do you still eat pepperoni pizza?'

Seb smirked. 'Only when I'm depressed.'

'Are you thinking of going back to the *Rangers?*'

His smile disappeared. 'I think you know I can't. They kicked me out after ninety days in the brig. I don't blame them. They could probably have lived with me going AWOL, but when they heard I was involved in some... *altercations* – well they *threw the book at me*.'

'I'm sorry. Really I am.'

'Maybe you could have helped me out, Jaz. A word or two of support from the FBI could have saved me some...'

'There was nothing we could do,' cut in Jaz. 'It was best to let it all play out the way it did.'

'Whatever,' shrugged Seb dismissively. He glanced around the room before finally meeting Jaz's eyes again. 'So, what do you want with me now?' He hoped they would just get on with it, whatever *it* was.

Jaz leant forward onto her elbows and rested her chin on interlaced fingers. She had stopped smiling. 'That *shit* that went down in *the cove*, it had what we call a *ripple-effect*.'

'Not my problem, whatever you mean by that.' Though Seb instantly knew what she meant, he wasn't about to make it easy for them.

'We follow threads of evidence, wherever they may take us. Let's say, those *ripples* have taken us all over the country - even to places beyond our borders.' Jaz paused to see if any of what she was saying was remotely interesting to Seb.

'So?' Seb shrugged.

Jaz pressed on, 'There's a very select group of people who know what happened at the *cliff house*. Even within the FBI, the circle of knowledge around that particular case is very tight. You understand?'

'Yeah, I guess it would be.'

'That leaves us with some issues.'

'Who's this?' asked Seb, staring at the agent sitting across the table. 'He just here to get your coffee?'

'I'm sorry. This is special agent Harvey.' Jaz glanced sideways at the man to her left.

Harvey just stared at Seb, his expression unreadable. There was no offered handshake or even a pleasant smile. Seb guessed then that this meeting wasn't his idea at all.

While Seb did his best to return a flat stare back at Harvey, he spoke to Jaz, 'I see you made it out of the basement. I guess you have your own team now?'

'Yeah, the *cove* case was my making,' she admitted. 'Reputation counts for a lot in the bureau. Nobody there knows any details of course, but they know it was a big case. I now have my own team, a fifteenth-floor corner office with a coffee machine and most important of all - my own approach. Yeah, I can do things my way from now on. And…that's why you're here. I wanted you on this with me.'

'Good for you, Jaz. Really, I'm happy for you. But you didn't answer my question. What if I didn't come in? Would you have arrested me?' Seb reclined, trying to appear relaxed.

Jaz glanced at Harvey. 'If it was up to me - no. But my influence only goes so far. I know what you had to do… to get your sister out of that situation, and I know you were defending yourself when you…*eliminated* those people. But some important folks consider your response was a little… *heavy*.'

'They had it coming.'

Jaz continued, 'Ultimately I guess it would be up to a court to decide – if it came to that.'

Seb slowly shook his head, before that still, cold gaze locked onto hers. Jaz could feel the predator that lived behind those eyes, when she looked past the façade of relaxed indifference, beyond the calm exterior he habitually projected. Here was a soldier who had served three tours in Afghanistan and had risen to the rank of Captain. She knew that Seb's demeanour could instantly change if he was put in the wrong place at the right time. And yes – he had been in plenty of *wrong* places, where he'd proven himself to be the right man for the situation.

Jaz sipped water from her glass, and with a steady hand, placed it back on the table. 'When it comes down to it, you didn't have a choice. The statute of limitations on charging you with manslaughter hasn't run out, and as you might know – there is no statute of limitations on murder.'

'Then charge me,' invited Seb, crossing his arms. 'Put me on the stand and I can tell the world all about what I saw.'

Jaz threw Harvey a side-glance. The look she gave him was an *I told you so*. Perhaps Harvey had talked about using *strong arm* tactics to get him in on whatever they were about to propose. Jaz had guessed that Seb would call their bluff, that he wouldn't be intimidated or manipulated that easily. She'd told Harvey what to expect and Seb had not let her down.

Agent Harvey's mouth firmed, then he said, 'No, that's never going to happen. There will be no court cases, no prosecution, and no chance for publicity. You know the deal with that. Let's just say, we have a new problem, and you are the man to deal with it. You have a history with our situation - we don't need to explain to you what this is all about. And we need to keep the circle small.'

'And off the books, right?' guessed Seb. 'Why else are we meeting in some old warehouse near the docks? You didn't even want me signing in at an FBI office. No one is supposed to know about us meeting at all. So, that tells me you probably have a CIA problem too. You can't bring them in on it because you don't know how far your...what did you call it...your *ripple effect*... how far it has gone?'

'I told you he would *cotton on*,' said Jaz, glancing at Harvey. 'Yeah, the CIA knew about McTaggart. What they knew, and what they had to do with him is anyone's guess.'

'So, *if* I help you, with whatever *this* is, what do I get out of it?'

'Knowledge that you are once more serving your country,' said Harvey.

Seb chuckled before making a sound like a game show buzzer when someone gets the wrong answer. 'I've done that. Try again.'

'How does fifty grand sound?'

Seb thought for a while. He leant forward on his elbow. 'It sounds like you could try a little harder.'

Then Jaz said, 'Fifty thousand now, and when you return, another fifty thousand. You could live off that for a long time, Seb. I know you need the money. I've seen your bank account.'

Seb initially appeared surprised, then looked annoyed. Jaz was right, his bank account *was* looking pretty bare since he'd set up Angel in her own house far away, where he hoped no-one would ever find her. 'Return? You said, *when I return*. Where *the hell* do you want me to go.'

'That's the kicker,' said Harvey. 'You're going on a cruise, my friend. We'll pay you a hundred grand to take a vacation. You'll just have to do some surveillance work for us. It will be a very straight forward job.'

Seb crossed his arms over his chest. Jaz smiled as she now knew he was interested. Seb was recalling the pizza joint in *the cove*, and how soon after meeting Jaz the first time that everything *got real*.

Harvey sensed that Seb was still unsure. Turning slightly, he asked Jaz - 'Are you sure he's the right one?'

'He's our guy. This is my call,' said Jaz firmly, looking straight ahead at Seb.

'How do you know I'm your guy?' Seb shrugged. 'I'm no spy.'

'You seem to be able to make the right calls when the pressure's on.' She sat back and flipped open her leather briefcase. 'I've seen your army record too. Making the right decisions under extreme pressure is in your DNA, Seb. The Rangers loss is my gain.'

She produced a paper file and turned it to face Seb. He could see that it was his military record, or a copy of it. Jaz pointed at the report – 'This is what sealed it for me. See right here, this is what your former CO had to say at your disciplinary hearing. It says *he can think on his feet; adjust and react. He is reliable under pressure*. I know I'm right about you, and I *know* you're right for this.'

Seb stared at his file. 'Yeah, well, we all have a *use-by* date, don't we? Maybe mine was up.'

'Are you saying you're a *burn-out?*' asked Harvey.

'If I was, I'd still kick your ass, Harvey.'

The two men regarded each other cooly until Harvey finally looked away.

'Are you boys finished?' asked Jaz into the silence. 'Because we have a real opportunity here.'

Harvey and Seb looked at Jaz, before Seb allowed a smile. 'I *could do* with a hundred grand. But I'm not convinced I can actually do what you want me to. Tell me more.'

'Okay, well as you know, our guy McTaggart was one of a clandestine syndicate. Even though he's dead, his operation was part of a much larger scheme, one that our intelligence suggests is still operating. The video that came into our possession...'

'*That video*,' said Seb.

'Yeah, *the Eric Winters video*,' continued Jazz, 'showed the faces of a number of...shall we say...interesting and powerful people.'

Seb was suddenly reminded of the film he'd watched in the hidden loft at St Anthony's Church. Some of the details were fuzzy now. 'You mean the film taken at the party... at McTaggart's mansion?' At the time he'd viewed it, his only consideration had been finding and rescuing his sister *Angel*.

Jaz nodded. 'The trail goes deep and long on this. We have billionaire tech business tycoons, we have a connection to an art dealer who also collects rare and precious antiquities, we have mafia bosses, maybe foreign government officials...' Jazz trailed off, but Seb suspected that her list had others she had not yet mentioned.

'And what does all this have to do with a cruise?' asked Seb.

Harvey said, 'After McTaggart's mansion went up in flames, his associates began consolidating. After all, they had an operation to recover.'

Jaz said, 'Most of the people I just mentioned will be aboard. They are all going to be in the same place at the same time. Something very big is underway, something that requires them to actually meet in person. Unfortunately, it isn't on US soil. Our legal options are very limited, but I don't want to give them a *free pass*.'

'I see,' replied Seb. 'You want me to get *eyes on* these people, then do some surveillance.'

Jaz nodded enthusiastically. 'A group of diverse individuals like these can only meet in a couple of places without drawing major press coverage. The ship…the *Estrella De Mar* is one place they can gather, and it looks natural – a vacation where they all just happened to be. We need to know the purpose of their meeting. We think they are closing a deal of some kind, but we don't know what. After what happened at *the cove,* we should try to discover the nature of their relationship and business ties. And…there could be more of them… more we don't yet know about. Having someone there, listening in, getting some intel, well…the value can't be understated.'

'So - I look, listen in and report? Is that what you want?'

Jazz smiled broadly. 'For someone with your skillset, this should be *a walk in the park*. Just a 14-day cruise out across the Pacific Ocean, on one of the world's most prestigious luxury liners, and at the end you get paid handsomely.'

'A hundred grand? Well, you make it sound pretty good. But what if things get out of hand?' asked Seb.

'This isn't that type of mission, Seb,' explained Jaz. 'There would be no possible reason why things will get *hot*. It's a recon job, with surveillance thrown into the mix. You can do that… I know you can.'

Seb frowned and then made a gun with his finger and thumb. 'I could take em all out…yeah get them while they're sitting together at the bar. Blow em all to pieces.'

Harvey paled, then flushed as colour came back into his face.

But now Seb was chuckling. 'You should see your face, Harvey. It was just a joke. Try to relax.'

Harvey turned to Jaz, 'Is he really the choice for this operation?'

Jaz smiled. But the look she shot Seb suggested he should take it more seriously.

'Okay,' said Seb. 'You want me because I'm not on your payroll, and if it goes bad, you can disavow me. Am I right?'

Harvey and Jaz glanced at each other. Then Jaz nodded. 'Yeah, that's part of the reason too.'

'Okay then, I'll do it.'

'Just like that?' asked Harvey.

Seb ignored Harvey, instead focusing on Jaz. 'Benson died because of those *sons of bitches*.'

Jaz nodded slowly, picturing Rebecca Benson lying on the ground under a clear night, blood running from her mouth. It was her last memory of the Crab-Tree Cove police officer. After a while, she finally met Seb's eyes, then changed the subject. 'How is Angel anyway?'

'She's good, thanks for asking.'

'We could protect her,' offered Jaz.

'Maybe… but it's better if she stays hidden, even from you people.'

Jaz was about to disagree, but then just nodded.

CHAPTER 2

The rain was just beginning. It was an early summer storm all along the coast, sweeping in north and south of San Diego.

Billie Dakota was reading over a file, preparing a final bill for a client. Glancing every now and then out the second storey window of her office, she watched as the first fat droplets made trails down the glass. It was getting dark outside, so she switched the desk lamp on, casting the office in a warming gold glow.

She stared at the monitor, at a series of photos of a guy in bed with a young *hottie,* his hand extended toward the camera, trying to block his face, or perhaps pleading with the photographer. She sighed, remembering the moment when the guy's life began to unravel. She closed the file with a sigh. It had been a messy case - a cheating hubby, a young girl working at a country club, a divorce proceeding, and some collateral damage that she herself had caused.

Her office was a *home away from home,* a place where she spent hours almost every day. The wood panelling, potted plants, leather sofa, often used as a bed, all made her feel cosy and protected. Adding to the feeling were the many photos adorning the walls - mostly of her and her parents together. Some frames had pictures of her brothers and sisters. Others showed her in a gymnastic uniform, hanging upside-down. There were action shots too – her swinging on ropes or springing through the air whilst tumbling. One frame, a large silver one, displayed her most prized possession in the entire world - a certificate, showing she was a *bona fide* PI.

Her favourite pic though was of her and her dad, taken minutes after she won a junior karate championship. She was smiling, holding a way too large trophy, her dad kneeling beside her, looking immensely proud. That day that would live on in her mind forever.

Hearing rain, Billie looked out at the gathering murk. The street was nearly empty. Across the road, Pacific Beach was insubstantial, the surf just a low grey line. No-one was out there now. She imagined a couple walking hand in hand, not caring about the rain that was about to bucket down. Did people still do that? Was there someone out there in the wide world that she would do that with? She sighed again. Then, glancing down she saw a guy in a car outside. She had only noticed him because he had lit a cigarette. His face had bloomed into view for a moment only as he raised the lit match toward his mouth. It was the *collateral damage* she had just been thinking about.

'Mother...,' she breathed. She rarely used the second part of the expletive. It remained in her head, never on her lips.

Billie had intended doing some account work but seeing Jason *mother-f-ing* Clements in the car outside, her appetite for work dissipated. Would he come upstairs? If he did, how pissed was he? She had used Clements to get to someone, had betrayed his trust to a large degree. It came with the job, she reminded herself. Jason had been the conduit to finding out which young hottie at the country club her mark had been seeing. She had led him along – sexually, but without any kind of consummation. It had been the game, and Billie played it like a pro. That had been a week ago. Why was he still angry? Was he angry? Was he here to get closure?

She could hear the rain falling harder, slapping against the windows. The office's entrance was a simple wooden door with a glass pane. The name was on the door - *Dakota Private Investigations* had not changed in over half a century. It had been her mom and dad's business before they retired, and now it was hers. Hesitating at the door, she turned and went back in the office. Peeking through the blinds, she could just see the shadowed outline of Clements sitting in the car. The vehicle's window was cracked, to allow the cigarette smoke out of the cabin.

Billie picked up the landline, the same phone she remembered as a kid, the same one used in the office for the last thirty years. In these days of computers and cell phones, for some odd reason, she still liked to use it. To her, it was an anchor to an earlier, simpler life when her parents ran the business. She would watch them work, doing her homework, and listening to everything they said. Without realising it, she had started becoming a PI even before she'd left school.

She dialled the local police. As her call was picked up, Billie said, 'Hello? Yeah, I have some guy stalking me.'

The cop said, 'Do you know him?'

Billie said, 'No, I don't know who he is, and he's waiting outside in the car. I'm scared.' She paused, waiting, then hearing nothing continued, 'I'm really, really scared. He may be dangerous.'

'I know that it's you Billie,' came the cop's voice at the other end.

She hesitated for a long moment. 'Yeah.'

'Another happy customer?'

'Something like that.'

'So, *you do know* who it is? We have a lot of shit going on here. You can't be calling us like this every *Goddam* time you have some asshole with a beef hassling you.'

'John...'

'Nah, listen to me, Billie. Not tonight, okay. We have more than enough going on right now.'

She made a face. 'I'll handle it.'

'You handle it.'

'I will!' She slammed the phone back into the cradle.

Glancing once more into the street, she snapped the blinds

down, and went to the desk, to the top draw, and took the *Smith and Wesson* .45 from within. It went in her belt, tucked in the small of her back, under her denim jacket. She didn't really think Jason was that dangerous, but she was a girl that liked to always be prepared.

Billie left the office. She could have slipped out the back and *done a runner*. But it wasn't her way. The rain was heavy. Regardless, she walked onto the sidewalk, feeling the fat drops flatten her golden fringe. She began walking toward Jason Clement's car.

He opened the door, and called, 'Billie, hey Billie.'

'What are you doing here?' she called, her voice carrying over the spattering rain.

'You're something, you know that.'

'It was business. No hard feelings.' She hesitated. 'I'm sorry.'

'You don't want me?'

'No, Jason, I don't want you.'

His shoulders slumped. He looked at her through squinted eyes. 'I trusted you… you know that? Man, I'm so stupid.'

'Don't say that Jason. It was a job. I'm sorry.'

'You're sorry? I thought I was falling in love.'

'I'm sorry.'

'So, it wasn't real.'

Billie shook her head. 'You'll find someone, Jason…'

'Fuck you, Billie, if that's your real fuckin name.'

'Yeah, it's my name.'

Jason stepped back into the car, snapped the door closed, rolled the window down and lobbed the half-smoked cigarette out onto the road where it landed at her feet. Heavy droplets soon extinguished the butt. Then the car's lights came on and he tramped the gas, pulled out into the road, and drove away past her.

Billie stood in the rain, eyes closed, face tilted heavenward. For two full minutes she allowed herself to get drenched, like a kind of penance. She sighed again, walked back under the awning, and stood for a moment, hating herself. The guy wasn't angry. He was just upset. In her experience, that could be worse. She had hoped he was angry, mad-angry enough that she could justify not feeling too much guilt. That kind of hate could be dealt with more easily, at least for her anyway. Trudging back up the steps, the internal staircase kept her from the rain. It didn't matter because she was already soaked.

Returning to her desk, she hesitated only a moment before slipping through a door into the small bathroom behind the office. The bathroom remained exactly as it had always been since it was installed in the 1950s, with bottle-green tiles, brass taps and a small round metal mirror that extended on a hinged arm. Billie suddenly remembered her father shaving in it, his face covered in white foam that smelt like menthol. On big jobs, he would often stay and work all night in the office. He had kept some spare clothes in the bathroom on a shelf for these occasions.

Running the hot water, she climbed into the shower, allowing the cascade to wash away the chill. Minutes later she emerged, rubbing the mist from the glass, and regarded her reflection as she towel-dried her hair. She was thirty something, but she never admitted her age, to anyone – least of all herself. At the moment, her hair was longer, and blond-streaked. In her work, she often changed her appearance. Sometimes, a red head, very occasionally she went toward a brunette. She couldn't do much to change her other features though, other than wear high heeled shoes to make herself appear taller. But that was more to do with vanity than effecting any kind of disguise.

Considering her wet clothes, she decided to hang her denim over the shower rail, and her other things on hooks on the back of the bathroom door. Dressed only in a towel, she walked back into the office.

There were two guys sitting there in front of her desk, waiting patiently. One of them was dressed in an immaculate grey suit, with a white open necked shirt. He was handsome, with a mane of dark hair and chiselled, clean-shaved face, which regarded her with some embarrassment.

The other guy was bearded, balding on top, with a long greasy ponytail that trailed behind him. Gold earrings adorned both ears. He had a craggy face and bulging eyes that goggled at the sight of her.

'I didn't hear you come in,' said Billie, adjusting her towel, and wishing now that she had put her wet clothes back on.

The guy in the suit smiled, his eyes turning away from her. 'I'm sorry. It appears I caught you at an inopportune moment.'

Her eyebrows shot up. 'Well, I *was* going to wander back out here in my *birthday suit* - so it could have been worse.' She sat behind the desk, which at least gave her a slight feeling of protection. She would be damned if she was going to skittle back into the bathroom to change back into wet clothes.

The handsome guy in the suit said, 'We saw the light was on. I know it's outside normal business hours. Maybe we should come back tomorrow.'

Billie smiled, trying to show that everything was fine. She knew a couple of things *off-the-bat*. This guy was loaded, and he must be in a hurry. That meant cash. Maybe her next proper job.

'It's ok.' She allowed the towel to sag just a little, showing a hint of cleavage. It couldn't hurt to make sure that the guys would stay long enough to tell their story. 'What brings you two here? Are you lost or something?'

'My name is Sam Forsyth. I would shake your hand, but I think your hands are rather full.' Billie heard a mixed old school Hollywood accent – a pleasing blend of posh English and local Californian. It was what in the Hollywood movies of old they used to call *Transatlantic*.

'And this is Brian Gillespie,' continued Forsyth, glancing at the guy with the ponytail.

'What can I do for you gentlemen?'

'I think we are in a spot of bother,' said Forsyth.

'A *spot of bother*,' she repeated, testing the phrase, attempting an English accent. She pulled herself up. 'I hear an accent…sometimes I like to hear myself try it on for size …sorry.'

Brian Gillespie was staring openly at Billie, constantly glancing down toward her chest. 'We…are here to ask for your assistance.'

'You came to the right place,' said Billie, adjusting the towel upward.

'I hope so, Ms Dakota,' said Forsyth. 'I'm a promoter, and Brian here, is the manager for a band. Do you know *Manson Villa?*'

Billie knew them. If she had been living under a rock for the last three years, she may not have. 'Of course. Who hasn't heard of them?' She smiled. 'They're great! I love the latest album – what was it?'

'*Don't shoot the messenger*,' said Brian, a smile creasing his bearded face.

'Yeah, that's right,' said Billie. She had heard some of the tracks on the radio recently. *Manson Villa* were red-hot right now.

Forsyth continued, 'Our lead singer…'

'Janie Reichenbach,' cut in Billie. She could picture the singer, raging around the stage, cropped blond wild hair, skin-tight purple leather cat-suit, belting out a song with a voice that was unusually powerful.

'JR,' said Brian, 'to her friends.'

Forsyth glanced sideways and then rolled his eyes. 'We've had some letters. They are not the usual fan letters.'

'She's had threats,' chimed in Brian.

'I assume you've gone to the police,' said Billie.

'Yes, of course,' said Forsyth. 'The police are aware of the threats. But as they rightly point out, most high-profile celebrities are threatened at different stages in their careers. They all attract unwanted attention from time to time.'

'Is that all it is?' said Billie. 'Attention?'

'This has been going on for a while now. The threats have increased in frequency, and intensity.'

'Why come to me?' asked Billie.

'We think we know who is sending the letters,' said Forsyth. 'His name is Carlton Meeks. He's an ex-boyfriend of Janie's.'

'He's an arsehole,' said Brian. Billie noticed that Forsyth winced as Brian made the comment.

'You've told the cops?' asked Billie.

'Yes, we elucidated our suspicions to them,' said Forsyth. He looked annoyed as he recalled the memory. 'They said they needed more than our suspicions to go arresting someone.' He got up and walked to the window, looking out at the rain. 'You see, Carlton was a nobody, from a wealthy family. Just a playboy with money, running around getting himself in trouble, mixing with the beautiful people in the clubbing scene. He wanted to be seen with anyone important or famous. Janie eventually understood what a loser he was, and she broke it off.'

Brian enthusiastically interjected, 'Then her career really took off. She put out a few hits – *bam, bam, bam,* one after the other.'

'Brian is correct,' said Forsyth. 'It was at that point, when we think that Carlton felt he had lost out on the one person that was meant to make him famous. He tried to get back with her. Janie laughed in his face and refused to return his calls. Soon after, the threats began.'

'The old *if I can't have her, no one can* routine,' said Billie.

'Quite,' agreed Forsyth.

'You want me to confirm that it is him… or not?' clarified Billie.

'And gather the evidence if you find any. If the police have more information, perhaps they will see fit to act,' said Forsyth.

'Okay, that seems clear,' agreed Billie. 'How sure are you that it's Meeks?'

'Fairly,' said Brian.

'Very,' said Forsyth, almost at the same moment.

Billie smiled. 'How dangerous do you think he is?'

The two men looked at one another. Forsyth said, 'I think he's an idiot looking to make trouble for Janie. I don't think he would actually carry out the threats.'

'If in fact it's him,' said Billie.

Forsyth reached into his suitcoat and produced a business card. It simply said – *Sam Forsyth, Promotor* with a cell number under his name. That was it.

Billie opened her desk draw and produced her own business card, which she held out, but neither man wanted. 'We know where to find you, Ms Dakota. Call us when you have something to share.'

'Do you want to know my rates?' asked Billie.

'It doesn't matter. We'll pay your usual rates, and reasonable expenses plus ten percent. Text me your bank details, and I'll pay two weeks up front. Find me something on this Meeks, something that will guarantee that we can *send him packing*.'

Billie nodded. Forsyth walked to the door, Brian Gillespie following a half pace behind. She wondered how such obviously different individuals could be attached to the same rock band.

Forsyth turned as he opened the door. 'Keep everything confidential. Janie shouldn't know anything about any of this. Neither should the media. Her career, the band's popularity cannot afford any negative publicity.'

Brian said, 'And she needs to be focused. Her performances are a notch higher when she has no distractions.'

They left the room without glancing back. Billie waited, then looked out the window, down at the street below. As Sam Forsyth and Brian Gillespie appeared, a driver opened the door to a Mercedes, and came hurrying across holding a large umbrella, which he held over Forsyth as he escorted the man to the car. Brian was left to hurry to the far side of the car, getting drenched in the process. The door wouldn't open for him for several long seconds, and then he too entered the car.

Billie closed the blinds, turned, and clapped her hands together. 'Yes!'

CHAPTER 3

As there was no-one waiting at home, and as Billie was suddenly elated at having landed her first high-paid, potentially high-profile job, she ordered Thai food delivered to the office.

After the meal arrived, she decided to settle in for an evening of a game called *find some shit on Carlton.* First stop - his social media posts. Nine times out of ten, people said things on their social accounts that would give her something juicy to work with.

For the harder to find stuff, she could use her contacts in specific locations – the police, the DMV, the electoral office, two banks, and a country club. Maybe not so much the country club - anymore. She was pretty certain that her and Jason were no longer on speaking terms.

On the PC, she began searching Carlton's name, looking to get a feel for the guy. The photos she found showed a tall man with brown flowing hair, a 70s style moustache, blue eyes, and fit looking. She trawled through his various threads across several different social media platforms. Nothing he said seemed too political, and there were no extreme views being expressed. His posts were carefully controlled and seemed to show a man who just liked a *good time.*

Carlton was in his forties, living the life of a guy in his twenties.

He enjoyed outdoor sports – cycling, jet-skiing, snow-skiing, parachuting, you name it – he liked to show the whole world the kind of adrenaline junkie he was. He looked like a confirmed bachelor, a guy with time on his hands, a terrible show-off with plenty of money to spend. But there was a recurring theme - the girl that showed up throughout, in every second photo - *Janie Reichenbach*. Billie knew that the relationship between Meeks and Janie was over, but to a casual observer, it appeared that she was still his *main squeeze*.

If she hadn't heard in so much detail from Sam Forsyth, just the kind of person Meeks was, she would not have arrived at the conclusion that he was possibly dangerous.

Billie cleaned up the last of the Pad Thai, wiped her mouth with the back of her hand, and set aside the chopsticks, feeling slightly overfull. She belched loudly with satisfaction.

Looking down at the file, she reviewed what she had managed to uncover in an evening. She had written down a list of Meek's associates, his address, his ride's details including make, model, and registration tag; checked his credit rating, tracked a couple of previous addresses, and discovered he couldn't spell. Not a bad night's work, but hardly any *smoking guns*.

Billie glanced at the clock, hesitated, then video called her friend, who was also her technical expert. His face popped up, and he bent toward the webcam, his three-day growth salt and pepper, his hair wild. He smiled when he saw who had called.

'Hi Harry.'

'Hey Kid. To what do I owe this pleasure?'

'I have a job, if you're interested?'

'You know I am…always. More *love-rats?*'

'No, no, no. This is big! Well, big for us.'

'The suspense is killing me. Hang-on.' Harry's background shifted, and Billie got a view of his aging video tape hire store as he walked to the back room. The store was now stocked with a library of nearly defunct VHS tapes and ex rental DVDs. His suburban shop had a second business relating to computer repair, which Harry himself ran from a back room. He supplemented the store's income with several aging gaming machines, which meant the place attracted a certain eclectic clientele, from older guys to young hipsters. His customers all had one thing in common – they all felt an emotional attachment to the 80s and 90s. Harry had moved the laptop to the back room and seated himself, with a view back into the main part of the store.

'Is it quiet?' asked Billie.

'Fuckin terrible, Billie. What have you got for us?'

'I'm gonna text you some details about a guy called *Meeks*, okay? I need whatever you can get on him.'

'Okay, so a *deep dive*,' said Harry.

'Yeah, I want you to hack the shit out of this guy, Harry.'

He winced. 'I prefer *deep dive*.'

Billie grinned. 'Just get me what you can. My client will pay anything pretty much. So, *don't spare the horses*, okay.'

'Who is he?'

Billie texted Harry the details of Meek's name and address, as well as some links to his social media accounts.

'A guy who might be sending death threats to Janie Reichenbach.'

'You mean the Janie from *Manson Villa*?' asked Harry.

'You know them?'

'I'm old, but I'm not quite that old, Billie.' He hung up.

CHAPTER 4

Seb left his hillside apartment, which overlooked the San Francisco Bay. He was sharing the accommodation with three other people who he barely knew, each person scraping together enough money to pay their portion of the rent. Considering his finances, and how tight money really was becoming, he realised he didn't even have the cash to buy any new clothes. At least, Seb now considered, he felt comfortable in the faded blue jeans and T-shirt he was wearing.

His dog, *Ripley*, was now living with Angel. Seb thought the two of them needed each-other, and the apartment was no place for a dog anyway. Since his discharge from the army, he had been a landscape gardener, a cleaner at a school and then a dishwasher. It was hard to settle anywhere, and everything he did seemed pedestrian to a guy like him, who was used to jumping in and out of helicopters or being shot at.

He strode, full of purpose, down-hill three blocks, intrigued about the job Jaz had set up for him. The FBI agent had said that she needed to find him a cover for his place on the cruise. On the phone, she hadn't really elaborated about what that cover could be, but there was something in her voice that hinted at amusement or at least self-satisfaction.

As he entered the little cafe, Seb found Jaz waiting near the counter, looking as smart as always, a half-smile on her glossy lips. She ordered three coffees as Seb waited, his eyes taking in the room. Then with her order complete, without pause, Jaz turned and walked. And he followed as she led him between small tables where people sipped coffee or hovered over plates of pastries and salads, all the time aware of a fresh scent that seemed to trail off her.

At a small table located as far from everyone else in the café as possible, Jaz finally stopped. 'This is Brian Gillespie. He's the only one on the cruise who will know you true identity.' Then glancing at Seb, she said, 'This Seb Bonney. He's the one I was telling you about.'

Seb Bonney. It was the first time Seb had heard his alias on anyone's lips, and he smiled.

Brian, a middle-aged guy with a ponytail coming down off a balding pate stood up from his seat and shook Seb's hand. It was forced and quick – and conveyed a lot about how Brian felt. Seb noted that Brian's eyes shifted, never staying in any spot for too long. His beard was greying, and he wore a black vest over a white t-shirt. There were a few gold chains hanging around his neck and they matched the gold rings in both ears. The whole outfit reminded Seb of a modern-day pirate.

'Seb Bonney?' said Brian.

Seb nodded, then he and Jaz sat in their seats.

'Like *William H Bonney?*' asked Brian.

Seb stared back at him flatly.

'*Billy the kid.* That was his name,' Brian clarified.

'Whatever,' said Seb with a shrug.

'I'll call you *the kid.* Is that okay?' asked Brian.

Jaz said nothing, though Seb thought she looked amused. Again Seb shrugged.

'That's what we'll call you when you start,' said Brian.

'Start what? You better explain what my cover is,' said Seb.

'Brian had an opening. Do you know who he is?' asked Jaz. Seb looked across the table at Brian, who affected a sort of a side pose.

'I don't know who he is,' admitted Seb. 'Why is he sitting that way?'

'Brian is the manager of the rock band – *Manson Villa*.'

'I've heard of them,' allowed Seb, looking at Brian, who now had a big smile frozen on his face. 'They're okay, I guess. So, Brian, why are you helping us out.'

Jaz interjected, 'Seb, you don't need to know.'

'Oh, but I do, Jaz, I do. If my ass is on the line in any way, I need to know who I'm dealing with.' Seb turned to Brian. 'Why are you doing this for Jaz?'

'*Manson Villa* are playing. We're the headline on the cruise.'

'Ok. But why you?'

Brian looked down. He dropped his voice. 'I'm the manager…'

'And?' pressed Seb.

'I was caught with some cocaine. The charges will be dropped if I do this one thing,' said Brian.

'Okay, now I get it,' said Seb.

Jaz said, 'Brian is cooperating with us to avoid prosecution, and negative publicity. But the cover he can provide is perfect for you, Seb. No-one will look twice at you. You will be one of two bodyguards for the band.'

'You can do that, can't you,' said Brian.

Seb ignored the remark. He looked at Jaz. 'Tell me he doesn't know what I'm doing for you onboard the cruise.'

'He doesn't know, and under no circumstances are you to tell him,' said Jaz.

'This is gonna be great!' said Brian.

'Why couldn't I just get a ticket?' asked Seb, meeting Jaz's gaze.

Jaz explained, 'The tickets are worth sixty-five thousand dollars each. In any case, there are none left. Only the fabulously rich or famous can get on-board this cruise. It's pretty much an invitation only situation. Trust me, this is the best and easiest course of action to get you on the ship and into position. *Manson Villa* were already booked to play the cruise six months ago. The cover is better than we could have expected for you.'

'Are you going to kill someone?' asked Brian.

'No,' said Seb. 'And no more questions, Brian.'

Brian shrank back in his seat just as the coffee was delivered to their table. No one spoke for a while. At last Seb leant forward, and, staring at Jaz, said, 'I hope you know what you're doing.'

CHAPTER 5

It was late in the afternoon. Billie had spent the day tying up some lose ends in a couple of earlier cases. Her view from the window over the beach drew her out of her chair. She watched as a group of female joggers ran along the edge of the waterline, tight short-shorts and nylon sports tops struggling to keep everything from moving about. *'So that's how you get a date around here,'* she breathed before she flipped the venetians closed.

During the day, Forsyth had texted her several times, making polite enquiries about anything she may have found out about Meeks. But Billie hadn't yet heard anything back from Harry, and she wanted to give him some time to do his thing.

Forsyth on the other hand - had supplied her with some details he had gleaned himself, from people who knew Meeks socially.

The last text, received just fifteen minutes before, said - *Meeks will be at a restaurant called Pascoe's.*

Then a minute later – *he's meeting someone there at 6 pm.*

Billie considered that last message. She had already formulated a plan which involved using Harry to hack into Meek's email account and his private messaging within his social media. Her assumption was that Meeks would have mentioned his threatening letters to a close confident or maybe even colluded with someone he trusted.

He may also be using some fake accounts that would be hard to trace directly to him.

But Billie had not anticipated Forsyth providing her with intel that Meeks was going to be at a particular place, possibly for the whole evening. If the information was accurate, she could leverage that and approach things in a way that would potentially fast track the investigation.

Billie went to her filing cabinet, unlocked it, then retrieved the small black gym bag she kept hidden inside. She thought of it as her *bag of tricks*. It contained a bunch of items that over the years she had found invaluable. Snatching it up, she made sure it was fully zipped before plucking her car-keys out of the desk drawer.

On the way out, she took a hoodie from the coat rack, checking the jacket's pockets. Satisfied she was ready for the evening's events - Billie exited and locked the office behind her.

Emerging from the concrete internal stairs into a shared garage space beneath the complex, she sighed as she saw her small, red, mechanically dubious Suzuki soft-top, which hadn't been washed or serviced in months. It was parked in her usual space, a fine coat of dirt covering it. The fluorescent lighting in the garage showed every mark, every imperfection on her vehicle. On the windscreen, written in the dust with someone's index finger was Billie is a slut. She was no expert, but she thought she recognised the handwriting as Jason's.

She stopped and considered the vehicle. Inside, she knew the footwells were littered with fast food containers and paper coffee cups. As long as the windows remained down, the smell wasn't too bad.

Billie knew where to find *Pascoe's*. It wasn't the most expensive restaurant around, but it wasn't that far off either. Small portions, and large bills. It was only ten minutes away.

She made it in eight minutes and pulled up under a spreading eucalypt tree fifty yards down the block from the restaurant. Her unwashed, slightly dented car stood out like an ugly duckling amongst Porsches, Audis, BMWs, and Teslas.

She had a camera with a 400mm zoom in the gym bag. The front of Pascoe's was glass. The place was packed with patrons, as were the other cafes and restaurants lining either side of the street. Although she looked down the viewfinder, she couldn't see anyone that resembled Meeks.

Couples walked past, hand in hand, the girls in high heels showing lots of leg, the guys in suits, swaggering. The whole area was rocking, with a distinct singles vibe. She could smell a cocktail of various colognes and perfumes, hanging in the air, and behind that, occasionally wafting aromas from kitchen restaurants. But then the crowds shifted, and she could see him, sitting opposite a red head, leaning over a table, pouring her some wine. Through the viewfinder, the redhead laughed, throwing back her head. Billie mumbled, mimicking her voice – '*Oh, Carlton, you know how horny I get when I drink.*'

From the black gym bag, she took a tracking device. It was small enough to fit into her palm, and had a magnet affixed to it. She had memorised Meek's license plates and knew he drove a dark blue Mercedes. Satisfied that Meeks wasn't likely to be leaving his table any time soon, Billie left her car, walked along the sidewalk, dodging people who seemed more interested in talking loudly than watching where they were going. She found his car parked about a hundred yards from Pascoe's. As she came up to it, she glanced around once, pretended to bend, and tie a shoelace, then quickly placed the tracking device up under the rear wheel-arch, where the magnet held it firmly in place.

From there, she backtracked to her car, and jumped straight in. Opening her phone, she used an *app* to keep tabs on where Meek's car was going to go. The app displayed a map showing streets, and a small red dot tracked the location of the device attached to Meek's car. Satellite technology combined with the tracker would give her up to the minute intel on where his car was at any moment. Laying the phone on the seat beside her, she pushed out into crawling traffic and drifted away from the area, close to the red-tail lights of the cars in front, heading for her next destination for the evening.

Carlton's house sat on the top of a hill in La Jolla, with views back toward the ocean. It was a high-end property. Billie parked down the street in a neighbourhood that seemed quiet. She took a lock-pick set from her gym bag and pushed them down into her pockets along with a pair of gloves. As she wandered from her car, looking around, she could hear sprinklers chittering in the evening warmth. Further along the sidewalk, the soft scent of jasmine mingled with late meals, wafting from the kitchens of residences fancy enough to have live-in chefs. The soft glow of interior lights spilled out into the night, suffusing the street in a warm glow. She pulled the hood of her jacket forward over her head and face, keeping her head down.

Meeks' property was highset. It was a modern place, with tropical gardens. A couple of lights had either been left on upstairs or had come on with security timers. *Birds of paradise* grew thick all along the frontage, including either side of a door in the outer wall. There was a buzzer and intercom set into an alcove. The door was a heavy, solid-looking timber. Beside the door, there was a keypad with glowing blue numbers. She pressed the intercom, said 'Hello…hello.'

There was no reply. She glanced down at her phone. The tracking app showed that Meeks had not moved from the restaurant. He was probably on his second course.

She tried it again. Still nothing – no cooks, no housekeepers, no-one answered the door. Assumptions had to be made. There might be cameras, so she had to take care not to show her face. She looked at her phone again. Meeks hadn't moved. Maybe Pascoe's was slow on a Friday night. Billie walked along the fence-line. The wall was solid brick, around seven feet in height. The whole area was so damned civilized, and quiet. No cars, no kids, nothing moved in the street.

Then she saw it – a big shiny blue trash recycle bin. It was across the road, sitting ready or perhaps not taken back into the neighbour's property after the last collection. Billie crossed the street, and returned, pulling the bin behind her - right up to Carlton's wall. She pushed it as flush as she could, stepping amongst the shrubs. Then in one quick jump, climbed onto the bin. She wasn't tall, but she was just tall enough to see over the fence. There was a pool, a really nice one with lights shining under the surface. Billie climbed over the wall and dropped into a shrub on the other side. It wasn't a *Goddam* normal shrub though, was it? It was a *mother-ing* bougainvillea with big, hooked thorns.

'*Mother...*' she hissed as she stumbled out of it, nearly toppling into the really nice pool. Through her jeans, she felt some pain, and her arms had a few cuts. She made it to the back door of the house. It was glass, and inside it was dim. There was a kitchen decked out with black stone benchtops and black stainless appliances. A lamp had been left on, casting a green light. It was probably one of those smart lights, because as she watched, it changed to purple, and then a minute after that, it was blue. In the light of the lamp, a Doberman sat watching her, rock still, unblinking. It didn't growl or bark, but gazed at her closely, right into her eyes.

'Nice doggie,' said Billie. She glanced around, but didn't notice any cameras. The new ones were easy to install, and were wireless, using a Wi-Fi signal to a base station which could be located anywhere in the house. She backed up, the Doberman watching her closely. Billie went around the side of the house, and found another door, which probably went into a laundry. She could hear snuffling from the interior. It was looking impossible. A barking dog would have sent her away, straight back to her car. A big dog, which would attack if she managed to get inside was going to be a big problem. She stopped and tried to get her bearings. She looked at her phone and saw that Meeks was now on the move, driving slowly, probably in the direction of his home. He would arrive in...Billie screwed up her face as she thought...maybe forty-five minutes. It was enough time, to get inside and have a quick look around.

She had broken into a few houses in the past, once as a teenager, and perhaps twenty times as a PI. It was pretty simple really. Most windows on the second storey were left unlocked, with many homeowners wrong in thinking that top storey windows could not be reached. That was mainly true, but Billie was a great climber, with wonderful balance. But what made it possible was her light weight, a childhood filled with gym camps, and… drainpipes.

She just had to get the angle right – it had been a while. She took the climbing gloves from her hoodie pockets and put them on. Then she found the drainpipe, leant back, and began a steady climb, her skate-board sneakers finding purchase. Her gloved fingers wrapped around the pipe. Slowly she ascended, right beside a window, and yep – it was open. She slid it back, her muscles straining. Then she used her head to push through the flyscreen and flopped into the room beyond, rolling neatly onto her back, breathing hard. 'Billie scores a three out of ten for her dismount,' she said as she stood. It was a hard trick that one. Despite the whole climb lasting barely a minute, it left her exhausted, her arms burning. The room was a spare bedroom. She looked at the cell again and saw that Meeks was on his way, progress slow, probably stuck in traffic. *Good.*

Entering the upstairs hall, she saw a door at the far end. The Doberman was throwing itself against it, over and over, its claws scrabbling between the thumps. Billie crept into the main bedroom nearby, her hood pulled low over her face. There was a picture of Carlton and some young woman, framed, sitting in a wall unit. She was smiling up at him, and he was looking at the camera. It was a selfie, taken from close-range, inside a café somewhere. She started searching in his cupboard, carefully picking through his stuff. Expensive aftershave, a *Padres* baseball cap, shoes, clothes, underwear, robes, but not much else. No miniature Janie voodoo doll with pins sticking in it, no collages of Janie with eyes cut out. There was a compact camera sitting on a shelf, facing the bedroom.

It wasn't on. Billie had used similar devices. It was very small, a device easily concealed on bookshelves or amongst nick-nacks.

She left the room, heading down the corridor, using her phone's light to show the way. There were two more rooms along the corridor - an upstairs bathroom, and another room, this one locked. She could handle internal doors with conventional locks. In a moment she had her lock-pick tool out and was working on the lock. Any door that Carlton had left locked when he was out was worth investigating.

A minute.later, the lock popped, and she let herself in. It was an office. There was a large desk, and a liquor cabinet. Billie searched the desk. The only thing of interest was a laptop computer. She set it aside, continuing a search inside the two draws. There were bills, receipts, all kinds of bits of paper. An envelope with fancy filigree drew her eye. It was like a wedding invitation. But when she opened it, she found two tickets, with a different name printed on each. One was for *Carlton Meeks* and the other was for *Candy Rainbird*. The tickets were for a cruise on the *Estrella de Mar*. She returned them to the envelope.

This was interesting. Was Meeks going to follow Janie onto the cruise? She left the tickets where she found them, then picked up the laptop. Retreating back along the corridor, she headed for the window she had entered through. She was out of time. Carlton was now only five minutes out. Going back down a drainpipe was infinitely easier, but she had to carry the laptop and she really didn't want to drop it. Stuffing it inside her shirt and zipping up the hoodie, she began the descent.

She retreated the way she had come, out to the backyard. The Doberman had returned and was watching her from the kitchen, through the glass door, its teeth now silently bared, saliva dripping from its mouth, giving a good impression of the xenomorph from the movie *Aliens*.

She found a deckchair and dragged it over to the fence close to where she had entered the property. Avoiding the bougainvillea shrub, she used the chair to vault onto the top of the wall. As she did so, two things occurred. Two cops came running across the street toward her, and in fright, she allowed the laptop to slide out of her top and fall back inside the wall. Her legs were dangling to the outside of the property, and she felt hands pulling her all the way down off the fence.

'Get on the ground, right now!' said an officer, her pistol pointed at Billie.

Billie slid down onto the recycle bin, trying to keep her hands in the air at the same time. She dropped to the grass where she was told to kneel with her hands on her head. Then they cuffed her, and pulled back the hood, exposing her face.

'Anything sharp in your pockets?' asked the other cop, his hands already patting her down, copping a good feel.

'Easy there, partner,' said Billie. 'You could buy me a drink first.'

'What's this?' said the male cop.

'Size *B*,' said Billie.

But the cop had pulled her lockpick tools from her hoodie's pocket and was placing them in a zip sealed bag.

'More like an *A*, if you ask me,' he said and swung her towards the police cruiser.

CHAPTER 6

When Seb entered the abandoned warehouse, escorted back to the same fifth floor room where he had earlier met with Jaz and Harvey, he found the whole floor transformed. The old red brick was there in the background, but there was now a huge flat screen monitor which took up half of one wall. Where the old desk had been, now stood a shiny new conference table. There were leads running around the floor, hooked up to computers, and around the outside of the room, several workstations had been hastily thrown together. Things were ramping up.

Harvey stood across the room, talking with someone, and he looked up as Seb crossed the floor. Jaz was seated at the conference table, looking over some papers, a small laptop beside her. He could also see several new faces, all dressed in jeans and t-shirts. These were her team of new technical people he guessed. Somehow, highly trained, IT folks always got away with dressing for work however they liked. There were three of them, a young woman and two guys.

Seb's memory flashed back to an earlier incident, a gun jammed in the faces of three terrified people, a bank of monitors, and on one of those monitors, the image of his sister sitting huddled with another woman in a cell. These three looked much the same as the three people he'd left dead in that room at the Cliff House. He didn't realise he had stopped and was gazing at them until Jaz invited him to sit opposite her at the conference table.

'We have a lot to get through Seb,' she said.

'Before we get into this, can you tell me how you found out about the rendezvous?' asked Seb.

'We've been bugging their phones, and other places for a couple of months now,' said Harvey, who had come to join them.

Jaz said, 'The information came up, in a call between Anson Mulgrave and Hillary West. The idea of the *Estrella de Mar* cruise was raised by West.'

'They never say anything incriminating over phones,' said Harvey.

'They do take a great deal of care. They assume that after McTaggart went down, they could be somehow implicated,' said Jaz. 'One thing we learned – although they are all together, they won't start their dialogue until day 7.'

'What do you mean?' asked Seb.

Jaz said, 'The exact phrase used, I believe, was *negotiations will not proceed until day seven, when all of us are present.*'

'Which means,' said Harvey, 'at that point, someone will join them, and whatever the negotiations are, will then begin. That's what we need to *really* know about.'

'Day seven puts them somewhere around Hawaii,' said Jaz.

Seb slowly nodded. 'Okay, so I'm on a timer of seven days.'

Jaz focused on her laptop, used it to begin to navigate through images, which showed on the flatscreen mounted on the wall.

'Let's go through the cabal's members one at a time. They seem to be a small group, well known socially, but secretive about their dealings with each other. Seb, you remember the video that you saw, taken by Eric Winters at the McTaggart place? At one point, the kid had walked past a room where a guy was talking loudly on a phone. He was arguing with someone. We never saw who that was, but we now know the voice belonged to retired army General Raymond Kennard.'

'I know of him,' said Seb.

'He's one of our marks, one of the *syndicate* as we refer to them. What he was doing at McTaggart's place, we can only assume,' said Harvey.

Kennard's face appeared on the screen, and Seb saw a male in his sixties, angular face with an almost shaved head staring arrogantly at the camera, without a hint of a smile. He stood beside a wife and two daughters in his formal parade ground uniform.

Jaz continued, as the next image flashed up. 'This is Lord Anson Mulgrave, our second member of *the syndicate*.' The image showed a man in his thirties, holding a double barrel shot gun, hunting-dogs arrayed around him, posing for the camera in a country setting.

'Why do I know that name?' asked Seb.

'He's appeared on a documentary or two. He's been invited into some important social circles. We know for example that Mulgrave has business ties in Japan, and academic ties to most eminent universities and museums around the world,' said Jaz.

'What is he exactly?' asked Seb.

Jaz flicked to the next still, a frozen image from the Winter's video, showing a large group of people standing near the pool at McTaggart's mansion. She stood, walked to the screen, and pointed to a slightly blurred image of a man standing a few feet from McTaggart. 'Here he is – Anson Mulgrave. To answer your question, he's an art collector. But he also collects artefacts… any ancient object of value he can get his greedy hands on. His collection's worth is estimated at over thirty million dollars.'

Harvey now moved to Jaz's vacated seat and took control of the presentation. The next image that showed on the screen was a Japanese man dressed in a suit. Caught mid-stride, he was moving toward a black car, with two men, obviously bodyguards on his flanks.

'Hiro Yuki… a Yakusa boss,' said Jaz. The next image was again a still from Eric's video. 'Here he is,' said Jaz, again pointing to another person standing near McTaggart. Hiro was over six feet tall, with thick dark hair. 'McTaggart had ties with Japan, and Hiro is one of them. Now that McTaggart is deceased, Hiro's status seems diminished within the cabal.'

'I always assumed that Eric was killed for what he found under the *cliff house*,' mused Seb, staring at the screen. 'But the people he filmed at that party may have been the real concern for McTaggart.'

The next image that came up made Seb smile. It was the instantly recognisable, smiling face of the tech queen, and billionaire – Hillary West. Her brand of mobile phone was now the third most used in the world. She had branched into nearly every field of technology in some way in the last few years. In the previously male dominated tech world, she was the new, big player. In this group, Hillary was easily the most famous, and likely to be the wealthiest.

Harvey said, 'Born Claudia West, she changed her name to *Hillary*. In an interview, she said she changed her name to honour the mountaineer, *Sir Edmund* Hillary, as her career felt like she too was conquering Mount Everest.'

'Are you sure she knew McTaggart?' asked Seb.

'Yes,' said Jaz. 'She was there, at the party.'

The next image to be displayed showed Hillary West, seated near the pool at the mansion, looking like an executive in a grey suit, sipping at a drink, staring from afar at McTaggart.

'But you don't know if any of these people had any real involvement with McTaggart's operation,' said Seb.

'No, we don't,' allowed Harvey. 'But they were there. It seems clear to us that some of the serum produced was going to these people. While the night crews were injecting large amounts of the stuff directly, the serum is also able to be imbibed in small quantities where the effects are diluted, and from what we hear – quite impressive at slowing down the aging process.'

'They are drinking it?' asked Seb, eyebrows raised.

'We know Anson is, and we think others may be too,' said Jaz. 'The whole operation is about that serum. It is about where it comes from, and where they can market it in complete secrecy.'

The flatscreen went blank.

'So - you have four marks for me to look at?' said Seb. 'And they will all be on this cruise?'

'Yes. They are all going to be together. But remember - there could be others. There is every possibility that McTaggart's syndicate was wider than we know,' said Harvey.

'But not too many,' said Jaz. 'An operation like this, the circle would not be too wide. If it was, something would have cracked open – someone would have talked. Remember, this is about the manufacture of a secret formula. McTaggart was the chemist. He needed funding. There were people enabling him, people protecting him, and people buying from him.'

Seb nodded. 'Okay, so I get close, try to plant some bugs. Record anything and everything they say, especially to each-other.'

'Yes. It will be the first time that they are gathering together,' said Harvey.

'You mean, since they were filmed by Eric Winters,' said Seb.

'Possibly,' Harvey nodded.

'That you know of,' said Seb.

Harvey nodded again.

'We've covered the targets,' said Jaz. 'Now, let's talk *comms*. You won't have a lot to carry, Seb. You will have a total of ten bugs available to plant. You will be doing that yourself, so they won't be anything too sophisticated.'

One of the techs brought in a small, hard, black case. It was then placed carefully in front of Seb on the table before he backed away.

Jaz said, 'We have your prints on file. This only opens with your biometrics.'

Seb pressed his index finger to the reader and unlocked the case. Inside were several compartments. One held the listening devices.

The other compartment held a laptop computer, some over-ear earphones, an in-ear earphone, a lock-pick device, a microphone attachment, and a camera.

'Is this everything?' asked Seb.

Jaz nodded. 'When you get on board, you need to start the laptop, and leave it powered on somewhere. While the ship is in range, our people will make the initial connection using it. They will then try to make a connection to the ship's Wi-Fi system, and hopefully from there, hack into the ship's main communications system.'

'You can do that?'

Jaz nodded. 'The ship's long-range satellite tech is needed to talk to us back here once the ship gets further out to sea. If we can establish that link, remotely, you will have a communication line back to us here through the laptop when you need it. Don't let anything happen to this laptop whatever you do. It's all configured, ready to go.'

'Then what?' asked Seb.

'You try to get into a position where you can place the bugs. We suggest trying to get one into each of the target's suites. If a meeting takes place, it is very likely to be in one of their private rooms,' said Harvey.

'Okay,' said Seb. He looked uncomfortable.

Jaz noticed. 'Listen Seb, I think you can do this. And we have to try. This cruise is somehow important to them. My gut tells me that they are meeting for a good reason. What that is, we don't know.'

'It's important that you get eyes on them too. That's the second element of the surveillance,' said Harvey. 'Knowing who else they are meeting with aboard that ship is just as important to us as what they are saying to each-other. Their group could have more members. We need to know who they are.'

Seb nodded.

'We are interested particularly in any mention of *subject Alpha*,' said Harvey.

'The thing from the *cliff house*?' guessed Seb.

'Yeah,' agreed Harvey. 'But we like to think of it as a species as yet unknown, or the first of its kind we know about – hence *subject Alpha.*'

Seb still dreamed, just occasionally of the creature he had encountered in the *cliff house* as they made their escape. He knew what it had done to McTaggart too. They were very dangerous, and still an unknown commodity. No-one knew what they were, where they came from, or how they came to be in the possession of McTaggart's lab. 'Call it whatever you like,' said Seb, 'I just hope I never see one again.'

'They may have their own name for it,' mused Jaz. 'Without those things…they *have* no operation. They must know what the species is, and its origin.'

'Anything else?' asked Seb.

Jaz said, 'As far as intel goes, there's one more thing. We want to know about the scientists McTaggart had in his lab. One was killed, but there are likely to be others. Listen for anything about them. We want to know who they are and… where they are.'

'Okay,' said Seb.

'Any questions?' asked Harvey.

'Rules of engagement?' asked Seb.

Jaz looked at Harvey and then made eye contact with Seb. 'The rules are - you listen, observe, report. Nothing else, okay?'

'So, no gun?'

'No gun,' said Harvey.

'What if I'm caught? What if they find out I'm listening or something?' asked Seb.

Jaz looked down. Harvey said, 'Make sure that doesn't happen.'

'With respect, that's not an answer,' replied Seb.

CHAPTER 7

Billie hadn't slept all night inside the police precinct's watchhouse. She had shared the cell with three women - one toothless, one angry, one sad, all of them including her in need of a hot shower.

Slumped forward, she sat very still on the edge of a bunk, sunken eyes tracking the comings and goings of police officers, busily processing fresh arrests. Never having been arrested before, Billie felt embarrassed, and a little uneasy. If she went before a judge, she'd have a lot of explaining to do.

When Sam Forsyth walked in, just behind a female police officer, his hair neatly combed, cleanly shaved, fresh pale linen suit, wafting a summery cologne, Billie felt relief washing over her.

Sam wasn't smiling though. 'I posted your bail money,' he said.

'You can go, for now,' said the police officer, opening the cell door, handing Billie a sheet of paper. 'These are your bail conditions. If you don't show for the court date, a warrant may be issued to bring you before the court. Do you understand?'

Billie nodded.

'I need to hear you say it,' said the cop, her face a blank mask.

'I understand.'

'Good. If you fail to appear in accordance with your bail, you can be charged with a separate offence.'

'I understand.'

'I know a good lawyer, Billie,' interjected Sam Forsyth. 'The charges will be dropped.'

They walked out through the cell area, and the female officer swiped them through a secure sliding door. Then they were in the foyer of the police precinct. Forsyth continued, 'I know they will drop the charges, and you won't need to appear in court. Do you want to know why?'

'Why?' asked Billie.

'Because Meeks hasn't agreed he will press the charges. He won't make a statement that you were even in his house at all.' Sam turned and looked at her as they walked onto the sidewalk outside the precinct. 'What is it that you found? I hope it was worth it.'

'Two tickets on the cruise,' said Billie.

'He's going on the same cruise?' asked Sam, his eyes wide.

Billie nodded. 'Sure looks that way.'

Sam appeared dismayed. 'Anything else? I must say, I didn't think you would get inside his house when I told you he was going to be at the restaurant,' said Sam.

'I took a chance. It was risky. But I think it paid off, don't you?'

'Yes, and it was rather brave,' said Sam, giving her an appreciative pat on the arm.

'There was also a laptop computer. It was in a locked room. There could be information on it that could tell us what Meeks is up to. Unfortunately, I dropped it inside his fence when the cops took me into custody.'

'They didn't mention anything about a missing or stolen computer. And neither did Meeks,' said Sam thoughtfully.

'Maybe there's something incriminating on it. He may not want the police to take it as evidence.'

Sam nodded. They started for his car. Billie could see his driver waiting at the Mercedes, the door open for her.

'Does he know who I am yet?' asked Billie.

'Meeks? I don't know. I deliberately avoided coming here until I knew he wasn't going to be around,' said Sam.

'If he knows I'm a PI, he may think someone's on to him,' said Billie.

'Perhaps. But he wouldn't know for sure who hired you. It could be any number of reasons why someone is looking at him.'

Sam climbed in behind Billie in the rear seat. The driver closed the door and then they were in motion.

'What did you do with the tickets?' asked Sam.

'I left them where I found them.'

'And the laptop? What did you say happened to it?'

'It dropped inside the fence. My intention was to get a friend of mine to break into it and hack every last shred of data on it to see if he had deleted any of his threatening messages. Meeks has probably found it by now though.'

'Not necessarily.' They drove several streets in silence before Sam continued. 'The cruise departs in under forty-eight hours from Acapulco. I don't think he will back away from whatever he's planning.'

'You should tell Janie. She should know she could be in real danger,' said Billie.

He shook his head. 'I won't tell Janie anything - not yet. She has some big performances coming up and any word of this will make her lose focus. These cruise contracts are worth a lot of money for us all.'

'How much?'

'Enough that she and everyone in the band could take the next two or three years off. It has to go ahead, and she has to be ready. If she was to breach the contract, back away from performing, it would break us financially.'

'Okay, so what now?' asked Billie.

'You're the detective. Please - feel free to advise me,' said Forsyth.

Billie said, 'I think we need to stay on Meeks.'

Forsyth turned away, shifting his gaze out the window at the San Diego morning, but Billie knew he was also thinking. Finally he asked, 'Do you think that Meeks is really a danger?'

'I assume he's paid a lot of money for those tickets. He's following Janie onto the ship. You tell me what that says to you, Sam.'

The promoter nodded but said nothing for the next ten minutes as they drove. 'Maybe he just wants to scare her. If he disrupts her performances, it could ruin her.'

'But he doesn't know that she hasn't seen the letters,' said Billie. 'He could be trying to scare her, and if he thinks he is failing, he might escalate to something more serious.'

As they approached Billie's office, she could see that her car had been driven back to the building and had been left on the street outside.

Billie paused as she opened the door. The driver promptly approached her side to hold the door open for her.

'My associate, Mr Gillespie, has taken the rather prudent step of hiring an additional bodyguard for the cruise. But I think it might be best if we send you on board too. What do you think?'

Billie climbed out and stood at the open door to the Mercedes. Leaning half into the car, she said 'Can you get me a ticket?'

'Not a chance. But perhaps we can arrange for you to replace someone in our entourage. Prepare yourself, Ms Dakota. You will be there to shadow Meeks, learn what you can, and we'll get him. But don't say anything yet to Janie. Not a word.'

As the Mercedes drove away, Billie stared after it, wondering what Meeks was planning for Janie. Her guess was that he would try to frighten her, the aim to disrupt her performances if he could. Worst case scenario – the guy was totally unhinged. On reflection, she didn't see anything at his house to suggest he was a psychopathic killer. It didn't quite fit.

Back in the office, she glanced at the clock, hesitated, then poured a bourbon into a glass. Then she opened her laptop and called Harry.

His face appeared. 'Jeez, Kid, it's too Goddam early...'

'Harry, that thing in the sky outside – the big yellow thing – says it's time to get out of bed. Don't you have a business to run?'

He sighed. 'I'm sure they're queuing up outside the door as we speak. What time is it anyway?'

'Do you sleep with that thing beside your bed?' asked Billie.

'The laptop? I like to read before I go to sleep. Hey – what are you drinking?' asked Harry.

'Orange juice.'

'I don't have anything yet, Billie. So far, the guy is clean.'

'That's not why I'm calling. I need you to do something else. But it involves you getting out of bed and getting in your car.'

'What? Why?'

'There is a laptop I left somewhere. I need you to go and get it. I have to pack some bags. I'm going on a cruise.'

Billie explained about her breaking into Meek's property and her subsequent arrest. She detailed how she was going to continue to shadow Meeks on-board the cruise ship.

'The laptop I dropped inside Meek's fence, inside the wall, is probably sitting in a bougainvillea shrub.'

'How do you know?'

'I didn't hear it smash, and I didn't hear a splash either. It must be there somewhere.'

'Huh?'

'Just go and look over the wall. I bet it's still there.'

'Why don't you go there?'

'I'm on bail. A condition is that I stay away from him and his property. And I have to get my ass down to Acapulco to make the cruise. Time is short.'

'Okay,' he sighed. 'How high is this wall?'

'I'm sure you'll work it out. Thanks Harry.' She hung up.

CHAPTER 8

Day 1

A sea of people surged along the docks, some walking, others seated in golf-carts piled with luggage, forced to crawl along with everyone else. Seb could not see the band, but the brass instruments sounded live, rising above the cries and shouts of an excited crowd.

Lifting his eyes above the throng, Seb paused, taking in the sight of the *Estrella de Mar* where she was docked, her crisp white hull shining in the morning sun. Her windows, and every other glass surface was either mirrored or tinted a deep blue. The ship towered above them, a leviathan, dwarfing the buildings around the docks. She was almost a replica of one of those classic luxury-liners from the 1920s era, he thought. As he neared the ship, Seb realised that the *big band* music was probably playing from one of the upper decks.

Several television crews had positioned themselves around the docks, trying to snare interviews as various celebrities with their respective entourages determinedly pushed forward, sometimes jostling the fans and tv crews aside.

'Keep moving people, don't stop,' said Sam Forsyth. Seb had met him briefly and had not yet seen the band's promoter smile.

Janie ignored Sam and stopped for a news crew. Seb tried unsuccessfully to interpose himself between Janie and the news crews, who pushed eagerly toward her, shoving microphones in her face. Christian Murdoch, another of her bodyguards stood on the other side of her. He was an ex-marine, who liked to telecast the fact. Sporting a range of tattoos across an impressive physique, he had kept the buzz-cut, despite having left the Corp years ago. Brian waited also, basking in the sudden buzz surrounding Janie. His face turned as each reporter asked questions, nodding eagerly as Janie responded.

'Are you looking forward to the cruise, Janie?' said a reporter, his face flushed.

Janie smiled and glanced up through oversized sunglasses at the *Estrella de Mar*. 'Isn't she beautiful. Oh yeah - I'll be enjoying this cruise, for sure,' she said.

Seb watched the rest of *Manson Villa* start to climb the gangway to the ship. The band members, including a couple of sound engineers, and Janie's new personal assistant had not stopped. All along the ship, other gangways had been extended and people were slowly moving aboard, heading up ramps toward hatches that had been opened in the side of the ship.

Sam Forsyth paused about halfway up the gangway, and was glaring back at Seb and Christian, his hands on his hips, as if they, rather than Janie were holding the procession up.

*

The woman, dress a bright red floral, with matching floppy hat, slipped away from her partner and looked down at the crowd gathered on the docks. She waved at people, and many waved back, not because they knew her, but because she was quite beautiful, perhaps famous, and they were in the midst of a euphoria born of expectant adventures and dreams about to be fulfilled.

Behind dark sunglasses, she watched as Janie Reichenbach and her entourage meandered through the crowd. There was music playing, but she wasn't sure if it was real or imagined. She became still. Below, Janie hesitated, the cameras drinking her in, the world opening around her, and her smile. The watcher pretended to wave once more.

She continued waving, now at Janie, and she called her name, but the crowd drowned out her voice. She called again, and for a moment, Janie might have looked up at her.

An arm looped into hers, and he held her hand. 'I didn't know where you went.'

'Who's that down there?' she asked.

The man frowned. 'Janie Reichenbach.'

'Do you think she's beautiful?'

'Not as lovely as you.'

*

Janie smiled a bit more, posed for a couple of selfies with some young girls, and answered some more lame questions which were no doubt being broadcast to a local tv breakfast show somewhere. Seb wasn't really tuned into Janie's responses. The background noise was pressing in, and he was watching the crowd. Although a pretend bodyguard, he was aware of Janie's fame, and everything that could come with it.

Janie eventually broke away, waving over her shoulder as she made her way up the gangway. Seb followed her close. She was not tall, nor was she short. She was shapely, but lithe at the same time, with a frame built on great genetics and regular workouts. With a classic movie star face that reminded him of Grace Kelly from the golden age of Hollywood, her presence was undeniable. Her outfit, a blue leather jacket and matching pants, was outrageously tight, and matched her eyes perfectly.

'You keeping your eye on the package?' asked Christian.

'What?' grunted Seb. 'Yeah, Christian, you *could* say that.'

'You should be watching them, not her,' said Christian, eyes flat.

As they arrived in the vast foyer, Seb realised that this ship was the most glamourous he had ever seen. He was reminded of a palace from an age long past. Marble competed with reflective glass, softened by lustrous polished timber. This was no ordinary cruise ship, and he stood in mute awe, looking about. The idea of a replica luxury liner from an earlier age had been stunningly realised.

The fact that the ship could afford such large open spaces, demonstrated that the number of passengers was significantly less than standard cruises. Everything felt spacious to his eye. It was the last thing that Seb expected.

Seb finally went and stood before a map on the wall – noting the general layout of the ship. Scanning the diagrams, he counted around 14 restaurants and bars, seven swimming pools, a gym and surprisingly – a library. A poster above the map showed Janie posing in the middle of *Manson Villa*, and the concert dates and times.

On the other side of the foyer, there was an uninterrupted view through to the open ocean. He could see a promenade deck, and chairs carelessly scattered about. Along one side, a polished timber bar with gleaming brass edgings, reflected natural light off a thousand coloured spirit bottles. The ship wasn't festooned with gaudy waterslides or other attractions that made some ships feel like giant, floating side-shows. The *Estrella de Mar* was elegant, a state-of-the-art piece of nautical engineering, as tasteful as any great ship could be. Glancing around he realised there were no kids anywhere, just lots of rich people, some with personal retinues.

'Incredible,' Seb breathed.

'Isn't she,' said Janie, suddenly at his side. 'But you're supposed to be following me, not the other way around.'

'Sorry.'

'Are you new at this? Brian said you had *some* experience.'

'Yeah, I've watched some important people before,' lied Seb, meeting her crystal blue eyes.

Janie gave him an appraising look. 'Good thing you're easy on the eye, Mr Bonney. I have a feeling you may not be a great bodyguard.'

Over Janie's shoulder, Christian was staring. The rest of the entourage had gathered in a group in the middle of what Seb thought could be a dance floor. They were listening to a ship's steward, who was pointing this way and that. Janie's dogsbody, the new personal assistant, was watching Janie too, Seb noted. She was obviously waiting to be told to do something. Seb sensed something odd about her - what was her name? Yeah, that was it – *Billie*. She wasn't dressed exactly like the others in the band. Attired in jeans and a denim jacket, she somehow didn't fit with the rest of the entourage. She was kind of short, and her eyes were always busy. He wondered what a personal assistant might do, and how such an ordinary little woman was given the role.

Billie stopped a female attendant as she sought to go around them. Seb saw her lean forward and whisper something into the woman's ear, and then barely a moment later, press what he thought was money into her palm. The attendant smiled, and the greenbacks disappeared quickly into a coat pocket. Then the attendant was examining her electronic tablet, typing something in. She said something to Billie, who in turn, typed something into her phone. It was all done in seconds. Seb wondered what information she had asked for, and why Billie had needed to pay for it. Caught staring at Billie, for a moment he could have sworn that she made a weird, cross-eyed face at him. He quickly looked away, pretending he didn't notice. Then Billie was turning away, taking a call. Obviously being onboard a floating palace was no big deal for her.

Billie took her cell phone from a pocket and put her index finger over her other ear to block the background noise. 'Hello?'

'It's me, Harry.'

'What was on the laptop, Harry?'

'Good to hear your voice, too, Billie.'

'I'm sorry, Harry. It's been less than twenty-four hours. So good to hear your voice,' said Billie, rolling her eyes.

'Yes, I found the laptop, and it was exactly where you said it would be. I have the wounds to show for it. The laptop didn't have anything about Janie. No threats, no conversations, nothing. I was able to find every *nook and cranny* on that hard drive and everything in the cloud. There's nothing about her.'

'Are you sure? It's him, we all know it.'

Harry breathed out a disappointed sigh. 'There's nothing about her. No conversations, no threats, nothing remotely violent.'

'So, it's not him,' said Billie, almost to herself.

'It certainly doesn't seem so. But I need more time.'

'Then why didn't he press the *break and enter* charges? I stole his laptop.'

Harry chuckled. 'I know why.'

Billie waited, but Harry seemed intent on making her ask the question. 'Tell me.'

'He had a bunch of movies on there. Ones that could get him in a lot of trouble.'

'Really?' Billie thought she knew what was coming next.

'He had secret cams set up in his bedroom, and judging by the angles, he had them all around the room, including in the light fitting directly over his bed. I'll say this for Meeks, the guy knows how to edit a movie.'

'Sex videos?'

'Do I have to spell it out? Yeah – a bunch of them. Every girl he ever picked up is on there. He has a whole library...including Janie. He probably thinks you will try to extort him at some point.'

Billie nodded. 'I wish it *was* him.'

'Why?'

'Because now I don't know if she's in danger, or how close someone could be getting. Thanks Harry. I gotta go.'

Billie ended the call, glanced across at Sebastian Bonney, and then at Christian Murdoch, the ex-marine, with his tattoos and buzz-cut. These two were all that stood between Janie and whoever was sending the threats. The two men appeared different, in most ways, though both had a certain look about them too. Christian seemed hyper-tense, and exuded menace. On the other hand, Sebastian was almost the opposite. He was leaning back, looking very relaxed, taking in the scene around him. Billie wondered if she would have to play the roles of both bodyguard and investigator if Sam and Brian refused to tell Janie she was probably in real danger. Maybe Christian already knew about the threats. He always looked ready, as if something might happen at any moment, while Sebastian... looked like he was on a paid vacation.

CHAPTER 9

On the very top deck of the ship, in the open air, the five stood at the railing in a tight group, gazing down at the crowded docks, while basking in sunlight. The four men and a woman, with eclectic skin colour and of similar ages, were all dressed in shabby-sheik holiday clothes. Lean, muscular, tanned, they radiated confidence behind dark sunglasses.

Darian lifted his sunglasses and settled them onto his shaved head. Directing striking green eyes toward his team, making eye contact with each member, he asked, 'Are we set?'

'Yes, Major,' said Jonty.

The other three just nodded.

'Not Major. Just boss or guv, or something – but there are no military ranks here,' said Darian.

Clive Richards, a tall, solidly built Jamaican man, said, 'Let's enjoy ourselves for a while. We have plenty of time to think about business later.'

'Yeah, he's right. Let's kick back and have a good time,' agreed Wayne, speaking with his country Australian drawl. His streaked blond hair pushed away from a round face as a gust of wind rushed over them.

A short Indian – English woman, Robyn Dev, lifted her hands

into the air as she performed a little jig. 'This is going to be unreal!' she spun around, shimmied sideways, moving with music that existed only in her mind.

Wayne grinned, and attempted his own dance, trying to emulate Robyn's fluid movements.

Clive began laughing quietly, all white teeth, and squinting eyes. 'You look like you're having a seizure,' he grinned.

'Okay, we can all chill for a while,' said Darian. 'And if anyone asks, we're all just old school chums. That's our cover.'

'What fucking school did we all go to?' asked Robyn, her face breaking into a grin.

'Just pretend we all went to a boarding school in England,' said Darian, absently rubbing his head, testing the level of stubble.

'Who's going to ask us anyway, Major?' asked Jonty.

'Are you a bit slow, Jonty? Didn't I just say to you to stop calling me that?' Darian turned and looked down at the crowd below, with many frantically waving as they spotted friends already onboard the ship. The gangways began to creep back toward the docks. 'We will be underway soon. Try not to get in too much trouble.'

'We're gonna be rich, we're gonna be rich…' Robyn was dancing again, repeating the phrase over and over.

Wayne smiled and again tried to join in with her, his dance moves making Robin double over with laughter.

Darian was about to rebuke them, but he spied a waiter and called him over. He just needed a drink to calm his nerves, he told himself, reaching for the high-ball glass sitting amongst the glittering tray of cocktails. They would enjoy the cruise and try to keep a low profile, and that meant blending in with the other passengers. There was no reason to expect that anyone would recognise them, he considered. Smiling as he sipped a Mojito, Darian said, 'Anson wants no contact whatsoever with us until the seventh day, okay. We don't know him, and he doesn't know us.'

'But we know each-other, right?' asked Jonty.

Darian rolled his eyes. He opened his mouth to suggest that Jonty should start taking everything seriously but was interrupted by the ship's horns as they started to blare. At that same moment they could feel a deep vibrating thrum as the ship stirred to life. The leviathan was waking, her massive propellors churning blue water into white, as swirls and eddies appeared around the hull. At the rail, they watched as far below, three tugboats manoeuvred into position, jockeying to nudge the *Estrella de Mar* away from the docks.

CHAPTER 10

Seb and the others in Janie's party had been kept waiting for an hour while Janie met and mingled with various people, including the ship's captain. It was after dark when he finally swiped his key card, walked into his cabin, and examined the cramped space with its single bed, and fold down desk. To one side Seb gazed with disappointment on a cramped shower, basin, and lavatory. Although there was no balcony, there was a port-hole window that he could open. His bags were waiting there, and the all-important black hard case was sitting in the one cupboard provided within the cabin.

Relieved that the luggage had been safely delivered, Seb placed his thumb over the biometric reader pad and opened the case. One by one, he examined the items that Jaz's team had showed him two days prior. They sat, protected in black foam, each with its own compartment. He took out the laptop, powered it up, then plugged the power cord into a wall-socket and watched as it immediately initialised some protocols. Seb walked away, unaware of what was happening on the screen, but trusting that the techs knew what they were doing. He hung up some clothes and shoved his toiletries into the bathroom space. Examining the clothes which Brian Gillespie had chosen for him, he was dismayed to find them all much the same. Each shirt was white, collared and button-up. Each pair of trousers was gray. There were two jackets, one white, the other navy. He stripped off his T-shirt and dropped it carelessly on the bathroom floor.

Distracted by the gadgets in the case, he returned to them for a closer look. He examined each more carefully now, putting them on the bed beside him. Laying out each listening device, he picked them up, and one at a time, switched each one on. They had enough battery life to last the cruise and months after, according to the techs back at the warehouse. They needed just ten minutes to individually hook into the ship's Wi-Fi system and would parasite off it for the remainder of the cruise. The laptop would act as the hard drive for all recordings and as long as all components remained connected via the ship's Wi-Fi, the range between the bugs and the computer would not be an issue. The bugs would lie dormant until they detected sound and then would switch on and begin recording. Or at least, this is what he had been told.

Satisfied the case was emptied, and each piece of kit examined, he sat back on the bed. He was pleased to see they had included a nice little telescope, with a switch for night-vision. But there was no pistol. He sighed with disappointment. *So,* he thought, *I really am unarmed.* How could he be a bodyguard without a gun? But he wasn't really doing that anyway, he reminded himself. He thought about Janie, the way she walked, and her faint, mysterious perfume. He considered that in another life, perhaps he could have been a real bodyguard to someone like her. After all - it was a *rather nice* body to guard, given the choice.

A knock on the door caused him to carelessly pile the kit items back into the case before quickly shoving it in under the bed, and out of sight.

'What is it?' Seb asked, opening the door. Janie's PA, Billie was standing there, arms crossed over her chest. He was immediately aware of how short she was, and how she had to tilt her head up at him to meet his eyes. Then she tried to look past him, as if Seb's room might have been better than hers. 'Just wanted to see your cabin. Mine's just as small.' She looked satisfied about that, thought Seb.

'Yeah, well, we're the *help*.' Seb gave her the once over, trying to make it appear casual. She was definitely petite...but there was *something* he liked, something hard to define. It was a look in her eye, the tilt of her head, the set of her jaw, or all three together. Whatever it was, it was... *something*.

Billie was staring openly at his chest, he realised. Seb was aware now that he was shirtless, having been interrupted while dressing. But instead of backing away, he leant on the frame of the door, cocked his head to the side, and waited for her to speak.

'What's that?' she said at last, pointing.

He hesitated for a second. 'That's from a bullet hole.'

Billie glanced up to see if he was joking, and then looked more closely, her eyes narrowing. 'Were you cut here?' her index finger pointed close to his flat stomach, along one side.

He chuckled and gave a little shake of his head. 'That's just where the appendix was removed.'

She lifted her eyes higher. 'What about that one?' she said staring at an odd-shaped scar where his neck met his shoulder.

'Knife wound, or maybe a bitemark. Both happened within about thirty seconds of each other.'

'Bar-fight?'

'No, a girl called *Krystal*,' he said.

Billie gave a snort of laughter. 'Good one.' Her eyes took him in, and she seemed to have no problem just staring. 'I thought you'd have some ink,' she said at last.

'Disappointed?'

She smiled and began to back away. 'Sam sent for you. He wants us up in Janie's suite in fifteen minutes, okay? I bet it's better than our crappy rooms. Oh, and he said to wear the blue suit coat.'

'Great.'

Billie walked away as Seb closed the door. He returned to the laptop. The device had finished doing whatever it was doing because he heard Jaz before he saw her.

'Who was that?' came her voice.

Seb bent before the laptop, then plugged in the headset and mic. 'Her name's Billie. She's Janie's personal assistant.'

'You'll have plenty of time for *that* later, Seb.'

'For what?' He tried to suppress a grin. 'She's not my type anyway.'

'Right now, you need to focus on getting those bugs into position. Remember, you turn them on and place them wherever they won't be seen - under tables, in light-fittings, any place you think they will pick up a conversation, okay?'

'Yeah Jaz, we've been over this. You said I have until day seven,' said Seb.

'Yeah - but it's just you, so you'll have to start getting them into position early. We don't know where they will hold the meeting on that day. And we might over-hear some useful information before then.'

'I know,' he tried not to roll his eyes. 'This isn't my first rodeo, Jaz. I've done over a hundred recon assignments.'

'It is your first attempt at spying. Ever planted a bug?' asked Jaz.

'You know I haven't.'

'Stick to the assignment.'

'And improvise if needed,' he reminded her. 'Stop worrying.'

Jaz nodded. 'Leave the laptop on - but lock the screen. Check in with us each evening when you get back to your cabin, or at dawn, before you leave.'

'I remember,' said Seb.

'Good luck.'

Seb smiled at Jaz, then locked the screen. He went to the cupboard where he took down a white shirt, and a blue jacket. In the bathroom he ran his fingers through his hair, smoothing it back with some water, and a comb. He had a three-day growth, but no time to shave. He considered himself in the mirror. The coat looked good with the collared shirt. This seemed to be a revelation. Maybe he needed to dress like this more often.

As he was about to depart, he hesitated, then returned to the hard case where he fished out three listening devices and slipped them into his jacket pocket. At the door, he hesitated again, then took the electronic lock-pick too. It was a palm sized device - black, flat, and rectangular, perhaps three times as thick as a normal swipe card. Jaz had reassured him that it would work on any of the ship's cabin doors. This he slipped into his other jacket pocket as he finally left the cabin.

*

When Seb entered Janie's palatial suite three decks above his, he couldn't help but stare in amazement. Billie was correct in her assumption that the rock-star's rooms would far surpass their own accommodation. Her suite was grand, but in an elegant way. His eye was drawn from the gleam of oiled wood-panelling to the luxurious textured rugs that invited bared feet and wriggling toes. There were plush lounging chairs comfortable enough to sleep on and around them all - space to move. She had her own generous balcony, and large windows all along one wall. Through a doorway, he spied her bed – which was large, piled with an assortment of pillows. Walking forward, craning his neck, Seb could just see Janie's bathroom off to one side, and it alone looked larger than his entire cabin.

But it was on Janie that his eyes finally rested, seated on a blue velvet chair in front of a mirror, applying makeup. She looked a little nervous, thought Seb. Her back was straight, but with a certain tension. Locked, firm, her jaw carried that same tension all the way from her slender neck.

Without turning around, Janie said, 'We were waiting for you, Mr Bonney.'

'He was making himself pretty?' commented Christian.

Seb glanced at Brian, who was standing off to the side, his ponytail neatly tied, wearing a tuxedo suite. The outfit didn't look right on him though. Maybe it was too tight, or perhaps it was the way Brian kept tugging at the collar with his index finger, trying to make more room for his bullish neck.

Billie was also there, and Seb thought she looked pensive. The PA's phone was in her left hand, as if she was waiting on a call. She had changed into an evening dress, a simpler version of something Janie might wear, Seb thought. Again, he found himself wondering who she really was, what she was thinking about right then. This was because her eyes moved constantly, from Janie to her phone, and back again. If she was a personal assistant, she seemed distracted from her duties. Perhaps feeling Seb's eyes on her, Billie glanced up and met his gaze.

Janie finally stood, and walked into the middle of the room, doing a twirl to see how the dress moved. It was a flowing piece, flame-coloured, and with very tall high-heels, she looked every part a diva. Her makeup matched her hair, each having red-gold embellishments, specially added for the performance she was about to provide.

Seb was suddenly aware of several scents in the air. From the open balcony, the freshness of salt on the breeze mingled with Janie's perfume, and perhaps whisky, recently imbibed to steady the nerves of several in her entourage.

Sam Forsyth walked in from a balcony, suddenly appearing through the curtains that billowed in the wind. The promoter was in an immaculate blue suit, with a matching tie. Behind him, the moon sat orange in the evening sky, hovering over a flat sea where the waves rippled past with hardly a sound.

'Are we ready?' Sam asked. 'We need to make a good impression. I don't need to tell you this, do I?'

'I'm ready,' said Janie. Seb could tell she was by the way she moved, her energy almost seeming to make her glow.

*

One deck below them, another woman was preparing for the evening. She looked into the bathroom-mirror, staring into her own eyes, frightened at what she saw when she rested in those depths. Her scalp was shaved to a stubble. Sweat beaded upon it as she had just performed exactly one hundred sit-ups, followed by a hundred push-ups. She would have done more, but the tiled floor was slippery after her shower, and there wasn't room for many of the other drills she used to maintain peak fitness.

The makeup went on, and her face slowly became tanned, her eyes cleverly accentuated. She applied blood red lipstick, then pouted at herself, and bared her teeth. No lipstick stained them - they were white and straight.

She regarded the rest of her body. There was nothing now to be ashamed of, nothing of her old self remained. She was lean, muscular, as muscular as any man. Her small firm breasts sat proud, her stomach flat, and in the shadow between her legs, she was waxed. The area between her breasts had a small tattoo of an ace of spades, and on her back, across the shoulder blades - large angel wings unfurled, in dark sapphire ink.

Her upper arms were also delicately inked, with roses, and thorns, entwining around each bicep. On her left upper arm, a name – *Mathew* sat inside a blood red heart.

'I'm going to kill you,' she said to her reflection. Then she said, 'You're going to die.' She smiled, and looking at the pose, dropped the angle of her jaw, and lowered her eyes. 'Would you care to dance?' Then with a slightly deeper, huskier voice, 'would you care to dance?'

There was a banging on the door, and a man growled, 'I need to get in there. Are you ready yet? What are you doing?'

She stared at herself in the mirror, and in the voice she had last affected, said, 'One moment. I just need a second.'

She opened the door. Her flat, expressionless gaze would not have looked out of place on a mannequin.

He stood there, naked, a towel in one hand. 'What the fuck were you doing in there so long?'

She said nothing.

'Where's your hair? You should be ready to go. I'm sick of your bullshit.'

She stabbed him then, the scissors jutting into his throat. His hand went to his neck, his eyes widening in shock. Then she withdrew the scissors and hammered them into his chest, and again. He fell back under the onslaught, trying to fend the blows. But the first strike had been lethal, and he was now fighting for a few more seconds of precious life.

He retreated into the bedroom, ragged, wheezing breaths hissing, his back to the balcony, blood pumping steadily from several wounds. Legs wobbling now, he stared at her as she stalked after him, naked, the gleaming scissors held low in her right bloodied fist.

'No…' his left hand went up, open palm. His right hand was clamped to the side of his neck, trying to stem the flow.

She lined him up, then launched a solid round-house kick that punched into his chest, designed to shove him powerfully away. He fell back, his spine cracking against the rail as he somersaulted with hardly a cry, gone even as he hit the almost black waves.

CHAPTER 11

The dining hall was set, an array of large round tables placed about the outside, each able to seat around twelve people. In the middle, a large open space was left to allow people to dance. Above, a domed glass ceiling let the night sky in, reminding Seb of an observatory.

On either side of the hall, Seb could see open doors leading onto balconies, allowing fresh, cool air to flow inside. It was a ticketed event only. Men in formal black suits, and women in gowns were gathering, smoking cigarettes or cigars, talking in groups of three and four, cradling champagne glasses, looking like they had stepped out of a portal from 1912.

It was an intimate venue as far as *Manson Villa* were concerned. Familiar with playing stadiums, they now occupied a small stage at the end of the hall, just large enough to allow the band to set up and not much else. After a few minutes of sound checks, plucking cords and tweaking dials on amplifiers, Seb saw Janie take the stage, and although she had only picked up the mic, the crowd turned and watched her, conversations all but ceasing. That was the kind of performer she was.

Christian was standing on the other side of the stage, eyes narrowed, mouth set, closely watching as people settled into their seats at the tables.

Billie also hovered beside the stage, standing close to the back wall, near where the serving staff were coming and going from a kitchen area, carrying trays of drinks. She was still holding her phone, as though waiting on a call she didn't want to miss. Her hawkish eyes followed the movement in the room, taking in every detail, Seb thought. Though a small smile played across Billie's lips, Seb knew that she wasn't the kind of girl that would miss a thing… *not a damned thing.*

Manson Villa started playing, with just their instruments for a full minute, before Janie decided to join them, her voice filling up the hall, the band falling into time with her. It was a cover, of an old song by Cole Porter – *Anything Goes.* It seemed to fit with the mood of the crowd, because several couples immediately went to the dancefloor.

There was polite clapping before they followed with a few of their own rockier tracks, which Seb had heard on the radio a few times. The room was dark, with most lights directed toward the stage. Seb took the opportunity to move into the middle of the room, surveying the tables, casually, like he was looking for someone or had forgotten his seat.

Of course, he *was* looking, trying hard to see if any of the marks he was meant to eyeball were present at the performance.

Then Janie slowed the show down, with an old song that sounded familiar to him. Janie had moved onto the dancefloor just in front of the band, a spotlight falling across her face. The lights dimmed, and Seb almost collided with a waiter, who barely held onto a drinks tray.

'Sorry.'

'Why don't you take your seat, sir,' suggested the waiter, before hurrying to a table where a group of men sat.

Then Seb was moving away as couples took to the floor, enjoying the slight upbeat Janie afforded to *Moondance*, just a little faster than the original by Van Morrison.

Then he saw them, seated at the same table, gathered together, looking nothing like what he knew they really were, the diabolical brethren of the late Stirling McTaggart, the wanna-be Shogun of Crabtree-Cove. He recognised them, each seated in an arc, watching Janie, talking quietly. Lord Anson Mulgrave, his hair slicked back off his forehead, was leaning close, talking to Hillary West, the tech Queen. Handsome Anson, with his slender features, clean-shaved, and striking blue eyes. He was younger than Seb expected too – perhaps no more than late-twenties. Hillary West was middle-aged, with dark hair cut into a bob. Around her throat glittered a bold necklace of diamonds and sapphires.

Seb kept walking, trying not to stare, playing idly with a bug in his coat pocket, while his fingers became familiar with its size and shape. He took a drink of champagne off a passing waitress's tray, without her noticing, and sipped. Then he stopped, and looked over his shoulder, back at the table where the *syndicate* were chatting quietly. The room was too dark to see exactly who was gathered there, but now Seb knew where at least some of them were seated. General Kennard came to their table, arriving late, his solid frame unmistakable. He smiled and shook hands with Mulgrave, and then with Hiro Yuki. Then he sat beside someone who Seb didn't immediately recognise.

A voice asked, 'What are you doing here?' Seb turned and saw Billie standing next to him, looking up. She smelt good he thought. Perhaps she had stolen some of Janie's perfume.

'Just looking around.'

'But Janie's over there,' Billie said, pointing one little finger in the opposite direction.

'Yeah, I can see that.'

The spotlight followed Janie, and she was drinking in the hundreds of eyes that were on her, her voice comfortably filling the hall.

Billie snatched the champagne from Seb and took a swig.

'You're welcome, I guess,' said Seb.

'You shouldn't be drinking. You're her bodyguard, Seb.'

'Hey, who's that guy at that table to my left. Try not to stare. He looks familiar.'

Billie turned and stared openly. 'You're kidding, you don't know him?' Billie laughed and turned away. 'That's Kyle Beacon.'

'No...no?'

'Yeah. You know the movie star, and all-around *great guy*,' said Billie, wrinkling her nose.

'I know who *Kyle Beacon* is, but are you sure it's really him?'

Billie looked again, saw Kyle laughing loudly and leaning across the table. 'Oh yeah, that's him alright. Why are you scoping them out anyway?'

'Who said I was?'

'Come on! You're talking to me, I *know*...' Billie stopped and drained the glass.

'You *know*...' prompted Seb.

'Oh...nothing,' she said, giving a brief shake of her head.

Then there was a drum solo, a new song slowly gathering momentum.

'Did you know that they played these songs?' asked Billie, her foot starting to tap.

'No, I didn't,' admitted Seb, also feeling the beat.

'*Fly me to the Moon*,' said Billie.

'What?'

'The song. My folks loved this,' said Billie.

'We should dance,' suggested Seb.

'Huh? I don't...'

Seb grabbed Billie's hand and steered her into the gathering couples, guiding her onto the dancefloor. Billie initially resisted, but then tried to gather herself, and allowed Seb to lead. Within a couple of steps, she was spun around and memories of her Mom and Dad dancing around the living room to this exact song transported her back in time. While she preferred Frank Sinatra's original, Janie's cover was better than okay. She found herself smiling, and looking up at Seb, saw something then that stirred a strange feeling within her. *Why did it have to be this song,* she thought.

'We need to get closer to that table,' said Seb.

'Why?'

'Just do me the favour, okay?' said Seb, and they spun closer to where he knew the syndicate's members were seated.

Janie and Manson Villa played yet another cover – *Tangled Up* which Janie announced was a song by an artist she admired, – Caro Emerald.

'If you want to meet them, just go over there,' said Billie.

Seb stared at her for a moment. 'No, believe me, you don't want to meet with *them*.'

Billie stared over his shoulder as they spun, her eyes narrowing.

'How would I get a bug onto their table without them seeing?' asked Seb. The words were out before he could think about it. *What was it about this woman that made him so careless?*

Billie just stared at him. Obviously, she had heard him, but didn't know what to say.

He smiled, and they slid between two couples. 'I'm serious,' he continued.

'In this room, with the music and the background noise, you wouldn't pick up much conversation,' said Billie, twirling and slipping back into his arms. 'Trust me.'

Now it was Seb's turn to stare back at Billie, wondering how she would know something like this. 'Okay then. And you would know that...how?'

They danced in silence for a short time, Billie giving him a strange look, like she was trying to work out who the hell he was.

Janie saw them dancing and she smiled, but Christian's look was cool, perhaps angry.

'What's your angle, Seb?' asked Billie.

'My angle?'

'Come on!' They spun and worked back toward the table that Seb was interested in. Billie met his eyes. 'What are you really trying to do?'

'We're just dancing.'

Billie smiled. 'You *know* what I mean. The idea of bugging those people.'

'Can I trust you?' asked Seb, though this time he didn't look at her as they moved.

'If you tell me what you're doing, maybe you can trust me,' she said.

They were moving more in sync now. Jaz had encouraged Seb to improvise as needed. Surely this was what she would call *improvising*. 'You play along with this, and I can share some details.'

Billie smiled, and Seb mirrored hers. At that moment she felt an instant gravitational pull, which surprised her, for it seemed to come out of nowhere. The idea was shocking, and her smile dropped away with her eyes, now to the floor. Then she heard herself say, 'I could help you.'

'I need to hear what they are talking about. Some of them I don't know at all, and I need to.'

A waitress was passing, expertly slipping between couples. Billie pulled away from Seb, who reluctantly let go of her hand. She stopped the waitress and handed her the mobile phone. 'Photo please.'

'Okay,' said the waitress, reluctant at first, but obviously told to play along with these requests. The waitress took the phone.

'Over here, *babe*,' said Billie, dragging Seb to his left. They posed for the photo. 'Make sure you get the whole scene.'

The waitress took another couple of snaps and handed the phone back to Billie. They continued to dance. Billie lent in and breathed close to Seb's ear, 'See how I did that?'

'The table was in the background,' noted Seb, delighted. He liked the satisfied smile she gave him that went all the way to her eyes.

'I have skills.'

'I can see that.'

Billie whispered, 'I think we need to talk…after this… in private.'

Seb nodded. 'Yeah, sounds great.'

Billie looked at him, eyes narrowed. 'Easy big boy – I don't mean *like that*. I mean a *real* talk.'

'Oh…sure, I know what you meant.'

The music slowed, and Janie began a cover of the *Lina* song that Billie recognised as *I'm Not the Enemy*. The night wore on. Seb returned to a position near the stage, where he could give the impression of being a bodyguard. Christian said something as he returned, but it was lost in the swell of sound. Seb could lip read though and he knew that Christian wasn't complimenting his dancing style.

Billie fetched water for Janie, and the band between sets. As midnight struck, every table popped champagne corks, pretending it was New Years. Seb flinched as the corks exploded from the bottles, but Christian practically dove on Janie, forcing her down to the floor, pulling a small pistol from an ankle holster. Janie looked amused at first, and a second later, realising her dress was torn, became furious.

CHAPTER 12

Day 2

Billie had woken feeling seedy. The sun shone into the cabin, directly onto her face, and she knew how vampires must feel when they were about to burst into flame. Her head throbbed from a lack of sleep, combined with too much champagne. *Why on earth had she drunk so much of it?*

In the shower, she allowed the water to revive her as it cascaded over her face and neck. Slathering herself with body wash, she breathed in the scents of lavender and pachouli, and eventually she concluded that she was not going to die after all.

Back in her room, she slipped into a pair of cut-off shorts, and a slim, body-hugging t-shirt. Then there came a knock.

Billie opened the door with a jolt, and said, 'I drank way too much last night.'

Chuckling, Seb strode inside, glancing around. He slumped into a chair where he could see Billie, who'd begun brushing her teeth in the bathroom. She leant forward a little over the sink, face close to the mirror, and he appreciated the view, her figure trim and tight. He wondered how something as mundane as brushing teeth could be sexy, but somehow Billie made it just that.

'Can I get those photos? The ones from last night,' asked Seb.

'Sure, I won't be long.' She spat water in the sink, and splashed cold water, trying to feel less wretched. A minute later, she walked from the bathroom and Seb smelt a soapy fragrance wafting from her.

'What *were* you doing last night?' asked Billie.

'Look, I got a little excited.' He glanced up at Billie, who was staring at him. 'Seriously, I just wanted some snaps of some famous people.'

'I can tell when people are lying to me,' warned Billie.

'Last night...I was just kidding around. But thanks for playing along,' he said.

'You said you wanted to bug them. That's what you said. Don't go changing your story now.'

He laughed nervously. 'I wasn't really serious. Honestly, where would I even get a bug?'

Billie stared at him for a long moment. 'Here, I'll send the photos to you.' She found her phone on the side table and within a few seconds had transferred them to Seb's mobile.

'You're playing games, Mr Bonney, and I don't know what they are.'

'It's nothing...really.'

'Then you need to leave.'

'Did I say something?'

'Just get out.'

'No...listen. I can't tell you too much, but I have something I have to do, and it involves some surveillance.'

'On Hillary West, Kyle Beacon, and a bunch of other super rich and famous people?' Billie's hands went to her hips. 'What the hell are you up to Seb?'

'Best you don't know. I don't want you getting involved...in case they work out what I'm doing.'

'You involved me last night.' She shook her head. 'Do you even know what you're doing?' asked Billie.

Seb shrugged. 'I'll get it done.'

Billie stared for a long moment. 'Whatever Seb, as long as you protect Janie, I don't care what else you do. I need you to leave now.'

Seb looked like he wanted to say more but instead closed his mouth and walked to the door. Billie shut it firmly in his face as he looked back.

Billie leant hard against the back of the door and considered the situation. She didn't like being treated like a fool, and that's what Seb had done. No-one treated her like a fool – *no-one*. And yet... *what was he up to?*

She sat down in a chair and rested her head in her hands, trying to ignore the hangover. His dancing was good though, she thought. Why did it have to be *Fly me to the moon? And why did he have to smile at her like that? Goddam it.*

*

Seb returned to his cabin, wondering what he had done to offend Billie so much. What did she care about why he needed the photos? Jaz had encouraged him to improvise when needed, and he had, with Billie's help and quick thinking. Without delay he uploaded the photos onto the laptop, and then switched on the comms app.

But it wasn't Jaz whose face suddenly appeared before him. Instead, it was Harvey. 'What have you got, Straeker?'

'Where's Jaz?'

'Not here, obviously. We weren't expecting a call quite yet.'

'I move fast, Harvey. You should try it some time,' said Seb.

'What is it?' asked Harvey.

'First photos, taken just last night. Look in the background,' said Seb.

Harvey waited as the photos uploaded. 'These aren't bad. I can see Mulgrave...Yuki, Kennard, and West. Who is this other...is that?'

'Kyle Beacon. Yeah. He must know Hillary West. He seemed to. I assume that her circle includes movie stars.'

'Who's the girl, the one you're posing with?' asked Harvey.

Seb shrugged. 'Just a girl. She's with the band.'

Harvey was already reviewing the photos. 'There are a few other faces at the table. The room is a bit dark. We will have to get someone onto trying to clean up these images. I can see a few others that we don't know.'

'The table was busy, and they were chatting. I couldn't get a bug onto it without being noticed,' said Seb.

'It wouldn't have worked if you had. Too much ambient sound.'

'That's what…' began Seb, then closed his mouth.

'Stick to the plan. The bugs go in their rooms. Putting them in a restaurant or theatre or anywhere with that kind of sound level won't be effective.'

Seb nodded. It was exactly what Billie had said. How did a PA know about using *bugs* effectively? There was a lot more to Billie than met the eye, he thought.

'It's a good start,' continued Harvey. 'Check the files. You will have some new ones. The code guys have accessed and copied the ship's full schematics. You now have a map of where all known target's suites are located according to the ship's current records. Remember, you hold the master key. Get in and place some bugs in their rooms. You're all set now.'

'That easy, huh?'

'Jaz said you could do this. I didn't think she was…'

'Thanks.' Seb hung up, cutting him off. He locked the computer and went to the shower, turning on the cold water taps to full. He needed to get ready for round two.

CHAPTER 13

Billie was preparing to leave her cabin and was standing in front of some clothes she had laid out on the bed. She considered Seb, and his reluctance to admit what he was up to. Maybe she would just have to work on him to prise open his secrets. And she would - one way or another. But right now, she had to think about Meeks, and what he might attempt to do to Janie. She had her own problems, and it had nothing to do with Seb Bonney, she reminded herself.

Her phone rang and she snatched it up. 'Harry.'

'Hi Billie…*good to hear from me* you say.'

'Hi Harry, great to hear your voice,' she said deadpan, rolling her eyes.

'No time for *chit-chat*,' said Harry.

'You have something on Meeks?'

'No – forget him, okay. There's someone else.'

'I don't understand. Did you find something else on the laptop?'

Harry said, 'No, forget Meeks, and his laptop. Did you ever look at anyone else?' asked Harry. Billie could hear him breathing a little faster at the other end.

'No, Forsyth said he was certain it was Meeks. It's been *tunnel vision* on Meeks the whole way.'

'So, you never thought to look into Janie's background?' said Harry.

Billie blinked. 'No...it all happened fast. The scope of the investigation has been Meeks, *all the way*. I wasn't hired to look at the client.'

'Can I ask when the threats started?'

'Around three months ago,' said Billie. 'They were pretty direct. The timing was also consistent with Meeks breaking up with Janie.'

'We may have someone else to worry about,' said Harry.

'What have you got?'

'I did some proper background on Janie. It turns out that ten years ago she was in a car wreck. Some friends died.'

'Okay.'

'One of her friends went to jail.'

'Go on.'

'Yes, well...the friend, Ashlee Donovan, was found to be culpable, criminally so, as she was *higher than a kite* when she ran into the other car, killing three of them too.'

'Jesus...'

'Janie gave evidence against her friend. It sealed the deal. Ashlee went away, did hard time. The friend was only eighteen years old.'

'*Mother...*'

'Yep. You could be looking at an Ashlee Donovan. She is out now. Recently released.'

'Do you have any idea what she could look like now?'

'I don't have anything I can send you. I'm not going to try and hack the Department of Corrections. Further enquiries will take time, I'm afraid.'

'I dunno, sounds like a long shot, Harry.'

'What have *you* got? Have you even seen Meeks yet?' asked Harry.

'No doubt he's skulking round somewhere,' said Billie.

'Kid?'

'Yeah?'

'Be careful, okay?'

'Oh Harry, are you getting soft on me?'

'Keep your wits about you, Billie,' he said, and hung up.

She was about to slip her phone away, but then saw that she had three texts on her phone. They were from Sam Forsyth.

Have you found Meeks?

Ten minutes later, there was second text. *Janie is on the war path about something. Have you spoken to her? Tell me you haven't mentioned anything.*

The last text, sent three minutes ago while she was talking with Harry said – *Can you please come to Janie's suite? She wants everyone there from the band and that includes you.*

CHAPTER 14

Janie sat, legs crossed on her blue velvet chair, facing the room like they were her audience. Sam stood outside, just beyond the billowing balcony curtains, smoking a cigarette, his eyes hidden behind blue lenses. The bright morning sun filtered in, along with salty fresh air. Seb thought the promoter was delaying, not wanting to come inside and face Janie.

Leaning against a wall, Seb had positioned himself in the corner, arms folded across his chest. His face was deadpan as he looked at his watch. It was only the second day, but he was aware that he had a great deal yet to do. Brian came and stood near him, with a concerned expression. Seb wondered what could possibly be bothering Brian, whose body language betrayed a certain stiffness.

Billie was looking serious about something too. Could it possibly be the same thing that was bothering them both? Seb observed that she seemed distant, as though she was thinking something over, and he would have liked to know what. Had he confided too much in her? Was she the kind of woman to blab? His involving her the night prior was a move based on instinct, a *spur of the moment* decision. Jaz trusted his instincts – she had told him as much. So why now was he feeling unsure?

Then the cabin door opened and in filed the entire band. Seb had been introduced to them before, and he nodded as Garth, Micah,

Lachlan, and Viola sauntered in. Then the backing vocals walked in too – Aria, Georgia, and Sophie, glancing around the room, wide-eyed. They were all dressed in a roughly 1960s Bohemian way, with scarves everywhere - on heads, around necks and around waists. The girls wore high leather boots to their knees just below miniskirts. The guys had paisley shirts in purple and green, opened to their chests, with a myriad of chains in various designs.

'I've called you all here because I want answers,' said Janie, cutting through their murmur, causing the room to fall silent.

Everyone looked at her. But no one spoke.

'Come on folks,' said Janie. 'I know you're keeping something from me. Billie here is hardly a personal assistant.' Everyone glanced at Billie who gave a nonchalant shrug that made Seb smile.

Eyes busily flicked around, looking at the faces of those around them. But still, no-one replied to Janie.

'Sebastian Bonney – what can you tell me?'

'I don't know what you mean, Ms Reichenbach,' replied Seb.

'Bullshit!' she exploded.

'Janie, you need to settle yourself…' began Sam.

'No – you need to shut up, Sam. I'm talking now.' Janie stood abruptly and went to the drinks tray sitting on a sideboard. 'Should I do this?' she said, looking at Billie.

Billie shrugged but looked a little guilty as Janie poured herself a drink. It spilled slightly, but she seemed unaware. 'What's going on? Christian watches me, all the time, as he always does, but…last night he leaps on me at the sound of some champagne corks popping. I haven't seen him smile in weeks. Billie is new, and no offence to you Billie, but you're a shit PA.'

'None taken.'

'And you,' she was looking at Sam, 'and him,' she pointed at Brian, 'are always standing around whispering behind my back. When I ask what's going on, you just stare, like I've caught you out doing something. I have though, haven't I?'

'Everything is fine,' began Sam.

'You're a bad liar, Sam,' Janie spat.

'You should tell her,' said Billie calmly.

Sam raised a hand, stopping Billie.

'Finally! Someone who has my back,' said Janie.

'We all have your back,' said Brian, his eyes unable to meet Janie's.

Several band members mumbled that they didn't know anything and simply looked embarrassed.

'You seem to know something, Billie. Why don't you tell me?' demanded Janie, deliberately facing her and turning away from Sam and Brian.

Then Sam spoke. 'I've employed Billie to look into some troubles we've had. Nothing to concern yourself with too much, Janie.'

Janie refused to acknowledge Sam. She continued to face Billie. 'Tell me Billie.'

'Billie works for me, Janie,' said Sam.

'And you work for me!' Now Janie rounded on Sam, and with clenched teeth said, 'You...work ...for...me!'

Sam swallowed. Brian slunk away.

'There were threats made, to the band,' said Sam.

'The threats were to you, Janie,' corrected Billie.

The room went totally still. Janie turned slowly and looked at Billie. 'What do you mean? Threats?'

'You have had death threats. They were to you, personally,' said Billie.

'Is that why you hired Sebastian? Extra security?' said Janie.

Sam nodded, while Brian simply looked helplessly at Seb. Seb shook his head just slightly at Brian. But now Seb wondered if he had two jobs to do after all. This was unexpected.

'What's your role, Billie?' asked Janie.

'I'm a private investigator.'

'All of you out of here, now!' Janie commanded.

Everyone began leaving the suite. Janie held up a hand, 'Except Billie, Sebastian, and Christian.'

'I should stay too,' said Sam. 'I need to explain.'

Janie glared at the manager but said nothing. When they were alone in the room, Janie sat once more and drained her whiskey.

'Who's threatening me?'

'We think it's Meeks,' said Sam.

'Carlton?' said Janie, eyes wide. She shook her head.

'He's on the ship,' said Sam.

'I can take care of it,' said Christian.

'But we don't know it's him,' said Billie. 'In fact, I don't think it *is* him.'

'Look...' began Sam. Janie raised a hand and he stopped and walked away.

Billie continued, 'Meeks...Carlton, doesn't fit the profile. He is not the kind of guy that is going to be obsessed with one woman.'

'He's a player,' said Janie. 'I can't see him being all that upset about our breakup, at least not for more than a few days.'

'But he's here, onboard,' said Sam.

'He is, but I think it's just a coincidence,' said Billie. She knew that Meeks was looking less and less like someone dangerous, and that something more was at play.

'How can you say that?' said Sam.

'Sure, we can watch him if you want. But I don't think he's our problem,' said Billie. 'My source has his laptop. He's gone through it, back to front and upside down. There's no evidence that he sent the letters.'

'I want to see them,' said Janie.

'That's not a good idea,' said Sam.

'I decide what is good for me,' said Janie.

Sam handed over his mobile phone, allowing Janie to scroll through several photos. As she did, the blood drained from her face. Billie poured her another drink and pressed the glass into her hand.

'Fairly direct,' said Janie.

Billie nodded. 'Do you know why someone would mean you harm?'

'I have no enemies,' said Janie. 'I can't think…no – why would anyone want to harm me? This is so ridiculous!'

'This seems very personal,' said Billie. 'If I was to guess, I'd say it's someone who knows you. Someone who has a problem with you, for a reason.'

Janie shook her head. 'No…there's no one like that. This is a mistake.'

'Has there ever been any phone calls?' asked Billie.

'No,' said Janie. Then the singer looked at Sam, 'has there?'

Sam looked at his shoes.

'Has there Sam?'

'Carlton called once or twice when you broke up with him. We refused to switch him through to you. You'd already blocked him on your phone.'

'Just say the word, and I'll go and fuck him up,' said Christian. The ex-marine rose from his seat and stood at Janie's shoulder.

'Anyone else?' asked Billie, ignoring Christian.

Sam looked at them. 'You do get other calls, Janie. We screen them from time to time. Sometimes it's a fan, who we know has become obsessed. It's the price you pay for stardom. It's just a part of your life. You get this kind of thing – all famous people do…'

Billie was gazing out the window. Janie was pouring yet another whiskey.

Christian lent in and said quietly in Seb's ear, 'You watch her. Do your job for once. I'm going to look for Meeks.'

Seb barely acknowledged Christian, instead returning his attention to Janie, wondering who could possibly have a problem with her.

The door closed, and Janie looked up. 'Where did Christian go?'

'He said something about finding Meeks,' said Seb.

'That's not the best idea I've heard,' said Billie.

Janie shrugged. 'He will ask him questions and probably scare the shit out of him. But Christian won't do anything to him. He's not like that.'

Seb noted Janie finally looked relaxed, reclining with legs extended, whiskey cradled in her hands which were resting on her stomach. But he wasn't so sure that Christian meant this *Meeks* no harm.

CHAPTER 15

Janie had fallen into a kind of petulant or sulky mood. Seb really did not want to be around her. He had to get away to think, to plan what he needed to do next. This nonsense with Janie, and her stalker, had nothing to do with him. And so he began following Billie as she started for the door.

'Stay with me,' said Janie, taking his wrist. 'I don't know where Christian went, and I should not be alone. Not now, when I'm feeling...when I'm feeling all upset.'

Seb stopped and turned. His shoulders slumped a little, and he reluctantly sat down near Janie on the blue velvet couch.

'Make yourself useful, Seb.' Janie lifted her feet and placed them in his lap. 'I could do with a foot massage. Yes, that would help.'

Billie abruptly left, making a face at Seb as she closed the door behind her. His eyes were on her as the door closed, and she could see his discomfort. She didn't know what the guy's problem was. Wasn't he supposed to be her bodyguard?

Then, drawn by the aromas of bacon and eggs, Billie took some stairs up a level to an open-air buffet restaurant, hoping to catch up with Brian. She piled her plate full, and poured herself a pineapple juice, before wandering around deckchairs and tables. At last, she spied Brian, sitting alone, his bald head already becoming red in the morning light. The upper deck had a large swimming pool, and Brian was pretending to look at the ocean vista instead of the array of young women taking their morning swim. Sipping her juice, she sat near him, blocking his view of the pool.

'Janie wasn't supposed to find out yet,' said Billie.

Brian shrugged. 'Not until we had everything in hand. But she's too smart for us. Perhaps it was best to get it all out in the open. I'm staying clear of her for a while though.'

'Sam is so focused on the band that he's keeping things to himself.'

'Like what?' said Brian.

'Tell me about the phone calls. The ones that were for Janie,' said Billie. 'I should have been briefed on them.'

Brian thought for a moment. 'We get some calls – men usually, sometimes women - some of them seem normal, and others - groupies, fans, whatever you might call them, can get… emotional. You know? Carlton tried to get through a couple of times just after they broke it off. We told him to *sod-off*.'

'Not him. Someone else,' said Billie.

Brian gazed into the distance and said nothing for a long time. 'There *was* a woman – crying… incoherent is what you might call her. Anyway, we could barely understand her.'

'How many times did she call?' asked Billie.

Brian shrugged, then shook his head.

'How many from this particular woman?' pressed Billie.

'A few, *if* it was the same woman. It was around the time she broke it off with Meeks.'

'Did she give a name?' asked Billie.

Brian shook his head.

'Did she threaten Janie?'

'No. But she was insistent about wanting to talk to her.'

'But Janie never did?' asked Billie.

'No. We never allowed that to happen. We try to keep her away from all this kind of stuff. There's no need for Janie to be thinking about calls from deranged fans. It's our job to make sure she stays focused. This woman was…not right in her head.'

'So – she never gave a name?' Billie sipped her drink, then said, 'have you heard of an *Ashlee Donovan?*'

Brian's face was blank. 'Who's that?'

'Someone Janie knew a long time ago.'

He shook his head. 'Janie's never mentioned any Ashlee. We know all her friends. I'd remember an 'Ashlee' – and she doesn't know anyone by that name. Why?'

'Show me the threatening notes,' said Billie.

'Why?'

'Because you never did, and I might see something you didn't,' said Billie.

He unlocked and handed over his phone. The notes were in his photo collection.

'Are these in order?'

Brian nodded. 'They aren't nice. It's why we brought you in.'

Billie looked at the first note.

I'M COMING FOR YOU AND I'M GOING TO KILL YOU JANIE.

Billie went to the next.

You are dead to me. Soon you will be dead too. I fucking hate you, and everything you did to me.

And the next.

Why won't you just talk to me? I've been calling…and calling. Fuck you, fuck you, FUCK YOU!

Billie brought up the last one.

I can't believe you can just go on, pretending like you have nothing to say to me, and nothing to pay for. I WILL KILL YOU – SOON. Time is almost up.

Billie handed Brian back his phone. 'Nice.'

'This is bad timing. I can't believe she found out.'

'It doesn't sound like Meeks, does it,' said Billie. 'I mean, unless he is deliberately trying to sound like a crazed fan. There's no mention of a break-up, or jealousy that she's moved on.'

They sat and enjoyed the sun, but both were occupied with dark thoughts. Then Billie said, 'what can you tell me about Sebastian Bonney?'

'He's new. Brought on to add to Janie's security.' Brian refused to meet Billie's eyes, and she noticed it straight away.

'Did you vet him?' asked Billie.

'No need to worry,' said Brian. 'He's okay. Trust me.'

'How do you know? He's hiding something.'

Brian smiled. 'Because I know. He's been checked out. The guy is *above board*.'

'I seriously doubt that,' said Billie under her breath.

CHAPTER 16

Garth, the bass guitarist from the band walked across the deck toward Billie and Brian, his face serious, blinking against the sunlight. The sky above them was clear and blue, and the breeze held a hint of salty freshness. A group were frolicking in the pool, throwing a volleyball, and yelling excitedly. Someone splashed Garth as he passed, causing the guitarist to shimmy sideways on the tiles.

'Funny fuckers!' he called out and glared at them before continuing toward Brian. He paused, flicking his lank, slightly dampened hair back away from his eyes.

'Hey.'

'What is it, Garth?' replied Brian.

'Have you seen Christian?'

Brian shook his head. 'Is he *missing in action?*'

'Yeah, well…Janie said she hasn't seen him for an hour. She said he went to confront Carlton,' said Garth.

Brian and Billie looked at each other. Then Brian said, 'He's not back yet?' He sighed, adding, 'We better go get him, before he gets into trouble.'

Brian and Billie left their seats, following Garth past the pool. Billie watched the group as they cavorted, laughing, smiling, splashing each-other in a mating ritual older than time. She noted that although the new group had a range of tatts, oddly, they all shared the same one on their upper backs, just behind their right shoulder-blades. The shared image was in the shape of an eagle clutching a serpent in extended talons. Billie thought their group consisted of three muscular white guys, a short Indian woman, and a tall black guy. The Indian woman was preparing to do a backflip off the shoulders of the tall black man. Her muscular legs were locked, bent at an angle ready to spring. The swimsuit clung to her, tight and more revealing than anything Billie might consider wearing.

Billie walked too close to the edge of the pool, and was nearly splashed, though she suspected it was quite deliberate. 'Hey!'

'Hey yourself, sweetie!' said Robyn, leaping off her perch and swimming toward Billie.

Billie stopped and observed the group, who were also watching her. She wanted to know their story, because somehow, they didn't quite fit with the usual crowd on this cruise. Billie's curiosity caused her to hesitate where she stood, eyeing them in a way she hoped was casual.

Robyn swam even closer, then rested her arms on the pool's edge and looked up at Billie.

'Nice ink,' said Billie, taking in the design – an eagle, wings flared, both legs stretched out, clutching a hissing serpent within the outstretched talons.

'You like it?' beamed Robyn, turning her glistening shoulder to give a better view. 'I could show you more of them if you like. I have several, hidden around the place.' She grinned.

Billie smiled, flushing just a little. 'Thanks, but…' then shook her head. *Must be part of some club* thought Billie.

'Hey baby! Come for a swim!' called one of guys. He slicked his long hair back off his face, using the movement to flex his pectorals, and show off his biceps as water ran across the muscles in sparkling rivulets.

'Leave her be, Jonty,' called Clive. The Indian woman had made her way back to stand once more on his shoulders in the shallow end, her smooth legs trembling as she sought to find perfect balance. 'Maybe you could get your swimmers later, hey,' she said, smiling at Billie.

Billie offered one last smile, then frowning, she kept moving, trying now to catch up with Brian and Garth. It was nice to get so much attention, she had to admit. But she could tell they were playing a game, perhaps even taking wagers on who could *pick up* next. She glanced at them once more over her shoulder, wondering where such an eclectic group had come from, who they were and why they each sported the same distinct tattoo.

'Do we have Meek's cabin number?' asked Brian as Billie caught up with them.

'Yes, I located him when we first boarded,' said Billie.

'How?' asked Brian, glancing over his shoulder

'I bribed an attendant,' said Billie. Garth looked shocked, though he said nothing. He merely nodded, glad that Billie was on top of the situation.

'We should go and get Christian then,' said Garth, 'before he gets into trouble. What if he beats the guy up?'

Billie took a deep breath and with Garth and Brian trailing, followed the signs to an elevator, and then descended several levels. She knew Meeks and his newest girlfriend had their accommodation on the *gold level* where they would probably enjoy a slightly larger cabin, bath and shower, and a nice open-air balcony.

They followed a narrow, blue carpeted corridor heading in the direction of Meek's cabin.

'Why didn't you stop him from going?' asked Billie, staring at Brian.

'Maybe it's a good thing he went to confront Meeks,' said Brian. 'If Meeks is the one, then Christian might put some fear into him, and make it all go away.'

'We don't know it's him, though Brian,' said Billie. They soon arrived at 271. 'This is it,' said Billie. She knocked on the door, wondering what she would say.

A young woman's face appeared from around the cracked door. 'Yes,' she smiled. She was pretty, heavily made-up, with flowing red hair.

'Sorry to disturb. We're looking for a friend of ours – 'Christian'. Have you seen him?' asked Billie, trying to look around the woman, who she assumed was *Candy Rainbird.*

'Why would he be here?' The woman looked confused. 'You have the wrong cabin.'

'No, I think he was looking for Carlton,' said Brian.

'You know Carlton?' she asked.

'Carlton's an old friend,' said Garth.

Nodding, her eyes flitted between them. 'Oh really? Well, I'm Candy,' she said, opening the door a little more to reveal the room behind her.

Garth smiled and tried an awkward attempt to shake her hand which ended up with him just bobbing his head, and Candy clutching the towel before it could fall. They could all see the intricate ink that enveloped her upper arms and clearly spread elsewhere.

Candy continued, 'Well, the poor dear is feeling seasick. I'm afraid I haven't been able to get him to leave the bathroom all morning.' Her painted on smile turned awkward.

'If you see our friend...' began Billie.

'Christian?' asked Candy.

'Could you call me?'

But Candy was already closing the door. Her face disappeared, and the door snapped shut.

'How rude,' said Garth.

'Strange,' said Billie, turning away and heading back the way they had come. Halfway down the corridor, she said over her shoulder, 'I think we have a big problem.'

'Carlton has good taste,' said Garth. 'First Janie, now Candy...'

They made it to the elevator, and Billie pressed the call button. 'We need the ship's police. Do they have police?'

Brian said, 'I think they have security…marshals maybe, but not police as such.'

'What's wrong?' said Garth. 'Why is there a problem, Billie?'

'I'm not sure anything is wrong,' admitted Billie. 'But she was weird, and…'

'What?' asked Brian, as they stepped into the lift.

Billie shook her head. 'Did you see the patch on the carpet in her cabin?'

'It could have been red wine,' suggested Garth, who had also noticed the huge dark stain on the beige carpet.

CHAPTER 17

In the middle of the lowest deck accessible to passengers, the ship's administration block occupied a half dozen small rooms with windows facing both to the port and starboard sides. Signs on the walls announced they were entering *Administration and Security.*

As Billie, Garth and Brian approached along the corridor, they could hear raised voices. Two men and a woman were arguing. One of them was their bodyguard, the ex-marine named *Christian.* There was a desk, which folded back, and beyond it, a few chairs, and workstations with PCs. Beyond that, according to the signage, a 'holding area', a nurse's station, a kitchenette, a breakroom, and a few storerooms – all occupied the area.

'Hey Christian, what are you doing?' asked Brian as they approached.

Christian turned, face flushed, mouth half-open in the midst of an angry tirade. 'These fuckers won't tell me where Meeks is hiding out.'

'As we've said, we can't tell you where a passenger's cabin is located. They're entitled to their privacy,' said the uniformed woman. She was short, with dark hair pulled back in a ponytail. Billie could see from the look on her face that she had probably been going over this issue for quite a while with Christian.

The other security officer, a man with a spreading girth barely held in check by a straining belt, and a dirty moustache, was as red in the face as Christian. He glanced at the group as they came up to the counter, eyes wary.

'We were looking for you, Christian. Janie's worried about you,' said Garth.

'*She's* worried about me!' said Christian, tapping his chest with his thumb. 'That's funny. That's too fucking funny!'

'Can you people shut up out there?' came a woman's pained voice from the rooms behind the counter.

The female security guard rolled her eyes. 'Go back to sleep in there.'

Billie glanced inside, past the counter. If she leant to the left, she could just make out a brig or holding room. On a bench she could see someone lying down, forearm crossed over their eyes as if to block out the lights.

'Just a drunk,' whispered the female guard. Billie saw a name on the uniform – *Ranieri*. 'She will be allowed out in a couple of hours. She was balancing on the rail.'

Billie looked horrified and Ranieri nodded at her.

'I'm glad you've come. They won't give me Meek's cabin number,' said Christian.

'It's G-271,' said Billie.

Ranieri turned to Billie, surprised and annoyed. The big security guard – name *Jackson* also turned. 'How did…'

'Never mind,' said Billie.

'Let's go,' said Christian, turning away.

'No – wait,' said Billie, grabbing his shoulder. 'There could be a problem.'

*

Jackson stayed behind with the drunk passenger. The other security guard – Ranieri, accompanied them all back to Meek's cabin on *gold* level. When they arrived, Ranieri knocked for a solid two minutes. It was clear that no-one was inside or if they were, they had no intention of letting in the ship's security.

'How many more security people do you have on-board?' asked Billie.

Ranieri glanced at her sideways. 'Why? Are you expecting a crime-wave?'

Billie shrugged. 'I just want to know in case you have to apprehend someone.'

'It's just Jackson and me,' said Ranieri. 'In case you hadn't noticed, this ship is a little special. The occasional drunk, a stolen purse... that's as bad as it gets,' she said. 'If we need help, the captain can call more police out to the ship.'

'We need to go inside,' said Billie.

Ranieri looked dubiously at them, shaking her head. 'Because you saw something on the carpet? That's not enough, nowhere near enough to invade a passenger's space.'

'I don't have time to explain,' said Billie.

A moment later, the door popped open, and the red head was standing just inside the door. Her face was flushed; her make-up having run just a little with sweat. 'What's the fuss about? You again? We were just having some fun in the shower - you know what I mean?' They could see she was having trouble holding a robe across her shoulders, which had been hastily thrown on, and not quite tied at the waist. Billie again glimpsed a large tattoo across the top of her shoulder, and a bit of nipple. 'What are you doing here again?'

'Is Carlton in there?' asked Christian. They could hear the hiss of water cascading from the shower.

But Ranieri interposed herself between Candy and Christian. 'I think we've imposed on Carlton and Candy's time enough, don't you, sir.' She pulled the door closed and walked Christian away, guiding him by the elbow.

'Leave them alone,' said Brian, trying to get Christian's attention.

'Why should I?' spat Christian, rounding on Brian. 'Who are you to tell me what to do?'

'Christian...' began Garth.

'I tell you what,' said Ranieri. 'You go near that couple again... I will lock your ass up for the rest of the cruise. You got that?'

Christian stopped and stared at Ranieri. Without another word, he stalked away, heading toward the elevator, back stiff.

'I need to write a report now, don't I. Can you tell me why Christian is so angry with this Carlton Meeks?' asked Ranieri.

Billie watched the elevator doors close, Christian's face a mask of checked rage. 'We think Mr Meeks might have been sending Janie...'

'It's nothing,' said Brian. 'Just a misunderstanding.'

Ranieri looked at them for a long moment, allowing the silence to build and become heavy. If Jackson was like a mall-cop, this Ranieri was more like a New York detective. 'Don't let it become more than a *misunderstanding*, or that brig will be very crowded, very soon. You got me?'

'Yup,' said Billie.

'Were they in the shower together?' asked Garth. 'How did they fit? Have you seen the showers?' He was looking back over his shoulder, a stupid grin on his face.

Ranieri entered an elevator, this one going down. Before the doors could close, she said, 'If anyone goes near that couple, without me in attendance, you know what will happen. You get that *Christian* guy on a leash...or I will.' The doors closed.

'Nice lady,' said Garth.

CHAPTER 18

Day 3

Seb knew that General Kennard was still talking with the movie star Kyle Beacon in a restaurant bar called *Endeavour* on the top deck. It was around 11 pm, and the moon was riding high above them. The night felt chill, the stars seeming close enough to reach out and touch. Subdued music was coming from a quartet of jazz musicians on a small stage near the pool. They looked bored, and tired. The crowd of around twenty people listened as they played but were in no mood to clap as the quartet finished each piece.

Kennard and Beacon were drinking whiskey worth a hundred dollars a glass, from a bottle that sat on the table between them. They were kept company - Beacon, by his twenty-two-year-old actress girlfriend, Olivia something or other, and Kennard, by two women Seb assumed were 'paid' company that were on board for his entertainment. The three women chatted quietly, long legs tucked up beside them on deckchairs, manicured, slender hands cradling brightly coloured cocktails, their shoulders draped with light jackets against the breeze.

Seb was positioned a discreet distance away, sipping a glass of his own ten-dollar whiskey, not really listening to them, but getting a feel for how long they were likely to stay.

'Can I join you?' The woman had approached without Seb having seen her. When he looked up, he saw a classically attractive woman in a long evening dress, which may have been a very deep purple. With blond, carelessly tossed hair, contrasting dark eyeliner, and blood red lipstick, Seb wondered if her look was what magazines called *vampish*.

'Please,' said Seb, gesturing to the vacant chair opposite him.

'How do you do, by the way. I'm Clarice.'

Seb filtered through the names he had compiled in his head from the mission brief, recalling that she was Anson Mulgrave's wife.

Seb looked past her, and across the deck, where he spied Anson with two other women, who were dancing near him.

'You were the only person alone. Am I interrupting? You seemed far away,' said Clarice.

Seb shook his head. 'Not at all. Are you alone?' he smiled.

Clarice threw a glance toward Anson, but then said without hesitation, 'Yes, yes I am.'

'A drink then?'

She smiled, 'Please - anything, as long as it's not wine.'

'Two negronis,' said Seb, catching the attentive eye of a nearby waiter.

'A classic drink,' nodded Clarice. 'So, what do you do?'

'Me? Nothing interesting,' said Seb.

'Everyone on this ship is here for a reason. Whether it's to be seen in someone's company... or... perhaps you are a journalist, looking for a story? There are a lot of famous people on this ship.'

Seb shrugged. 'Can't we just be passengers, on a vacation?'

'Cruises are to rekindle tired marriages...or to run away to forget your past, to try to hit the reset button.'

Seb wondered if she was talking about herself. 'Not me,' said Seb, with just the hint of a smile as he met her eyes. 'I'm just here for a *good time*.'

Clarice nodded. 'A *good time*? Life seems to be about nothing else, and nothing more.' Her eyes hardened as she sat staring at her husband until Seb interrupted her thoughts.

'Would you like to dance? I'm not very good, but perhaps...'

'No...thank you,' she said quickly. She met Seb's eyes. 'You are handsome, I suppose you know that. I just don't want to dance.'

The drinks arrived, served off a silver tray. They each took a sip and Clarice turned her cool gaze back to Anson.

They sat for a while, listening to the music, Clarice rhythmically tapping a finger on her knee. She looked back at Seb, smiled, then drained her glass in a gulp. 'I have to go. It was very nice meeting you. I hope you find your *good time*.' She stood and walked away toward the rail. Then she lifted her face to the wind coming off the waves.

Resisting the urge to go and join Clarice, Seb instead returned his attention to General Kennard and the actor Kyle Beacon. Satisfied the pair were still entrenched in a long conversation, he threw back the last of the negroni and walked past the group. Feeling bold, he winked at Beacon's girlfriend, who just stared back at him as he passed.

Seb descended to the *diamond* deck, and walked toward Kennard's suite of rooms, the details of the layout imprinted in his mind. Outside the door, he saw no guards, no security or indeed anyone. He took the *magic key* as he had come to think of it and held it near the door's swipe-card reader. He heard a click, and then used his own card to enter. 'I'll be damned,' he mumbled.

He had no way of knowing if anyone would be waiting within, but as a lamp had been left on, he could see the entire room at a glance. The bed was a mess. Women's clothing was strewn all over the place. A breeze blew in from the balcony, shifting the curtains. Other than that – nothing moved. He walked in, quickly ensuring that he was alone. Taking a bug from his coat pocket, he switched it on, saw a small green light flash once only, indicating it was active. If the bed was ever made, he could not risk them finding it hidden beneath it. He looked around. Why hadn't they told him where to place these things?

He looked down. A small coffee table sat in the middle of the room, several glasses as yet uncollected by room service scattered across it. Though made of glass, it had a metal frame. He bent and looked underneath. 'That will do nicely,' he mumbled, reaching in and sticking the device up under the frame where two pieces came together. As the frame was black, the device would not be easy to spot.

Seb retreated back to the door and left the suite. As he walked along the corridor, he saw Kennard coming the other way. The corridor on this level was generous, and he walked wide around the trio, glancing out at the moon-dappled ocean through the windows. The two young women, one dark, the other a blond, were tucked under each arm, doing their best to look enthused at Kennard's groping hands. Seb barely glanced at them, and Kennard was too busy whispering into the blonde's ear to even notice him.

Seb walked into their wake, catching the mist of strong perfume mingled with good whiskey. Emboldened, he loitered for a few minutes and then walked to the other end of the ship. On the same deck, Anson Mulgrave's suite would be wide open. Rounding the curve of the corridor, he found a tall man standing outside Mulgrave's door. With a neck as thick as a bull, and a face that Seb could imagine plates being smashed on, he meandered past, enduring a challenging stare holding all the warmth of a medusa.

Feeling cheeky, Seb couldn't quite resist saying a quick 'Good evening.'

The hulking guard gave no reply, instead shifting his gaze to follow Seb's retreat along the corridor. So – Anson's suite of rooms was guarded, thought Seb, even when he was on another deck with his wife and girlfriends. This was disappointing. Anson's room was going to be tricky to get into.

Seb retreated to his own cabin, several levels lower in the ship, and collapsed on his bed. Knowing that the device was already recording Kennard, Seb closed his eyes and fell asleep within minutes.

*

It was two minutes past two in the morning. Billie couldn't sleep, her brain refusing to shut down. She was not seeing what was happening in this case, and it made her uncomfortable. Meeks was a *player,* someone capable of blackmail perhaps, but she could not see him sending actual threats.

It didn't help that the ship was in choppy waters, the movement making her feel vaguely queasy. Apparently, Harry was awake too, because her phone beeped, and she saw his name flashing green in the darkness.

'Sorry to wake you,' said Harry.

'I was awake.'

'Sorry if you were in the middle of something.'

'I was just lying here staring at the ceiling,' admitted Billie.

'I'm sorry.'

'Why?'

'Your love life is worse than mine, kid. When was the last time you had a real date?'

'Why are you calling?'

'Going to send you something,' said Harry. 'It's a compressed video file. I've gone through all those videos.'

'You've been watching porn again, so what's new Harry?'

'Meeks had thirty-three women on thirty-two tapes. One was a threesome,' said Harry.

'What a creep,' said Billie.

'The last one, something seemed odd.'

'Okay, how? What's your point Harry? Where are you going with this?'

'My point…yes…she was different from the rest of them.'

'What do you mean? She was actually into it?' joked Billie.

'No – she wasn't Meek's usual type…at all. The others had a certain look. They were all similar – longer hair, voluptuous…bigger tits.'

'I know what *voluptuous* means Harry. Go on.'

'The last one was kinda skinny… small breasts, tattoos, shaved head, and muscular. She looked like a punk. Not his usual taste.'

Billie thought about that. 'Who do you think she is?'

'I'm getting to that. Now…the time stamps on the video indicates it was taken around two weeks ago. I'd say it's his latest girl, Candy Rainbird. But it looks nothing like her – right?'

'Maybe he was fooling around. He's that kinda guy,' said Billie.

Harry said, 'Is it possible that she's…'

'Ashlee Donovan,' cut in Billie. 'You think she's *that* Ashlee.'

'Yeah, maybe.'

'The timing could be right – Janie breaks it off, then Ashlee shows up. She could have been stalking Janie before Meeks even broke up with her. Then she moves in on him knowing he's available, and knowing he is fairly loaded.'

Billie opened the video file on her phone. 'Stay on while I review this,' she said.

The video was grainy, shot in low light conditions. Like the other films, it had been edited, with angles obviously from a few cameras hidden around Meek's bedroom. The foreplay had been cut. What was left was a video of a thin woman with a nearly bald head having sex with Carlton Meeks in various positions. Her body was lithe, and she looked strong, getting herself into a variety of energetic poses, sweat trailing off her. At one point it looked like she made eye-contact with the camera, as though she knew she was being recorded.

Billie watched until the end. 'Okay, so she was the last one in the collection, and that was two weeks ago.'

'Yeah, a little over. So, this has to be Rainbird,' said Harry.

'Put a wig on her and it could be,' agreed Billie, trying to recall anything specifically about the red-head's face. But it was the tattoos on her arms that made her certain it was Ashlee. She was looking at the final frame, a frozen image of the face of Meek's lover, which she tried to zoom in on.

Harry said, 'The correctional centre refused to talk to me. They did give me a doctor's name – the psychiatrist that Ashlee Donovan was getting treatment from.'

'And?'

'Nothing–refused to talk to me. Patient confidentiality...*yada, yada.*'

'I guess it could be her.'

'It's her,' said Harry. 'I went into the prison itself and visited a couple of in-mates. I made out I was a relative. One agreed to talk to me, just to *chew the fat* with someone new. She told quite a story.'

Billie sat up in the bed, her phone hard against her ear. 'Go on.'

'Well...Ashlee went in a scared eighteen-year-old kid. She was picked on and abused, as can happen in a prison. She was beaten up a few times before she learnt how to play the game on the inside.'

'Poor kid.'

'Yeah, *poor kid.* Over time, she changed, and Ashlee started to fight back. Over the years, she became hard, both physically and emotionally. She ended up being the one everyone was scared of. The way she tells it, when the ten-year sentence was up, the psychiatrist said she was a danger to society and shouldn't be let out. But...they had no choice – she had done her time. She'd gone in a druggie who crashed a car and killed some people, and she came out something far worse.'

'What did she say Ashlee looked like?' asked Billie.

'Thin, muscular, covered in ink. A tattoo of angel wings spreading out on her back, and another of an ace of spades on her chest.'

'That's specific,' said Billie.

'Women's showers in a prison. I guess you can't hide that kind of ink.'

'How did she get tattoos in a prison facility?'

'She didn't. On supervised leave, once a month, she would see Dr Canning, at his offices. He allowed the tattoos to happen. He even arranged the artist to come to his offices when he had Ashlee there. He said it was part of her recovery from the trauma she was caused.'

'I wonder what else he did to her. Any more info?'

'She's dangerous, *very…fucking…dangerous*. Not my words, that's what the inmate said.'

'Harry?'

'Yeah kid?'

'She's here, on board. I've seen her. I have to go warn Janie and the others who we are really dealing with.' Billie hung up.

*

At 2:33 am, Christian left Janie's room where he had been sleeping on the couch. He locked the door to her room and set out to see Meeks. He just needed a few well-chosen words with the guy. It was a matter of principle.

He rode the elevator to Meek's level, and headed down the corridor, his shoes quiet on the carpet. The rooms on either side were silent, except for one where a tv was playing loudly. It soon dissolved into a distant hiss as he came to Meek's room. He paused. Should he reach for the gun in his ankle holster? Meeks was nothing to be frightened of, and he didn't want to be accused of drawing down on the guy. He could take him, just with his hands, if it came to it. He was about to knock, when the door opened a crack, and then wider.

It was the redhead – Candy. She was standing there, almost naked. A lamp somewhere in the room behind her shone through her patterned silk robe, left hanging open, exposing her small but firm breasts. One long leg protruded from between the robe, tanned and smooth. 'Christian?'

'Yeah,' he swallowed.

'He's not here. Carlton, I mean. He left. Did you want to come in?'

'I shouldn't,' he said.

She shifted just slightly, her hands on hips, legs apart, her robe gaping open a little further. She was cast in an amber light, her skin seeming to glow from within. She looked him in the eyes, daring him to look away, daring him to retreat. She held her face up, chin lifted, defiant.

For a moment he stared and walked into the cabin. 'Where is he?'

She closed the door behind him. 'Carlton? Not here, I told you that.'

'I need to talk to him.'

'Take off your clothes.'

'No. I'm not here for you.'

'Don't you want me?'

He swallowed. 'Can you turn on a light?'

'No- I like the dark.' She stepped in close to him, allowing the robe to fall away from her shoulders.

'We're not going to do that,' said Christian, gently pushing her away.

She stared, her eyes wide and unblinking. 'Are you one of Janie's bodyguards? I saw you on the docks.'

He nodded. 'I should leave. I shouldn't have come here so late. Tell Carlton that Christian wants to talk, okay?'

'Carlton left me. He's gone. He wants Janie back.'

'Where is he then?'

'Do you love her too?' She paused, staring at him for a long moment. 'Did you know that she took my boyfriend?'

'Carlton?'

'No – Matthew. He was mine, and she took him. Then she caused Matthew to die. It was her fault we crashed.'

'Matthew? I don't know any Matthew.' His eyes narrowed on her. Then he noted the tattoo on her shoulder – *Matthew.*

'He was mine. He loved me. When I die, I'll find him. He's

waiting on the other side. I have the wings already.' She turned, looking back at him from over her shoulder. She displayed her neck, her narrow waist, the exquisite sweep of her spine where it met the top of her firm buttocks. Though her nakedness was beautiful, it was the intricately inked feathers spreading across her upper back, strange, and lifelike that held his eyes.

'Do you also love her?'

'Janie?'

'Yes.'

'Always. I loved her from the day I began working for her,' said Christian. He had never told anyone before, and it felt good to say it aloud.

'She's not what you think she is. You can't ever trust her,' she said, advancing alongside him, her hand brushing his arm, then grazing his chest.

'No.' His voice was barely a whisper.

'You can pretend I'm her. You can say her name. I don't mind.'

As she walked to the bed, she maintained eye-contact over her shoulder. Her bare feet didn't make a sound on the carpet, so light was her step. Helpless, like a puppet, he followed, slowly peeling out of his shirt. By the time he was at the bed, she was seated before him, her blue eyes gazing directly into his, unblinking. He cupped her jaw, tilting her face up. She smiled, her tongue caressing her lips. He bent toward her mouth as her hand dipped between her legs, then tightened on something she had placed between the two layers of the mattress, something that glittered silver.

CHAPTER 19

Janie woke to something. At first it was part of her dream, but then as she stirred, she could hear banging. 'Oh my God - someone get the door.' The pounding continued, and she rolled onto her back, still in denial that she had to actually get up and see for herself what was happening. Flopping both feet to the carpet, she saw by her mobile phone's light that it was 3.30 am.

Billie pounded a fist on the door until Janie appeared, eyes bleary, a little red and definitely hostile.

'Where's Christian?' asked Billie, looking past Janie.

'How do I know?' Janie's hair was fluffed out, and without her high heels, she looked more like an angry teenager than a grown woman.

Billie glanced at the sofa, at the blanket, and the pillow. Christian had taken to sleeping in the same area as Janie of late. The wrinkled sofa and the blanket showed he *had* been there.

'What's this about, Billie? Can't this wait?'

'Do you know an *Ashlee Donovan?*'

It was as if Janie had been slapped awake. 'How do *you* know that name?'

'I think she's the one who has been threatening to kill you,' announced Billie.

Janie swallowed. Billie saw her pale a little. She took a long shuddering breath. Billie stepped in close thinking she might actually faint.

But Janie composed herself enough to sit down where Christian had been sleeping. 'That's a *blast from the past*.'

'I think she is on-board,' said Billie. 'She's Carlton's latest *gal*. She has been using an alias - *Candy Rainbird*.'

'She was sent to prison,' said Janie, distantly.

'She was…now she's out.'

'We didn't part as friends. I…had almost forgotten her. She was part of an old life…one that I had left far…far behind.'

Billie took Janie's hand, crouching before her. 'You could be in real danger, Janie. I suspect that she may have already killed Carlton.'

Janie shook her head, confused.

Billie went on, 'I haven't seen him once since we came aboard. But I've seen Candy…*Ashlee*…several times. What I've seen makes me wonder.'

'Why?'

'I know about the car wreck, and I know she went away for a long time. She may have been waiting this whole time for…'

'Payback,' said Janie, then gave a humourless short laugh. 'I never meant to hurt her. This was an age ago - *ancient history*, you know what I mean?' said Janie staring up at Billie.

'Not for Ashlee.'

'I never really got on with her, back then. I took her boyfriend – Matthew, and …it was something… I regret. I would never have admitted it then, but I did it just to show I could.'

'It's something young people do sometimes,' said Billie, thinking back on some of the games played between so-called friends during her high-school days. Some had been outright betrayals.

Janie nodded. 'I was young. I shouldn't have done it. Matthew died in that accident. Did you know that?'

'No.'

'Yes, it was one of the reasons I wanted her to go away. I couldn't forgive her. She was the target for my grief. I gave evidence against her. Not that they needed it. The blood tests showed how much shit was in her system when she drove into that other car.'

They sat for a while in silence, Billie allowing Janie time to wrap her mind around the news. Then Billie laid out what she thought had occurred. 'Ashlee only wanted to get close to Meeks because he had been in your orbit. Carlton's social media posts made Ashlee believe that he was still close to you. She was probably already stalking you, Janie. Her initial attraction to Carlton was because she thought he was your boyfriend.'

Janie rolled her eyes. 'It was a brief thing. I was not with him long.'

Billie continued, 'He was a steppingstone to get closer to you, and he has the money that Ashlee needed – all making him the perfect *mark*.'

'What now?' asked Janie.

'I think you are in immediate danger. I wasn't sure before, but certain events are starting to line up. You need to be especially careful from now on. That's why I came here now. This couldn't wait til morning.'

Janie's phone began ringing. Billie picked it up from the coffee table, and looked at the caller ID. 'It's Christian. Here, take it.'

Janie answered, putting the call on speaker. 'Hello, where are you?'

'Janie?'

'Ashlee?'

There was silence for a few seconds. 'Where is Christian?'

'He's here…with me. After all this time, you remember my voice?'

'Put him on.'

'He's mine now, Janie.'

'What does that mean? Put him on…' repeated Janie, staring now at Billie, her eyes round.

'You took Matthew, and I took your Carlton…and Christian.' They heard a silvery, demented laugh echo at the other end.

'What have you done?'

'Come and see,' she whispered breathlessly.

'Where are you?'

'In Carlton's cabin.'

The phone went dead. Janie threw the mobile down on the sofa and held her head between her hands, over her ears, 'What just happened?' Then Janie looked up. 'She had Christian's phone. We need to go…'

'I'll get the security people. Ranieri is capable…' began Billie.

'No! Get Seb. He will know what to do.'

'With respect, Seb is…'

'What? Lazy? Never around where he's supposed to be?' said Janie.

Billie nodded. 'He should be here with you. If Ashlee comes looking for you, he needs to be ready.'

'Get him out of his bed. Then get the police,' said Janie.

Billie had Seb's number in her phone from when she had shared the photos with him. She called. After only a few seconds, he answered.

'Get up here – now!'

'Where's here?'

'Janie's room.'

'Sounds fun.'

'No – we have a problem,' said Billie. 'Do you have a gun?'

'No.'

'What kind of a bodyguard doesn't have a gun?' asked Billie.

*

Though it was barely two minutes later, the knock on the door made Janie jump, bringing the singer from a deep reverie. A voice called - 'It's me, Seb.'

Billie let Seb in, and Janie rushed over to him and threw her arms around his neck. Billie stood back - eyes wide. Janie was acting the *damsel in distress*. Maybe it was something in her DNA, but she had decided that Seb was her best chance of staying safe.

'What's this?' mouthed Seb over her shoulder to Billie.

Billie mouthed back, 'I don't know,' and shrugged.

Seb walked Janie back to the sofa and sat her down, disentangling himself from her arms. He found the whiskey decanter and poured her a drink, then paused and poured himself one as well. 'What's happening?' He placed the glass in her trembling hand.

'We know who is sending the death threats,' said Billie.

There came another knock at the door. Billie went and answered it. 'Who is it?'

'Ranieri.'

Billie knew her voice. She admitted the security officer, who looked a little annoyed. 'It's…' she glanced at her phone, 'four am.'

'Christian is gone,' said Billie.

'God-damn-it!' said Ranieri. 'I told you what would happen if he went back there.'

'No, Ashlee called on his phone. There's only one way she could have Christian's phone,' explained Billie.

'Ashlee?' said Ranieri.

'Candy…Rainbird…is actually a woman called Ashlee Donovan,' said Janie.

Ranieri shrugged. 'So?'

'Try to keep up,' said Seb, a slight smile on his face.

'This is serious,' said Billie, rounding on Seb.

Ranieri turned to him. 'Who are you?'

'I'm her other bodyguard,' said Seb, pointing at Janie.

'Someone explain to me *what the hell* the problem is,' said Ranieri.

Billie said, 'Janie's been getting death threats. I think it's the woman in Meek's cabin. She goes by the name *Candy Rainbird*, but her real name is *Ashlee Donovan*. We just spoke to her on the phone…on Christian's phone. She made a threat against Janie.'

'What did she say?' said Ranieri.

Janie looked at Billie helplessly. 'She said she's 'taken' Christian.'

'What does that mean? She slept with him?' said Ranieri.

Impatiently, Billie said, 'Can you just go and see where he is?'

'You want me to go back to that red haired lady's cabin? And see if Christian is in there?' said Ranieri, pasting on a fake smile.

'You don't know the history,' said Billie.

'Stop! Let's go and take a look. Christian can tell us all about it.' Ranieri took Billie by the elbow, and they started toward the door. 'This is ridiculous. Rich people make me sick.'

CHAPTER 20

Day 4

The sun was just coming up when Ranieri and Billie approached Meek's cabin door. Ranieri knocked sharply, causing the door to slowly creak open. There was an acrid odour – coppery and pungent. Billie knew what it was before they entered. They went in, flipping on the lights. Ranieri drew a Glock from her hip holster and swung it around the room.

Christian lay on the bed, naked, pale, facing the ceiling. His groin had been sliced wide open; the femoral artery having released a torrent of blood across the white sheets. The second cut had been across his throat. His eyes were staring, a look of surprise still on his face. Billie felt a chill sweep across her as she palmed her phone and dialled Seb.

He picked up. 'How's Christian doing?'

'Not so well,' said Billie. 'Do you have eyes on Janie?'

'Yeah, she's just here. Why?'

'Christian's dead. Don't leave Janie's side.' She hung up.

Ranieri was standing in the corner, face pallid. Billie was pretty sure she was about to puke.

'Did you check the bathroom?' asked Billie. 'Hey, Ranieri, did you check the bathroom?'

Ranieri looked over at her. 'No. Wait here.' The security guard made her way to the bathroom and with the Glock extended in front of her, then rushed the room. 'Nothing in here.'

'We need to find Ashlee,' said Billie.

Ranieri was making a hacking sound and then Billie heard her throwing up the contents of her stomach into the toilet.

'Ahh jeez,' Billie said, heading for the balcony, feeling her own stomach beginning to lurch.

*

Just after lunch, Captain Jacques Phillippe walked into Janie's suite. He was a tall, slender man in his sixties, distinguished by a short grey beard and an immaculate white uniform. The shirt had captain's epaulettes on the shoulders. He observed the room, staring around at each face, noting that most of Janie's entourage, including the whole *Manson Villa* band was present.

Satisfied everyone was present, he slipped his cap beneath his arm, revealing a balding head, and acknowledged Janie with a nod. 'I'm sorry for your loss, madame.'

Janie had stopped crying, though her eyes were red. She was sipping at another whiskey, her fourth for the day.

The captain continued. 'Your...*Christian,* has been moved to the morgue. We have a doctor...Dr Shepherd ...and she will conduct an examination of course – though we know what happened.'

'What can we do about Janie's safety?' asked Forsyth.

'I only have two security guards for this whole ship. I have communicated with the cruise line's executive, and they have instructed me to continue the cruise as planned, and to keep this situation from disrupting our planned itinerary. They were clear that we are to hold course and maintain vigilance.'

'So that's it?' asked Janie.

'Madame, my hands are tied. There are many people on board who have paid a lot of money for this experience. Do not worry - the police in Hawaii have been contacted. Detectives will board when we arrive off Honolulu and conduct a thorough search of every inch of this vessel.'

'Is that really good enough?' asked Forsyth.

'I have my instructions. I can assure you that I have circulated this woman's description to all my crew and when she is found, we will subdue her. There are only so many places for her to hide. With her red hair, she will be easily recognisable.'

'What if she is wearing a wig?' asked Billie.

The captain looked at Billie. 'Why would you think that?'

'I think she is wearing a wig. She could have any hair colour, and any length,' said Billie.

'We are searching within the cabin. Perhaps we will find some clues. This *Carlton Meeks* is also missing, you say…though he could be hiding somewhere too.'

'He could,' allowed Billie, 'but I think he's dead too. So, captain, you have two murders, and a killer at large.'

He stared at her. 'No. We have one murder, and two possible suspects.' He turned to Janie and gave a very slight shake of the head. 'I don't know what trouble you have brought onto my ship, but I won't allow it to interfere with the other passengers.' Then he smiled, his crooked teeth showing for the first time. 'We must keep going, and you have more performances.'

'So, that's it?' said Janie as the captain exited the suite, softly closing the door.

'What do you want to do?' asked Seb.

'She will do what she needs to,' said Forsyth.

Janie took a long shuddering breath. 'I'm not sure yet.'

'Come on Janie,' pleaded Forsyth. 'There's a lot riding on this!'

Janie threw her remaining drink on him. He blinked as it splashed over his face and ran down onto his white suit coat.

'Get out now! Please.' Janie strode to the bathroom and slammed the door.

'Try to get her to see reason, old boy,' said Forsyth to Brian, before he too exited the suite. Slowly the rest of the band dissolved from the room, talking amongst themselves.

'How long did you know Christian?' Seb asked Brian.

Brian glanced toward the bathroom door. 'He came on around a year ago. He was a hot head, but Janie seemed to like him for some reason.'

'I never found Christian's phone,' said Billie, almost to herself.

'So, she might be calling again,' said Brian.

'Did anyone find Christian's gun?' asked Seb. 'He had one in an ankle holster.'

Billie lifted her shirt. Tucked there, against her belly, a small silver pistol sat nestled in the waistband of her jeans. 'You mean this?'

'Where was it?' asked Seb, looking pleased.

'On the floor, under the bed. Ranieri was busy yacking. I saw it and...'

'Can I have it?' asked Seb.

'Why?' she asked.

'Because I don't have one. And I'm supposed to be Janie's bodyguard.'

Billie took the small pistol from beneath her shirt and handed it to him. '*Supposed* to be her bodyguard? What does that mean?' She again wondered who Seb was, because he didn't seem to know much about being a bodyguard.

'Nothing,' said Seb. He examined the little automatic, turning it over in his hands. To him, it felt too small. Examining the weapon, he noted small print on one side – *Smith and Wesson - Chiefs Special.* It had blood on it, smeared across the handle.

'You said you were *supposed* to be Janie's bodyguard. If you aren't then who is? Or maybe you aren't a bodyguard at all.'

'He must have reached for it, but not had the chance to use it,' mused Seb. Sniffing the barrel, he said, 'It hasn't been fired recently.' He examined it more closely, pulling back the slide, and ejecting the magazine. Testing the weight of the trigger pull without the magazine, he then replaced it. 'I'll say this – those marine boys know how to keep a gun clean.'

'Don't change the subject! Tell me what's going on with you,' demanded Billie.

Brian went to a cupboard and dragged-out Christian's two overnight bags. Then after some riffling that went on for a few minutes, he came up with a small box of extra rounds of 9mm. He threw them to Seb. 'You should tell her, Seb.'

Seb stared hard at Brian, but the manager stared back defiantly. Then Brian continued, 'I think you need to get Billie involved in your mission, Seb. Things have gone awfully wrong for us so far.'

'Brian, I can't believe you failed to mention to Jaz what was happening with Janie,' said Seb quietly.

'Tell me what?' asked Billie. 'What mission? And who's Jaz?'

Seb refused to answer, instead turning his eyes on Brian. If looks could kill, then at that moment Brian would have keeled over.

CHAPTER 21

To calm her nerves, Seb and Billie kept refilling Janie's glass with whiskey. It was just after midnight by the time Janie finally fell asleep. Billie stood by as Seb carefully carried the diva from the couch to her bed, one arm cradling her legs, and the other beneath her torso. Placing her gently on the bed, he retreated from the bedroom as she began snoring quietly.

'I have to go now. She drank enough that she should sleep until morning,' commented Seb, glancing back at the sleeping form.

'You have to go?' asked Billie sarcastically from her seat near the coffee table. 'I suppose you have your *mission.*' Her tone was mocking, at least that's what she was going for. Whatever Seb was doing now could not possibly be more important than watching over Janie.

'Here, take this,' he said. Seb walked over and handed Billie the little automatic pistol.

She accepted it by the handle, though her eyes betrayed her annoyance. 'Where *are* you going?'

'I have some things I have to do,' he said cryptically. Seb glanced at Garth, asleep on the blue velvet couch. Brian was also dozing, a thin line of drool running from his half-open mouth. He was seated, propped on the floor, near Garth, his back leaning against the couch.

Neither man seemed to be worried about an intruder trying to enter the suite. Seb thought that they should be at least a little concerned, but he would not admit that to Billie.

He walked to the door, glancing back at Billie, who was watching him, disapproval plain in her gaze, the gun now resting within easy reach on the coffee table in front of her.

Seb said, 'Take the safety off. You know where that is, don't you?'

But she said nothing as he exited and locked the door behind him. The last thing he saw was her staring at him, with narrowed eyes, and a pinched tight mouth that probably hid gritted teeth.

*

Back in his own cabin, he seated himself before the laptop, staring at Jaz and Harvey, who were looking rather tired.

'This bodyguard gig is a problem,' announced Seb.

'It's just a cover. Don't let it get between you and the mission,' said Harvey.

'Easier said than…'

'What's going on?' interrupted Jaz.

'Did Brian tell you anything about *a situation* when you leant on him to get me undercover?' asked Seb.

'No. What situation?' asked Jaz.

'So, he didn't happen to mention anything to you that might have made you think that this particular cover was a bad idea?'

'Nothing. Tell me what's going on,' said Jaz.

'Janie Reichenbach is getting death threats. Someone is getting very close to making good on them.'

Jaz and Harvey sat back in muted surprise. After a pause, Harvey leant close to the camera. 'Stay on the mission.' He gave a small shake of his head as he said, 'She's not our problem.'

Seb smiled, though it was without humour. 'You're not here Harvey. Her real bodyguard is deceased. The guy, *Christian* was killed yesterday. He was sliced open in a couple of places that make breathing difficult – if you get me, and…well let's just say that the killer is not afraid to get dirty. And, you just want me to leave Janie exposed, while this psycho comes after her?'

Harvey angrily opened his mouth, but Jaz placed a hand on his arm. Jaz said, 'That leaves you as her only security?'

'And I'm no bodyguard,' admitted Seb. 'The cover is a problem. How am I going to get this done in time?'

'Do you know who the threat is?' asked Harvey.

'Billie thinks she knows.'

'Who's Billie?' asked Harvey.

'The one in the photo?' guessed Jaz.

'That's her,' nodded Seb.

'The little blond?' said Jaz, her nose wrinkling.

'She may be little, but she's not…if you know what I mean.'

'I have no idea what you mean,' said Harvey.

'I do,' said Jaz, now smirking. 'What's her angle?'

'She's a private investigator. She's chasing down leads, and she seems to know what's going on.'

They sat looking at each other across the ocean, but only feet apart. After a while, Jaz said, 'If you don't help them, then all of this could go sideways. Whatever you have to do, do it discreetly.'

'I think I know what you are saying,' said Seb.

Harvey looked at Jaz, turning slightly in his chair. 'Stop the recording,' said Jaz.

Harvey reached out, and a button was clicked. 'Okay.'

'You want me to take care of it?' asked Seb.

Jaz said, 'Whatever gets us back on mission. Capture or… *whatever*, if that's what it takes. And pronto.'

'You know, with that attitude, you people could be the CIA?' said Seb.

'Don't you ever say that,' said Jaz.

'Hard decisions get made in the field,' said Seb, rubbing his eyes, trying hard not to yawn. 'Sometimes a bad choice is the only choice,' as the yawn escaped him.

They all sat back for a while. Then Jaz reached out and turned the recording back on. 'Where were we? That's right. How many bugs are in place?'

'Just the one so far. It's in the general's room,' said Seb

'Kennard's room,' said Jaz.

'He didn't seem to have any security, so it was pretty simple. I hope they're all that easy.'

'Don't count on it,' said Harvey. 'Straeker, you need to get moving, pal. This is going along too slow. You won't make it at this rate. Get your ass into gear.'

'After Kennard's room, I tried to get into Anson Mulgrave's room, but it seems like he leaves a guard stationed outside even when he's not there.'

'Is there another way in?' asked Jaz.

'I hope so,' said Seb, but he couldn't think how.

CHAPTER 22

Anson woke, at first confused about where he was. The couch was an L shape, and he sat in the middle. Cool air billowed in past the curtains, fresh and tinged with salt.

Clarice, his wife, sat slumped over to his left, her nose sprinkled in a fine white powder, her eyes closed, and breathing deeply.

The glass coffee table was strewn with champagne glasses, empty bottles, and discarded clothing. Tara noticed that he was awake and though she watched Anson from the corner of her eye, she managed to lean in and place a lingering kiss on Marguerite's mouth. The blond stirred then, responding in kind. The pair sometimes did this because they knew it turned him on. They were still partially dressed, and as he watched, they removed each other's sequinned tops. Friends of Clarice, neither woman was supposed to be more than a companion to his wife, but somewhere along the way, they had taken to teasing Anson when Clarice was not paying close attention. It started as a kind of game but had slowly become a contest to see just how far they could push things.

At fifty-three, Anson could easily pass for twenty-eight. No-one really knew how he achieved this feat. The media speculated that he was getting very clever plastic surgery. Since he had met McTaggart several years prior, he had not only managed to stop the aging process but had actually peeled some years away. For years, Anson had financed a large part of McTaggart's operation. But that was then, and now the chemist was gone, he had to find another way to keep his lifespan on pause. Replacing the deceased McTaggart's operation was of paramount importance to Anson. It was vital that more serum not only be sourced, but that he had his own operation set up so that he was never again reliant on someone else.

Rising, he moved away from the two women, their bodies beginning to entwine. It was becoming more and more difficult to ignore them, to pretend he was not interested in their play. He poured another glass of wine, his back to the women. Opening a draw, he removed a small black leather case, then unzipped it, taking the last small vial, which was not much larger than a medicine bottle. It had an eyedropper attached to it, which he squeezed, allowing just two drops of blue liquid into the wine. Holding the small vial up before his eyes, he noted that it was still around three-quarters full. He then hid the precious object back where he had found it.

Anson observed his reflection in the mirror. The shirt, opened to his waist, revealed pectoral muscles that belonged on a younger, more perfect version of himself. His hair, shoulder-length and black, had lost the greys that had begun to take over ten years before, and had once more become lustrous.

He switched on the stereo, hearing the smooth voice of Bryan Ferry fill the suite. Walking to the shower, he stripped from his shirt and trousers, carelessly casting them aside. He drank the last of the wine in a gulp and felt instantly alive. The dose, though only small began to course through his veins like fire, and he trembled as it settled inside him.

A moment later, Tara walked in, peeling out of her remaining black underwear. She was tall, long legged, small-breasted, a little thinner than a ballerina, but with similar proportions. He turned the faucet, and water cascaded across them as she stepped in to join him.

'What are you doing? Clarice will...'

'She is asleep, yes?' replied Tara.

'What if Adam comes in here, or Kai?' Anson was referring to the two bodyguards stationed outside, in the corridor.

'I thought you were *the boss?*' she smiled, leaning in, and kissing him through the spray of water, then pressing herself firmly against him.

The truth was that Clarice would be jealous and would be livid if she now woke and saw what they were doing. Anson found this thought stimulating, as if he needed more encouragement than having just taken some of McTaggart's serum.

And then Marguerite was there, stepping into the shower. 'I would like some too,' she purred. Anson knew that she was referring to the serum. Both women had received the concoction on several occasions, and Anson knew that they were addicted to the stuff as much as he was. They would do whatever it took to remain in his inner circle, to share the precious potion.

'There isn't enough right now to share around,' he said.

'Okay.' Tara forced a smile, though for a moment Anson had seen her clear disappointment.

'Soon we will have more,' he soothed. 'Soon, we will have a new supply. That's why we're here. I'm making a new deal.'

In the other room, Clarice stirred. Remaining still, through slitted eyes she watched them showering together. She hated Anson for his infidelity, and she hated her so called friends for their betrayal. But she understood that each of them, herself included, were now trapped in Anson's orbit, and the thrall of the blue liquid that promised to keep them young forever.

CHAPTER 23

Day 5

Seb sat on the blue velvet couch in Janie's suite, listening as the singer belted out her latest songs while showering. He had reluctantly reached the conclusion that he needed Billie's help. Either she would take on the role of bodyguard to Janie, thus freeing him to conduct his surveillance, or she would help him to plant the bugs in each remaining room. It was, he now considered, the only way forward.

Billie entered the room with a bagel in hand, dripping sauce, which was somehow smeared across her cheek.

'What?' she said.

'Nothing,' said Seb, glancing away.

'You were staring at me,' said Billie, dabbing her mouth.

Janie's bathroom door was closed. They had the room to themselves. Seb decided to get to the point. 'I need your help, Billie.'

'With what?'

'You know who's sending the threats to Janie now. Your job is done…essentially.'

'I won't be happy until Ashlee is caught. Aren't you concerned about her?'

'Yeah,' he shrugged. 'If we keep an eye on Janie and keep her door locked, she's safe, I think. I have my own...*situation*.'

Billie said, 'Your job is to watch Janie.'

Seb was shaking his head, slowly but deliberately. 'No.'

'Huh?'

'I'm not here for her. That was Christian's job.'

'He's dead. You know that right?'

'I'm aware. My point is that I am not a real bodyguard and never was. It was a cover...my cover.'

Now Billie was shaking her head. 'This again? What are you doing? Are you trying to steal from those people. Are you a thief?'

'I'm not trying to steal anything. *I am here* to spy on them though.'

The silence in the room was complete, except for the sound of the shower. Although Janie had stopped singing, they could still hear the water running.

'You're so full of shit, Seb,' hissed Billie.

'I can prove it to you.'

'But why tell me? Shouldn't you be *keeping it secret?*'

'I have no choice. I can leave Janie alone and hope you can protect her, or I can continue to protect her the best I can.' He stood and continued, 'I can't be in two places at once. I'm running short of time. I need you to help with *my* job.'

'Spying,' said Billie, suppressing a smile that threatened to escape her.

'Yes.'

Billie finished the bagel. Seb could see her thinking as she digested his words.

'You're more qualified than I am,' he admitted. 'And I'm running out of time. I have to place the bugs before the seventh day.'

Billie thought *he's back to talking about bugging people*. She decided to play along now, just for her amusement. 'So, what happens on the seventh day?'

'A meeting.'

'Of this group…this syndicate?'

'They're a criminal syndicate, yes. They're bad people.'

'Bad people?' she chuckled. 'And who are you doing this for? The CIA or the FBI or…' This time she didn't bother trying to suppress her wide grin.

'The FBI,' interrupted Seb.

She blinked. 'And you can prove it,' reminded Billie.

'I'll be talking with my handlers later. When Brian, Sam and the others return, to watch over Janie, you need to come to my cabin. Okay? At 11 pm, you come and see me, and I'll prove to you that I'm legit.'

'I don't think so, Seb. This all seems… *off*. I'm not sure what you're playing at, or that I can trust you.' It was best that she was honest, even if Seb was not going to be.

Janie walked from the shower, dressed in a silk robe, a towel around her head. She paused and looked at Billie. 'There's something on your face. I think it's sauce.'

*

It was after dinner that Billie showered, washed, and conditioned her hair. Wrapped in a towel, she brushed her hair and then her teeth - all the while thinking about Seb, and what he had told her. He was an unlikely spy but then wasn't that the whole point – to seem unlikely. Her natural inclination was to want to know, to understand every little mystery in life that crossed her path. She had always been curious – even as a child.

It didn't hurt that she liked the way he moved, the way he talked, and how he looked at her when he thought she wasn't watching him.

On the other hand – he might just be a conman. He could be lying to her. That would be so very disappointing. Because then, she would no longer entertain any thoughts she had of…. *what?* Where did she see the relationship going anyway?

At 10 pm Billie was in her bed, watching a tv show, clicking aimlessly through channels, considering Seb's story. Was he a liar, and therefore someone to be wary of?

At 10.30 pm she clicked the tv off, dressed in her pyjamas and applied a moisturiser, staring at her reflection in the mirror. She returned to bed, turned the lamp off and crawled under the covers. When she closed her eyes, her thoughts again went to Seb, his infectious grin, those intense eyes. But surely he was certifiable, a bullshit artist, or at least a spinner of good stories.

At 10.45 pm she switched the lamp back on and swung her legs out of bed. 'He's so full of shit… isn't he?'

*

Seb heard a knock at the door at 10.59 pm and answered it. Billie was standing there, a robe wrapped around her. For some reason she was bare foot – like she'd forgotten to put something on her feet.

He pulled her inside by the hand, holding a finger up to his lips. Billie, playing along, entered the cabin silently. Seb gestured that she should sit in the corner on a chair, but not in front of the computer, where she could be seen by the camera.

Seb walked to the front of the laptop and sat before it. Outside, beyond Seb, Billie saw the moon riding amongst wispy clouds, it's amber light casting Seb's face in silhouette.

Billie was surprised when she heard a woman say, 'What's happening? You still have a lot of work to do, and time is running out. You need to get moving!' Billie sat forward, eyes narrowed, carefully listening.

'I know. Janie is convinced that Ashlee will attack her when she least expects. She won't let me out of her sight, most of the time,' explained Seb.

'I thought we were clear, Seb,' said a male voice. 'Janie is not your priority. You need to get the bugs set. Time's running out, Straeker. Janie will have to fend for herself.'

So, his name is Straeker. Billie watched as Seb nodded. 'Have you heard anything from Kennard's room yet?'

Jaz replied, 'Yes, we've heard things we didn't want to know about. That man is an absolute pig. But - he's had a conversation with Kyle Beacon which was ...enlightening.'

'How so? What did he say?' asked Seb.

Jaz said, 'It sounds like he doesn't like Anson - says the guy is holding out on them all. He doesn't trust Anson. Maybe none of them do.'

'Why?'

Jaz continued, 'He thinks Mulgrave has somehow located the remaining two scientists that were employed at the cliff house. The suspicion is that Anson is trying to set up his own operation and cut the rest of them out.'

'Why is he talking to Beacon? What does he bring to the table?' asked Seb.

Harvey answered, 'Nothing...really. He's a friend, that's all. Kennard is a big fan. He likes to tell people he knows Beacon. Goes to his opening nights – all that kind of stuff.'

'Beacon is probably getting something in return. Maybe a supply of the serum,' said Jaz.

'Should I try to bug Beacon's rooms?'

'No - Anson is the priority. You absolutely have to get a bug into Mulgrave's room,' said Jaz. 'If he does have the two scientists squirrelled away somewhere, we need to know where they are.'

'About that...' began Seb.

'Don't even think about it!' said Harvey.

'You don't even know what I was about to say,' said Seb.

'I do,' said Jaz. 'You want to use that girl – *Billie*. You want her to assist you. You can't. She isn't to be told anything. You understand?'

Seb stared at the monitor. Billie could see him thinking. Then

Seb said, 'How do I get into Anson's rooms? His bodyguards are always there. Even when he is somewhere else, he leaves a guard watching his place.'

'That means something,' cut in Harvey.

'Yeah, he must have something in there. Something he wants kept secret,' said Jaz. 'When you do manage to get in there, plant the device, but take a look around too. See what he's hiding.'

Seb, looking annoyed, said, 'Anything else?'

'That's it for now. Take care, Seb. We still have time. You can do this. Get it done. Janie's situation is regrettable, but she is not your concern.'

Seb reached out and hit a button on the laptop, ending the video call. He turned and looked over at Billie, where she was seated in the shadows.

'So, you aren't a liar,' she said quietly.

Seb stared at her. 'You sound surprised. There is so much you don't know.'

'You're last name – *Straeker*.'

'Right now, I'm Seb Bonney.'

'What's this serum they mentioned?' asked Billie. 'And what is the *cliff house?*'

'That is what this is *all* about. You wanted to know if they were smugglers. Well, that's kind of right. It's hard to explain. The serum… it's *a force of nature* – it makes you immensely strong, heightens every sense – might even stop the aging process!'

'It would be worth millions, if it were true,' said Billie, sounding amused.

'Billions, more like,' replied Seb. 'I've seen what it can do…you have no idea. It's incredible. The side effects are bad though – very, very bad.'

'What side-effects?'

Seb paused, trying to find the words that could possibly explain. 'With higher does, sunlight harms. I mean, they don't die in sunlight, but its unpleasant enough to stay out of it. It makes you aggressive too. After prolonged use, you begin to change.'

'Like an addiction?'

'Yeah, but worse than that. I mean an actual transformation… into something…it's hard to explain.'

Billie said, 'Do you have pictures in the file? This sounds crazy weird.'

'I don't know if photos even exist of what they look like.'

Billie stared at Seb. 'I take it you've see what *they* look like.'

'You would think I'm crazy.' Seb shook his head.

'That ship has sailed.'

'I don't know if I believe it myself.'

They sat in silence, Seb watching Billie's face, trying to get a read on her. She appeared to be contemplating everything about the conversation she had just heard, storing it all away in her head like a hard drive. After a while, she sat forward. 'I still don't know about any of this. Perhaps you should show me the files you have on this syndicate. If I agree, we will need to plan this, if you have a chance of getting those bugs planted.'

'So, you're in?' Seb asked with some surprise.

'I'm going to regret it, I know, but I could never walk away from something as strange…'

'As *exhilarating* you mean…'

'As *disturbingly, bat-shit crazy-weird* as this,' finished Billie.

Into the late hours of the night, they poured over the files, Billie enthralled by what she was reading. She was quietly absorbing all the information Jaz's team had pulled together for Seb to be able to place the bugs. Billie had a lot of questions, and Seb tried his best to answer them, though most of the time Billie seemed unconvinced.

After a couple of hours, Billie said, 'Why you?'

'What do you mean?' asked Seb.

'Why did they choose you for this? Why not send a team of agents if this is so important,' asked Billie.

'Jaz said they want to keep it quiet. The FBI don't have jurisdiction to operate outside of the states. So, they sent just little old me.'

'I think they are using you. This operation is definitely *off the books*. They have no legal jurisdiction.'

Seb tried to defend Jaz. 'They don't know who to trust. Jaz knows she can trust me...after what happened before.'

Billie looked at Seb. 'What did happen before?'

'The *Cliff House*...look, it's a long story.'

'If I am going to get involved, I want to know what it is I'm getting into. I need to know it all.'

Seb gave Billie an abridged version of his sister Angel's involvement with the gang known as *Dagon's Riders*. He explained to her his reasons for traveling to the town of Crabtree Cove to locate Angel, including how his efforts to discover her location had nearly resulted in his death. He tried to explain the gang's use of the serum that McTaggart had developed, and how it was harvested from a creature kept prisoner in a laboratory under the mansion.

By the time he was finished, Billie had a look of undisguised horror and disbelief on her face. 'I'm not sure I can swallow all of that,' she admitted.

Seb nodded. Her comment was fair enough. How could she believe it all when he was not sure he could either?

After a while, Billie said, 'I can help you get into their cabins to place the devices.'

'That's what I was counting on.'

'Show me the gear. What are we working with?' she asked.

Seb brought out the case and unlocked it. He showed Billie the small listening devices, and the *magic* door key that was programmed to let them into every single locked door on the ship.

Billie examined the gear and gave a nod. 'This is some good stuff alright. I could never afford any of this. It's not as high tech as what the CIA are rumoured to have, but it's high end all the same.' She replaced a bug neatly in the case. 'You mentioned that Anson

Mulgrave is a hard target. Maybe we leave him until last. Let's focus on the others – Hillary West, Hiro Yuki, and Kyle Beacon. Are there others?'

Seb nodded. 'We don't know if there are others involved. Kyle Beacon is just an associate of Kennard. Forget him.'

Billie nodded. 'With this key, it will be a *piece of cake* for me to get into those rooms, providing they aren't guarded. Perhaps I will go in as a maid. There are storage lockers all over the ship. Room service would allow someone like me to just slip in.'

'I can picture you as a maid,' admitted Seb with a smirk.

'Can you? Maybe later I could dress that way for you.'

Seb's face reddened.

Billie laughed, delighted that she had made him blush.

'Any ideas about how we handle Anson?' asked Seb.

'Not yet. There will be a way, though we may have to get creative when it comes to Anson,' she admitted.

Seb knew that Billie was now *on-board*. He could tell by the way she looked at him - there was no longer any hint of disdain, or uncertainty. Instead, she seemed excited at the prospect of helping him. She didn't understand that there was danger in being caught, or the consequences if they came for them. He considered saying something but thought better of it.

Jaz would not approve, and Harvey would be livid. But he needed her. She was here, now primed, and he had no doubt that she would not let him down.

CHAPTER 24

Day 6

Just before lunch, Hillary West left her suite of rooms, two steps behind her favourite bodyguard – Claudette, but two steps in front of her personal assistant, John. Her other bodyguard, Myles, a hulking, mountainous man, she instructed to remain outside her room. Hillary did not trust General Kennard, nor did she trust any of the syndicate. Myles was left behind to ensure that none of those people would try and leave anything untoward in her room. The syndicate was a group that needed one another, but it didn't mean that she would trust them, especially as such an important juncture was approaching.

Two minutes later, a short blond woman came along the corridor pushing a cart with sheets and towels piled atop it. The maid smiled at Myles as she approached, offering her best eye-contact.

'I'm here to change the linens.' Billie stepped up to the door, but Myles placed a meaty hand on her arm.

'You can't go in,' the voice seemed to rumble from within his massive chest and out of his thick neck.

'Well, alright, but Ms West said she wanted the sheets changed and a bit of a tidy up,' responded Billie. She paused, maintaining a steady gaze and ensuring that as she spoke, she did not avert her eyes. A good lie required direct, unwavering eye-contact.

Myles looked down at her, his height making Billie appear almost childlike. 'She said that?'

'She did.' Billie knew that Hillary West had indeed instructed the cleaning staff to attend while she was at lunch. Billie had spoken with a steward 30 minutes before and then had paid him a hundred-dollar tip to allow her a 'quick look' in the celebrity's room. Billie didn't lie to the staff member, but inferred that she was a reporter, looking for a scoop. The real cabin cleaner had initially seemed reluctant, but after another two hundred dollars was handed over, the deal went through, and Billie had quickly dressed in a maid's white uniform.

Myles nodded, then pushed the door open for Billie to bump her way into the suite. When the door swung closed, Billie walked in and found a very neat space, with hardly anything out of place.

Quickly, she pushed a chair over beneath a pendant light in the centre of the room. Then standing on it, she reached up and put the listening device inside the rim. She prodded the light, and it swung slightly, before the bug dropped out into her waiting hand.

But Billie had been expecting this. The room was set out similar to Janie's chambers, and she had thought about where she would put the bug when she was standing there an hour before. She had chewed gum since then, and now she took it from her mouth and used it to cement the bug on the inside rim of the light. When she pushed the light, it swung, but the device remained fixed. Satisfied, she climbed down off the chair, just as Myles stuck his head in the room.

'The light was filthy,' said Billie, shaking her head. 'No-one ever cleans these things.'

Myles stared at her. 'Hurry up.'

Billie dusted some surfaces in the lounge. Then she went into the kitchen, finding several empty bottles, which she placed in her trolly. She remade the bed, which had been left in some disarray. The bathroom was clean, but she spent five minutes wiping over the surfaces and generally trying to straighten everything out. She took the used towels and replaced them with fresh towels from her trolly. When she came back to the door, Myles was standing waiting for her, staring.

'You're a big boy,' said Billie as she pushed past the tall, muscular guard. Myles gave a ghost of a smile, as Billie wandered back down the corridor. Pushing the trolly before her, a slight, satisfied smile on her face, Billie hurried along the passageway and turned a corner. She leant forward over the trolley, where her cell phone sat amongst a tray of cleaning products. 'You can cross off Hillary West.'

'You did it,' replied Seb.

'Easy.'

*

The view from the external fire escape stairs over the bay, as she leant against the red brick wall calmed Jaz, along with the cigarette. She had given up the habit around 10 years before, but today, she seemed to just need it. She didn't want anyone to know she was having a smoke, and so she had stepped out, leaving Harvey alone inside.

Stubbing out the butt, and flicking it into the air, she then returned to the operations room to find Harvey sitting at a terminal.

'What is it?' asked Jaz as Harvey turned toward her, his face showing concern.

'The ship has changed direction, Jaz. We never saw that coming, and it bothers me. Where is it going?' Harvey brought up a map on his screen, a series of blips showing several ships in the sector of ocean around the *Estrella de Mar*. After a minute staring at the screen, he said, 'They are way off course now. If they keep going in that direction, they won't travel anywhere near Hawaii.'

'So where are they going? And why?' asked Jaz.

'If they hold course...' Harvey scrolled the screen sideways and zoomed in. 'There isn't much out there.'

'Day seven – where will they be if you project the course another day?' asked Jaz.

Harvey zoomed in and brought up a sector of ocean north and west of Hawaii. 'Somewhere around here I guess...presuming they maintain the heading.'

'These islands are small...' began Jaz.

'*Karabeki Island*...why does that ring a bell?' said Harvey.

'You know it?' asked Jaz.

Harvey's brow was furrowed. He stared at the screen. 'I'm sure I've heard that name. Let's find out what we can. That could be the destination.'

'For what?' asked Jaz.

'That's the question. Why go all the way out there for some damned meeting? Makes no sense.'

'There's a reason alright,' said Jaz. 'Someone is joining them, someone from that island is coming aboard. Then they will all be there.'

'If you're right, Seb needs to get *eyes on* whoever that is,' said Harvey.

'What if all these bugs are placed, and they choose somewhere else to have the meeting? What if they go ashore on an island out there somewhere and all our efforts are for nothing?' said Jaz.

Harvey shrugged. 'What were we supposed to do, Jaz? As it is, we're well outside our jurisdiction. The *Estrella de Mar* isn't a US ship, and they're not on US soil. We have no right to ask for additional resources – so you can forget that.'

'I know,' said Jaz, staring at the screen.

'This was always going to be a *long shot*,' said Harvey.

'Bringing Seb in on this was...' began Jaz.

'Risky' finished Harvey. 'But we had few options, and it was worth a try. He's an amateur. We needed a professional.'

'I know, but he will get it done, even if it's his way.'

'It was your idea Freeman,' said Harvey. 'If things go bad, we agreed you will take the fall. Why did you use Straeker? I could never understand your continued interest in him.'

'Look - Seb *is* a rule breaker. He knows when to follow the plan, but also when the plan won't work. I needed someone who will make decisions on the fly, respond when the situation evolves, regardless of whether you or I would approve.'

Harvey thought about all that. 'Okay.' But he didn't sound convinced.

CHAPTER 25

Seb followed Janie up the long sweep of stairs. The neon lights shining from beneath each step cast a golden glow onto Janie's calves. He was trying not to stare past her narrow waist at her perfectly formed backside.

Sure, there was a homicidal lunatic running around the ship, waiting for her shot at Janie, and sure he was supposed to be bugging the rooms of a criminal syndicate. But how could he ignore his surrounds? The *Estrella de Mar* was simply beautiful, from her polished timber handrails to her marble pillars. The cocktails that he was learning to appreciate, the seafood, the constant fresh ocean breezes…and walking around, two steps behind Janie, high heels showing off her long legs, perfume wafting back over him in waves, slipping from within her billowing silken robes that barely hid the bikini she had taken to wearing on her way to and from the several pools that she frequented – it was all so… *distracting.*

Then Seb thought about Christian, and his violent end. Ashlee couldn't just be hiding anywhere, thought Seb. Seb knew that her options were limited. The woman could not simply disappear into the bowels of the ship. She needed to eat, and her tattoos also made her conspicuous. Surely, she would be easily spotted by the crew. The captain of the ship - Jacques Phillippe, had so far refused to mention

Ashlee in any of his intercom announcements. He had not revealed what had happened to Christian either. Instead, the Captain had invited the guests to renew wedding vows or encouraged people to take part in one of the many games that his entertainment directors had set up around the ship. Where could Ashlee be?

When they arrived on the top deck, Janie walked around the pool, looking up at the blue sky, a smile touching her lips. She dropped a towel on a daybed and patted the next one over from hers, indicating that Seb should remain close.

The pool was occupied, by a group that looked familiar to Seb. Seriously muscled, tanned, they always seemed to be around somewhere. There was a tall, dark-skinned man, a short Indian woman, and three white guys – all around the same age, guessed Seb. They were rowdy, by his standards, but probably not when compared to a sorority house on spring break. Each seemed to have a tattoo on their shoulder, but Seb could not make it out clearly, as they splashed about and swam.

'Who are they, do you think?' asked Janie, slipping her sunglasses down her nose so that she could see them better. She was reclining on her pool chair, face tilted at the sun.

Seb bent his head to the side, squinting. 'They all have the same tattoo. I can't make it out, but if I had to guess – I'd say they were military.'

'Why do you think that?'

'Something military people do, especially if they come from the same unit…or have been through something together.'

Janie looked at Seb sideways. 'Do you have any tattoos?'

'I don't want anything to remind me of what I've been through.' He would have gone for a swim, as the water looked inviting and he was missing his morning runs. But he didn't want to show the scars on his torso, for he would have felt compelled to explain how he got each one.

Janie was about to say something, then thought better of it and closed her mouth. Seb was staring at her lips but caught himself and looked away.

Anson Mulgrave, naked from the waist up, waxed chest as bronzed as if he had spent his every summer swimming at an Italian seaside villa, walked onto the pool deck. Two women flanked him, neither of them his wife. Clarice walked a few steps behind them, her head slightly bowed. Seb had read Anson's file, and he knew that the blond was Marguerite, and the dark one was Tara. The two women, former models, were supposed to be Clarice's companions, but Seb could see in their body language that this was no longer strictly true.

Anson's file had him aged 53. Seb tried not to stare, because Anson looked like a young man in his late twenties. It didn't seem possible. Even Janie found herself staring as Anson and his entourage, now including a bodyguard, as they took residence in a group of nearby daybeds.

Seb saw the group in the pool, the *tattooed bunch* as he thought of them, suddenly depart, as if Anson was someone they didn't want to be around.

'Do you know who that is?' breathed Janie.

Seb knew, but he said, 'No, should I?'

'That's Lord Anson Mulgrave. Have you never heard of him? He's an art collector. I read an article on him once. I must say, he's much more handsome in real life.' Janie pulled her eyes from Anson, who had just slipped into the pool with barely a ripple, Marguerite and Tara sliding in near him, giggling at the freshness of the water.

Seb watched Anson's wife, and he didn't need to wonder what she was thinking. Clarice sat on a towel, her eyes following Anson, her expression stony. She was shorter than her companions, with a 1920s Hollywood hairstyle, pinned up in honey-coloured waves. Seb had heard Billie refer to photos of Clarice in the file as *vintage glam.*

Seb picked up his mobile, and texted Billie - *Anson on top deck. Room free?*

It was three minutes later that Billie replied. *No – still has a guard stationed...*then a frowny face emoji.

Seb locked his cell and put it on his towel. Anson was going to be *a tough nut to crack*. He looked up then and saw Clarice staring at him. He smiled, expecting her to immediately look away. Instead, Anson's wife returned his smile, her eyes locking onto his. It was a smoky, direct look that lingered.

Seb stood and walked to where Clarice was seated. 'Water too cold?'

She hadn't bothered wearing a bikini to the pool. Instead, she wore a short dress that showed off long tanned legs that were tucked up beside her. A delicate gold ankle bracelet caught the sun, drawing the eye. 'It's not the water that is bothering me.'

'Can I join you?'

Clarice looked over to where Anson was swimming with Tara and Marguerite. 'Can I stop you? You had your chance last time.'

Seb sat on a lazy chair and caught the eye of a passing waiter. Within moments he was holding a cocktail and had placed another in Clarice's hand. Her fingernails were long and intricately painted. It was a beautiful hand.

'You're with the band - Manson Villa?' she asked.

'I am. I get to guard Janie.'

'She's beautiful. Tell me, is she as much of a handful as I think she might be?'

'She is,' agreed Seb.

'So, has she taken you to her bed?' asked Clarice.

'No.'

Clarice gazed at Seb, as if she could read his mind. 'My husband sleeps with the help.' She turned her face back to Anson, who met her eyes briefly before looking away.

'I'm sorry,' said Seb.

She asked, 'What made you think you could just walk over here and talk to me?'

'Last time you joined me when I looked lonely. It was my turn this time.'

'Oh, how sweet. You came over to see if you could cheer me up.'

'I came over here to see if I could make you smile,' said Seb.

'That might be difficult,' she breathed. 'They are practically doing it in front of me. Those bitches.' She was staring at Anson, Tara, and Marguerite again, but she spoke to Seb, 'I wish I could somehow make him pay. But deep down…I'm not sure I care anymore.'

Seb glanced at Janie, who was staring at Seb from behind her oversized sunglasses. She was watching though she could not hear what Seb and Clarice were saying. 'Are you coming to the show? The band are playing again.'

'My husband and his new friends are coming I believe. I think I will give the show a miss.' She attempted a smile, but with eyes filled with sorrow, she only succeeded in looking as bereft as any woman he had ever seen.

'I think I will give the show a miss too. Perhaps we could have another drink?' asked Seb.

Clarice stared at Seb for a long moment, and her face changed. The sorrow fled, and in its place settled what might have been excitement and determination. Seb stood. 'Later then?'

Clarice said nothing, just watching Seb as he retreated to Janie's side.

'Did you get what you wanted?' asked Janie from behind the sunglasses, her face deadpan.

'She's lonely,' said Seb.

'Is that what a girl has to do? Look lonely? Here I was wearing my bikini to the pool, making you walk two steps behind me…and all I had to do was *look lonely*.'

CHAPTER 26

From halfway up the theatre's tiered seating, Seb observed the band practicing. The theatre could seat around 300 people he estimated, and had a high, lofted ceiling. Like any theatre on dry land, it had small balconies on either wing. *Manson Villa* had assembled at around 10 am, which for them, was early. They had spent an hour discussing with the young ship's entertainment director how she wanted the show to proceed and the arrangements for the sound and lighting set up. Seb observed that the timing for finalising these details was rather late, given that they were scheduled to perform this evening. Several members of the cruise staff had discreetly positioned themselves in the back rows to preview the forthcoming performance. Seb observed them seated in small clusters, engaging in quiet conversations.

Seb focused on the band, who were plucking strings, and testing the acoustics within the space. They were now performing a track, Janie lending her voice. Having engaged in a conversation with Billie until nearly 3am, he stifled a yawn, then tried to conceal it.

The concert was an invitation only event, and the second of Manson Villa's three planned shows for the cruise. Russian acrobats would perform on hoisted ropes above the stage in the second part of the performance. The show was billed as *a spectacle that no-one would soon forget.* The two impressively muscled acrobats, one male and one female, now swung above the band, performing flips and turns, balancing, and showing off generally. Janie only glanced up at them once as she sung, but Garth took the time to wave, his smile mirrored by the two acrobats.

Billie made her way up from the stage area, looking pleased. She sat near to Seb. 'I have the list of ticketholders. You can thank me later.'

'How is it that you can get these things?'

'I have talent. It's what I do. Anything can be bought on this ship. But this time I used my charm. I told the entertainment director, *nice girl* - that Janie had a special song planned for a guest, and she wanted to make sure the guest would be in attendance.'

'Sneaky.'

'Yes I am.' She looked pleased with herself. Seb could tell that she lived for this kind of thing.

'Are *they* on it?'

'All of them. Yep.'

'Good.' Seb nodded. 'We're going to switch it up. You will watch Janie tonight. I think I can get into Anson's suite during the performance.'

'That's bullshit! You should be watching her Seb – not me.'

'It's what has to happen.'

'You know as well as I do that Janie is going to be at risk tonight more than at any other time. Ashlee is bound to make an appearance,' said Billie.

Seb nodded. 'You're probably right. But I'm not going to get closer to getting into Anson's room than tonight. I have no choice.'

'I heard you chatted up his wife. Is that your big plan? Get into her pants while you get into her room?'

'Janie told you, huh? It was you who said to me *we would have to get creative*.'

'You're going to sleep with her?' asked Billie.

'The groundwork is laid. I've spoken to her…flirted a little. Are you saying you've never done something like that? In your line of work, you've never smoozed up to someone for a case?'

'Smoozed? What is that?' Billie shook her head in disappointment. 'Look, if Ashlee takes a run at Janie tonight, you want me to protect her? I don't like it.' Billie now recalled Jason, an employee at a local country club, and how she had used him on the last case. She had gained his total trust by sleeping with the guy, then left him cold. In hindsight she hated what she had done, and now – she hated that Seb was right.

'I've seen the way you handle a gun. You know what you are doing,' said Seb.

'That's target practice. I've never shot anyone,' said Billie.

'I made a connection with Clarice. I need to use it. I may not get another shot.'

'You're assuming she doesn't go to the show tonight,' said Billie.

'I am.'

'When this is over, you will owe me.'

He smiled, 'Yeah, I know, anything you want.'

*

The warehouse was buzzing. Harvey's techs were charting the *Estrella de Mar* on a large screen tv.

Harrison, an analyst with an impressive bushy beard, cleared his throat, causing Jaz and Harvey to look up. 'Okay folks, I'm ready now. If you will look at this.'

The radar image of the *Estrella de Mar* disappeared from the screen, replaced by a satellite photo of Karabeki Island. The island was dominated in the middle by a large, extinct volcano. It had formed a mountain that sloped down to thin beaches, and one or two areas of flat ground. In the image, ragged white cloud floated above the summit, and white beaches surrounded the island, with deep blue lagoons.

Their eyes were drawn to several ships coming into the harbour, long white wakes shown by a series of overhead photographs, taken from a satellite, and magnified. Harrison clicked to the next series of images, which showed the ships unloading large crates.

'What is this?' asked Jaz. 'What class of ship are these?'

'Container vessels. Big ones,' said Harrison.

'So, not navy?' asked Jaz.

'Not navy,' agreed Harvey.

'These were taken three years ago,' said Harrison. 'These…' he clicked to another photo, showing huts, 'were taken just weeks later. Whatever they were doing, they did it fast.'

'So, the island is now inhabited. By whom?' asked Jaz.

'I found no records of anything existing on that island. No navy outpost, from any country in the region, no resorts, nothing,' said Harrison.

Harvey was watching, his brow furrowed. 'But I recall a report. The name Karabeki is so familiar.'

Harrison smiled. He looked pleased with himself. 'These next ones I had a lot of trouble getting my hands on. I wouldn't exactly call it hacking, but…'

The screen now showed several boats being towed into the harbour.

'What's this then?' asked Jaz.

Harvey sat forward. 'I think I am remembering now. There was a report about refugees heading for Hawaii. They disappeared off the radar. Our government were tracking them out of the South China Sea and into the Pacific. They were originally thought to be heading for the Philippines, but they didn't stop there. The people smugglers were using ships to island hop, refuelling and re-stocking at each port.'

Jaz nodded. 'I seem to recall that. There was a flotilla of around twenty boats, all crowded with refugees. They disappeared. It made the news. The reports said they hit a storm…and just sank.'

'This is only a month after the huts were built. They never sank. We can't be sure they are the same boats, but I'm pretty certain they ended up here,' said Harrison. He clicked through several more images, showing the ships unloading, lines of people snaking off the vessels and onto the beach near the huts. Perhaps two hundred souls were living on that island.

'Well, someone had this intel, and sat on it,' said Harvey.

'Someone who could pull strings,' said Jaz.

Harrison stood in front of the screen. 'I did well to find this.'

'Yeah Harrison, you did,' nodded Jaz.

'This raises an awful lot of questions,' said Harvey.

'Like what are they doing out there?' asked Jaz.

'And who is doing it?' said Harvey.

'Why is the *Estrella de Mar* making for that island?' said Harrison.

Jaz ignored the question. 'We need to tell Seb something about this,' said Jaz.

'Like what?' asked Harvey.

'I have no idea,' admitted Jaz. 'But he needs to know that he is probably going to Karabeki Island, and we have no idea what's on it.'

'Harrison, we need more up-to-date images of the island. Something recent,' said Harvey. Then, staring at the screen, eyes squinting, he continued, 'And see if you can find anything about McTaggart having gone there. Come to think of it, cross-check all names from the syndicate against *Karabeki*. Do it now.'

'On it,' said Harrison, striding away.

*

In her security hub, Ranieri had received a call just twenty minutes before, complaining of an odour coming from a room on the seventh deck. Apparently, the smell emanating from within the rooms was so bad that the cleaner had not dared to enter. Instead, he had called security.

'You ready?' asked Ranieri, pausing as she gripped the doorhandle, and drawing her pistol. Jackson gave a curt nod, then used the universal room key to unlock the door with a click. They stepped inside, Ranieri aiming her weapon ahead. But nothing appeared, and all was still. Jackson closed the door behind them as a few inquisitive passengers from nearby cabins gathered outside, trying to peer past and around the two guards.

There was an unnatural stillness pervading the room. The air was heavy, redolent of copper, mixed with worse. Dim light filtered through green, opaque curtains at the far end of the room. They paused, listening for signs of life, but all that came back to them was a deep silence that filled them with dread.

'No-one could be in here now – not in this,' whispered Ranieri. She gave a cough, then quickly produced a handkerchief, which she pressed over her nose.

They walked the short corridor to where the space widened, allowing them a broader view of the interior rooms. 'Anyone here?' she called. 'We're security.'

In the middle of the living room, a figure sat slumped, propped in a chair, his head tilted forward. A gag had been placed in his mouth. Ranieri observed that a long, deep cut had severed his jugular vein, for blood had spurted and flowed down over the underclothes he had been dressed in. She moved forward, clearing the room, swinging the pistol left and right.

'This is Mr Johansen,' said Ranieri, pausing beside the corpse.

Jackson advanced on the bathroom, and kicked the door open, ready to fire his weapon. He paused there, lowering the gun, and Ranieri could see that he was composing himself.

'She's dead too.'

Ranieri pulled her phone. 'Captain, we've got two more murders. Two passengers – Mr and Mrs Johansen. I'll come back to you soon.' She ended the call before he could respond. The last thing she wanted now was to be told how to do her job.

'Was she killed first?' asked Jackson, turning away.

'I don't know,' said Ranieri, coming to the door and peering inside. 'How would I know? *Goddamit* – what the fuck is happening on this ship?' Unable to look away, she took another two steps into the room, noting blood splatter on the tiles at her feet. In the bath, her head at an impossible angle, eyes staring at nothing, the woman seemed to lay tangled in her own limbs. The bath was coated with trails of sticky, congealing blood, the pattern no doubt important, but beyond her ability to analyse. Like her husband, her throat had been savagely opened, creating a gaping wound from ear to ear.

Swallowing down a rising gorge in the back of her throat, Ranieri retreated from the bathroom, conscious now of further disturbing the crime-scene. She followed Jackson into the bedroom, where the cupboard doors had been flung wide. Clothing had been left scattered all over the floor. Bright sun dresses, in yellow and blue lay discarded amidst bikinis and skirts.

'His clothes weren't touched, but hers are all over the place,' said Jackson.

'We know who we are looking for,' nodded Ranieri.

They retreated to the exit and paused. Outside, the corridor was filling with people, the murmuring growing louder.

'When are we stopping at Hawaii?' asked Jackson, holding a cloth over his nose and mouth. The big guy was standing in the doorway, trying not to breath. He had opened the door a crack and kept putting his face into the corridor to get a breath of fresher air.

'Soon,' said Ranieri, peering back into the suite. 'Don't touch anything. But we need to find the knife she used - if we can. They will want to take prints off it. This room will have to remain as it is, locked up tight. We need to take some photos too – before the bodies are moved.'

Beads of perspiration had begun to form on Jackson's brow, whether from the uncomfortably warm, still air within the close confines, or the disturbing situation they now found themselves in.

'This would never have happened if folks were warned that we had a killer running around.'

Ranieri could not disagree, but she knew her orders. More passengers had gathered in the hall outside. Some were asking questions of each other about what was going on in the room.

'Don't let them in... don't let anyone see in here,' said Ranieri, grasping Jackson's arm. 'If you must go, you can stay out in the corridor. See if you can get them all to leave.'

Captain Phillipe had made it clear that no word of any murder should be allowed to circulate on the ship in case it caused a panic. So far, Jackson and Ranieri had managed to keep the killings confidential.

Ranieri lifted her radio to her mouth. 'Jemma, get two gurneys down to Room 709. And two boxes. We have two more homicide victims and they need to be moved. No...wait - we will move them tonight when no-one is around. Not a word to anyone, okay.'

Jackson stepped into the corridor, closing the door behind him. Though muffled, Ranieri could hear him pushing people away from the doorway. 'Nothing to see in here folks. Just a couple of passengers who are a bit ill. We are looking after them.'

She turned and walked back to the body strapped to the chair. Kneeling, she examined the corpse and began taking photos from different angles. 'I'm sorry,' she said sadly. 'You were in the wrong place at the wrong time.'

Ranieri flinched when Jackson said, close to her ear, 'Who are you talking to?'

'No-one...just talking to myself,' she whispered. 'This is so fucked up.'

'Ashlee can't hide forever,' said Jackson.

'Sooner or later the psycho bitch will show herself and we will have to do something about it,' agreed Ranieri.

Ranieri had pulled her gun before, a few times in her career, but she had never actually shot anyone, and she had certainly never killed anyone. Staring at the corpse, she told herself that things would get better soon, when the detectives from Hawaii could board the ship, and start a real search. It would be their problem then. In the meantime, she knew that they may have to subdue or even kill Ashlee, and the idea was not appealing.

'Before they take the bodies away to the morgue, we need to take lots of photos of the scene,' said Ranieri.

'Okay.'

'I'll stay and do that. I'll use my phone. You wait outside. Keep people away from the room. Tell them whatever you have to. Maybe tell them that there is sickness in here and that they could catch something if they hang around.'

CHAPTER 27

It was mid-afternoon, and Janie had retreated to her rooms after their lengthy rehearsal. Janie, Forsyth, and Brian were chatting about the upcoming show, debating what the opening song should be. Billie and Seb stood at the other end of the room, leaning against the wall, arms folded across their chests, engaged in whispered conversation.

Three loud chimes sounded across the ship's PA system, causing everyone to stop what they were doing. The voice on the intercom had a French accent, and by now, everyone knew who it was.

This is your captain speaking. Our scheduled stop at Hawaii has been delayed. We have changed course and will not stop at our next port of Honolulu. There is a hurricane forming off Hawaii and for the safety of the ship, and the comfort of passengers and crew, I have decided to take the Estrella de Mar around this weather event. If you have any questions, please talk to me or your nearest crew member. I apologise for this inconvenience.

'A hurricane?' said Forsyth, stepping out onto the balcony and looking up at the sky. He walked back inside. 'I can't see anything. What the hell is going on?'

Seb and Billie wordlessly looked at each-other.

Brian said, 'I wonder where we are going then. We need those coppers to come on board and find…you know who.'

'You can say her name,' said Janie quietly. 'I won't fly into a tizz, or anything.'

Sam and Brian exchanged glances. Then Sam turned to Billie. 'Can't you help the security people locate Ashlee? I think perhaps they could use your assistance.'

'We were told to stay out of it,' said Billie. 'They don't want our help.'

'But I'm paying you,' said Sam.

'I was paid to get to the bottom of who was threatening Janie, and I did,' said Billie.

'Now I wish to hire you for another purpose…' began Sam.

'Leave her alone, Sam,' said Janie, whose earlier anger toward Sam had only slowly abated. 'Billie's no cop – it's not her job to locate Ashlee.' Then meeting Billie's eyes, she said, 'I don't mind if she stays with us…with me.'

'What about Sebastian?' asked Sam.

'What about him?' said Seb. 'I'm no cop either.'

'He stays with us too, at all times,' said Janie firmly.

Billie went out onto the balcony and scanned the horizon. Seb joined her a moment later. 'Do you see a storm?' she asked.

Seb looked around. The sun was shining, and there were few clouds anywhere. 'The waves are the same as yesterday. There is no swell. If a hurricane was forming, within a hundred miles, you would see big waves. I'd say the captain is changing course for another reason.'

Enjoying the silence, the salt air and gentle breeze, Seb and Billie decided to remain on the balcony. They sat down on sunbeds, watching the waves from behind their sunglasses. Seb put his feet up, and fully reclined, his hands behind his head.

'There's no storm. Where are we going now?' asked Billie.

Seb was silent.

'Hey! I said – *where are we going?*'

Glancing at Seb, she noted that his eyes were closed behind his sunglasses. *How could he take a nap now?*

CHAPTER 28

In the early evening, Seb returned to Janie's suite, showered, and refreshed. He found Billie, Sam and Brian waiting for Janie to appear from her bathroom.

'I think Janie's nervous,' said Brian quietly, glancing at the bathroom door, which had remained closed for over an hour.

'She will be fine,' breathed Sam, though his face said otherwise.

'The next performance is in an hour,' said Brian. 'She doesn't want to do it. We may have to convince her.'

They all knew that Christian's death, and Ashlee's threats had Janie sitting precariously *close to the edge*. The alcohol she had plied herself with for days was no longer in her system, and the numbness was replaced by a strangely energised anxiety.

Janie suddenly burst from the bathroom, wearing only a bra and panties. Sam and Brian quickly retreated from the room, wordlessly closing the door to the corridor behind them. But Seb followed her progress, drinking in the sight. Her gold hair was up, pinned by something shiny, showing a long perfect neck. Even Billie goggled for a moment at the flesh on display before her eyes came back and rested on Seb.

Seb merely smiled and then finally dropped his eyes to the floor, or anywhere other than Janie.

'Where the hell is my outfit?' Janie demanded, striding around the room, flinging open cupboard doors.

'Which outfit?' said Billie. She was no longer technically her PA, but Billie wanted to help Janie get dressed as quickly as possible.

'The red one. The only fucking red outfit I have, Billie.'

'Umm, maybe it's down with the laundry, getting mended. It had a tear, remember.' Billie shrugged.

'Go get it, Billie. Why the fuck are you still here?'

Billie left the room as Janie stopped her pacing and stared at Seb. 'What?'

Seb, trying to look anywhere but at Janie, said 'you say *fuck* a lot.'

'Fuck…fuck…fuck-fuck-fuck!' she fired at him. 'I'm the *fucking* boss. You're the *fucking* help. I can say whatever the fuck I want, and there's not a fucking thing you can fucking say about it.'

'I should go,' said Seb, walking toward the door.

'Stay put, Sebastian!'

Seb stopped, halfway to the door, not bothering to turn.

Brian stuck his head inside the room, his eyes resting on Janie. 'Everything alright?'

'Get out, Brian,' she spat.

He goggled at the sight of Janie, resplendent in her underwear, and then shot a look at Seb, before pulling his head back out.

'You are my bodyguard if you hadn't noticed yet. You go where I go and do what I say.' She was standing close to him now, her head barely reaching his chest. He could smell something on her – something intoxicating.

'This doesn't seem right, me being in here while you get dressed.'

She walked away from him, toward the full-length mirror beside her bed, her panties opaque and sheer. She stopped and examined herself. 'Come on Sebastian, surely, you've guarded women before. You probably even slept with some of them.'

He stared at her, and she smiled. 'Are you saying you can't control yourself? Come over here.'

He hesitated.

'Come here, Sebastian.'

Seb walked over.

'When Billie returns, you will stand in the corner, out of the way. But right now, you need to scratch my back.'

'Huh?'

Janie turned, and looking in the mirror at Seb, said, 'I have an itch. Just scratch the middle of my back, ok?'

Seb scratched her back.

'That's not it. It's under the bra strap.'

Seb shoved a finger beneath the bra strap and scratched. Her back was flawless and arched inward beautifully.

She pressed back and sighed, 'That's better.'

Billie walked in at that moment, holding a glittering red sequined dress and stopped. At that moment also, Janie's bra popped off, Seb having accidently unclasped it.

But Janie caught it before it revealed anything. 'You men, always thinking you can get away with something.'

Seb walked away, his back turned. Billie came in and handed Janie the garment, but looking at Seb, her eyes flashing.

'Stand there while I get into this thing, Billie. I need someone to balance on.'

'I didn't mean to interrupt,' began Billie cooly.

'You didn't…' began Seb.

'You might have,' said Janie, and her laughter filled the room. She straightened, with Billie zipping the dress tightly from behind. Billie brought the matching shoes.

'How does this look?'

'*Fucking* awesome,' said Seb.

'Language Sebastian, what would your mother say?' said Billie.

Janie laughed. Billie didn't see the joke.

The door opened. 'Are we ready?' asked Garth, his head peeking in.

'Do you knock, you fucking pervert,' said Janie.'I could be getting dressed in here.'

Garth's head withdrew, and Janie said,'How is the makeup?'

Billie looked at her closely.'I don't think you need any.'

'Ohh, she's a love. What do *you* think Sebastian?'

'I'm your bodyguard, not your makeup artist.'

'Good with bras though,' said Billie, meeting his eyes briefly.

Janie laughed, her mood now having switched from nervous and angry to just nervous.

Seb's phone beeped, and he saw that Jaz had messaged him. *Need to talk ASAP.*

Seb glanced once at Billie, then slipped out of the room as soon as Janie went into her bathroom. He made his way back to his cabin.

No sooner had he sat down in front of the computer than Jaz appeared. Seb said,'What have you got?'

'We think we know where the ship is heading,' said Jaz.

'The captain finally announced that we are going around a hurricane. We're no longer going to Hawaii.'

'That's bullshit. There's no hurricane.'

'So, where the hell are we going?' he asked.

'We think they always meant to go to Karabeki Island,' said Jaz.

'Karabeki? Never heard of the place.'

'Me neither, until earlier today.'

'What's out there?' asked Seb.

'We don't exactly know...*yet*.' said Jaz.

Seb shook his head. 'Something feels wrong about this. They wouldn't be all the way out in the middle of nowhere without a good reason.'

Although Jaz knew that there was a definite connection between the syndicate and the island, she was not ready to start guessing what that was. Instead, she posed the question,'What do you think, Seb?'

'I'm just the guy who bugs rooms.'

'I'm asking you. I trust your instincts.'

'Do you? Cut the crap Jaz. I'm out here on this ship, in the middle of nowhere because I'm expendable.'

'I'm sorry you feel that way. The truth is – yeah, we can deny having anything to do with you if this all goes bad. But I wanted you on this because I know when it comes down to it, you will do the right thing.'

Seb looked at the time, and seeing it was late, went to the cupboard to retrieve a suit. He removed his T shirt and pants. 'You may not like what that is. The *right thing* I mean,' said Seb.

Jaz watched as Seb slipped on a white button up shirt, then changed into the suit. After a minute she said, 'I'll keep you updated...should anything come to hand.'

'Jaz, before you go - how does the captain simply change direction mid-way through a cruise and get away with it?'

'That's easy. Hillary West owns the *Estrella de Mar*.'

'The whole thing?'

'You don't own half a ship. Yes, we discovered she acquired it only four weeks ago. The captain will be doing exactly as she commands. She is also the owner of the whole cruise line.'

'She bought the cruise company?'

'These people are elites, Seb. They get what they want, when they want it. Don't forget that they will do anything to keep their secrets. You need to be careful.'

'I know...but there are two bugs left to place. Anson Mulgrave and Hiro Yuki. I have less than 48 hours.'

Jaz nodded. 'How will you do Anson's room.'

Seb grinned. 'I have a plan.' Seb reached out and hit the 'end call' button.

Seb went to the bathroom mirror to check himself one last time. Hillary West cared enough about the meeting to buy the ship, and everyone on it. She was the real captain of the *Estrella de Mar.*

He left the bathroom and gazed from the port hole out at the sea. He had never heard of Karabeki Island. But this was always the destination. If Jaz wasn't tracking the ship, no-one on board would have any idea where they were going.

No-one except the syndicate.

CHAPTER 29

M*anson Villa* were pumping, the volume blasting across the ship. The theatre was packed, the crowd noise lost in the music. Although dark, strobing lights flared and beamed around the stage and across the audience like lasers fired by alien spacecraft.

Five minutes into the performance Seb *eye-balled* Anson with his two girlfriends as they arrived late, moving along a row halfway up the terraced seating. Clarice was not with them.

Seb left his place at the side of the stage. As he strode away, he nodded at Billie, who returned a cool look. Seb had left her Christian's pistol. She was now Janie's last line of defence. As Seb left the theatre, he snatched a bottle of champagne out of an ice-bucket as it was being wheeled in on a trolley.

Taking the elevator down a level, he could distantly hear the thrum of the concert above. He followed the corridor to Anson's suite, finding a big guy standing guard. Seb walked up to him.

'I'm here to see Clarice.'

'Go away.' The guy was maybe six foot five, with a square, boxy head. He could have been a model thought Seb, if people were giants, and designer brands were made for gorillas.

'She's expecting me.' Seb held up the champagne bottle.

'You should leave, little man.'

Just then the door behind the guard opened. Clarice was there, blond hair and gauzy dress backlit against the golden glow from a couple of lamps within the room beyond. 'Let him in Kai.'

'Anson said...' began Kai.

'Mr Mulgrave to you,' she snapped.

'Mr Mulgrave...' began Kai.

'Is – not – here!' barked Clarice.

Kai looked over his shoulder at Clarice, his massive form still in front of the doorway that had now opened completely.

'Come in,' said Clarice sweetly, peering around Kai, smiling at Seb.

Seb stepped forward, and reluctantly, in slow motion, Kai stepped to the side looking displeased.

Clarice shut the door after Seb entered and locked it. Before Seb could say another word, Clarice took the champagne and set it on the table. 'I wondered if you would come.'

'How could I not?'

When she turned around, Seb stepped close. He only had a moment to wonder what she might do - as she reached behind his head and stretched up to kiss him, her tongue diving into his mouth. She pulled him back toward the bed, and collapsed onto it, her fingers quickly undoing his buttons.

*

Jaz had wandered outside, cradling a mug. She was taking a few minutes outside the warehouse to have a coffee, trying to relax, when Harvey called. 'Get up here. Something is happening.'

As Jaz entered the control room, Harvey and Harrison turned to her, excited expressions lit by the bank of monitors. Harrison cast the image from his screen up onto the large monitor on the wall.

Harrison said, 'We have a vessel approaching the *Estrella de Mar*.'

On the screen Jaz could see a blip, slowly coming into range of the cruise ship. It looked like it was still some distance away. 'How do you know? Could be anything. Fishermen…another liner…'

'No,' said Harvey. 'They are staying at the same range, matching the speed of the Estrella de Mar.'

'They're *shadowing* them,' said Jaz.

Harrison was nodding. 'Yep. Definitely.'

*

Afterward, Seb rolled over and drank some water from the bedside table.

'You know, I never asked your name,' said Clarice. She sat up in bed, her cheeks flushed, watching Seb beginning to dress. Seb looked back at her. She was lovely, with her hair mussed up, her eyes direct and playful.

'Call me Seb.'

'You could have lied. I can tell though that you didn't. That's *actually* your name.'

He put on his shirt. 'I can't stay long.'

'My husband is not a nice man. His friends…are not nice people either…but I sense you know that Sebastian. He calls them a *club*, like they are a team playing some game. Is it a game?'

'Maybe it is to him. But what they are doing hurts people. They hurt my sister.'

'So, they *are* bad people?'

Seb turned and met her eyes, then nodded.

'I will be punished for this liaison. But I want you to know it was worth it,' said Clarice.

'You could leave him,' suggested Seb.

'He may try to punish you too. I'm afraid Kai knows your face now. Tell me, Sebastian, did you come here for me…or Anson?'

He hesitated. 'I came here for Anson, and his friends. But I found you.'

'Oh, how sweet,' she laughed, 'but I am no fool. I knew from the moment we met the other night that you were not quite what you seemed to be. I've been around my husband's friends long enough to know when people are hiding things, when they lie, and when I can trust them.'

Seb reached into his pocket and took out a bug. 'Where should I put this?'

Clarice stared at the device for a long moment, then laughed. 'You are a bold one, Sebastian. How do you know you can trust me?'

'You're nothing like him. Men like him don't deserve women like you. You should get out before it's too late.'

'Give it here. I will find a place for it,' said Clarice.

*

Janie was bouncing across the stage, well into her fourth song, a cover of the Sheena Easton hit from the 80s – *Strut,* when the acrobat swung out over her head. It seemed strange, for the two Russians were not supposed to play their part in the performance until the second half of the show following the intermission.

She glanced up at a trapeze as it swung back, saw a woman looking down at her from perhaps fifteen feet, and instantly recognised the haunted eyes within the pale, white-powdered features.

Billie only glanced up after she saw Janie drop the mic and attempt to run off stage. At that moment, a figure landed on top of Janie with a loud *thud,* pinning her to the floor. Billie's hand dove into her belt, beneath the shirt, and brought up the Smith and Wesson automatic.

But it was Garth and his bass guitar that saved Janie, a forehand blow that knocked Ashlee's lithe form off Janie and rolling across the stage with a lingering *twang.* Janie began crawling away, desperately heading for the edge of the stage. The drums stopped, and a hush fell.

Billie's weapon was now up, and she took aim at Ashlee, holding her breath, but feeling a shake in her hand as she tried to steady herself. The audience was behind Ashlee. She couldn't afford to miss.

Ashlee was back on her feet, and she slashed out at Garth, her bald head gleaming in the stage lighting. Garth fell back, clutching his shoulder. Ashlee straightened, her eyes finding the crawling form of Janie. She strode toward her, the knife held low in her fist. Billie tracked her, trying to steady her aim, one eye half-closed as she stared down the sights.

Ashlee reached Janie, her left hand grappling her slender leg, halting Janie's departure, the knife coming up in the other hand.

There were shouts, and there were screams. Billie squeezed.

The shot, almost lost in the tumult, sent Ashlee buckling to her knees with a yelp of dismay. She let go of Janie and clutched her leg. Looking around, Ashlee saw Billie and snarled. Now it was Ashlee crawling across the stage. Billie got her feet moving, air suddenly coming back into her lungs. She rushed to Janie's side as Ashlee fell from view over the edge of the stage.

'Where is she?' shouted Garth, leaning out and peering across the platform.

Billie pulled Janie by the arm, backing away from the edge of the stage toward the band, who had now gathered around their singer.

'She's gone in there somewhere!' Garth pointed down over the rim of the stage into the darkness where a myriad of cables and cords jumbled amongst amps and switch boards. 'You should get her. Don't let her leave.'

'Where's Seb?' asked Janie, staring around her.

Billie advanced up to Garth, the pistol held out in front. She peered into the dark space beneath the stage, but she couldn't see Ashlee anywhere. The crowd was surging to the exits, a river of bodies fleeing the concert. From the moment that Billie had pulled the trigger, the spell holding the audience had broken. Ashlee could be amongst those fleeing for all Billie knew.

CHAPTER 30

Day 7

It was nearing 3am. There was no moon, and the night was quiet. The mercenaries gathered in Darian's cabin without speaking, and when they moved around, they did so quietly. Jonty walked onto their balcony, checking the balconies on either side of them were clear. He re-entered the room where Robyn was seated on the bed. She handed him a torch. Beside her, Clive and Wayne were perched on stools, nervously watching the sea.

Darian came in from the corridor, looking at his watch. 'It's time,' he said in a whisper, and stared at Jonty.

Jonty nodded, then turned back to the balcony. He raised the torch and shone it out to sea. Darian appeared at Jonty's shoulder - a small telescope raised to his eye. It had night vision capability, and he concentrated his view on the waves about a half kilometre in the distance.

A minute passed, and then another. 'Come on,' whispered Darian.

'They'll do it,' said Clive.

'I can't see the ship,' said Darian.

'In this light, I don't expect you will,' said Clive.

'What range are they? How do we know they are out there at all?' asked Wayne.

'We should radio them,' said Jonty.

'Keep the torch steady,' said Darian, glancing at Jonty.

'Sorry major.'

Then they heard it, a low hum. The sound was an insect-like buzzing.

'I have them now,' said Darian, looking once more through the telescope.

The three drones were no more than ten feet off the waves, travelling fast, one after the other in a line. Suspended beneath each craft was a large bag or case. They were virtually invisible to see in the darkness, at least to the naked eye.

The sound grew, and within moments, the first drone had lifted off the waves, rose before them, and then came directly toward the source of light. It hummed up onto the balcony, where Darian unhooked the bag from the carabiner clip. He tossed the bag inside where Clive caught it and placed it on the bed.

The drone flew back out to sea as the second drone repeated the approach, and the bag was delivered to their waiting hands. The third and final drone approached and dropped its cargo before flying back out to sea. Jonty switched the torch off.

Clive unzipped each bag, displaying an array of guns, ammunition, some explosive charges, a short-wave radio, and night vision goggles. 'We are set. It's all here.'

Darian sent a message to Anson on his mobile phone. *Standing ready.*

'Let's have one last drink, Major,' said Jonty, producing a bottle of scotch.

Darian knew that this was a ritual, something they had always done, ever since the first time they had been in combat together. In Africa, and in Iraq the team had guarded contractors, had even rescued hostages when governments had given up on them. This was their first heist though and seemed extra worthy of celebration.

'Give it here,' said Darian, swilling a long pull straight from the bottle. He passed it to Clive, and then around the circle of comrades until the bottle was close to empty.

'To Anson, the stupid *son of a bitch*,' said Robyn, as she took the bottle.

'If he only knew,' chuckled Darian.

'Did he say exactly what it is?' asked Wayne.

'He just said – *there was a fortune in the crates, and they would be coming from an island with an extinct volcano*,' said Darian.

'Could be Spanish gold…you know…from a galleon,' said Wayne. 'This island is roughly on a Spanish trade route. It *could* be, you know.'

'Thanks professor,' said Robyn mockingly.

'Well, I think Anson's rich enough already, don't you?' said Darian.

*

It was at about 5am that Seb took his seat in front of the laptop.

Jaz was already seated at her end. 'You did it. The bug in Anson's room is working.'

Seb nodded.

'How did you get in there?' asked Harvey.

'Clarice let me inside.'

'I bet she did,' said Harvey with a wink.

'You seduced her?' declared Jaz. 'I told you he could,' said Jaz, glancing at Harvey, looking a little surprised and pleased.

Seb didn't like what he'd done. It felt cheap, and he knew he was putting Clarice in danger by involving her.

'You have to try and get the last one into Hiro Yuki's rooms,' said Harvey.

'He's right Seb. As soon as you can,' said Jaz.

'Just so you know, there is another vessel about two clicks to your stern, shadowing the *Estrella de Mar*,' said Harvey.

'Another member of the syndicate?' asked Seb.

'I don't know,' admitted Jaz. 'If they were, why wait? They've been there a while.'

'They've left the area,' said another voice. It was a young guy.

'Who else is there with you?' asked Seb.

A man with a thick beard entered the frame, waved at Seb, and said, 'You may not remember me. I saw you at the warehouse. I'm Harrison.'

'Harrison? You were saying?' asked Seb.

'That other ship, it is leaving your vicinity even as we speak. They *were* following you though,' said Harrison.

'Who are they?'

Harrison shook his head. 'We have no way of knowing. Maybe a fishing boat? But somehow, I doubt it.'

*

Seb - showered, shaved, and freshly dressed, made his way back to Janie's suite. In the corridor outside her room, he heard raised voices. Sighing, he knocked, wondering what he was walking into. Billie let him in, her eyes wide.

Positioned in the centre of the room, dressed in a body-hugging silk robe, Janie stood with hands on hips, face flushed. Before her stood a rigid Captain Phillippe, hat tucked under his arm - and Ranieri, eyes downcast. They merely glanced at Seb as he entered and waited discreetly near the door.

'I want off this fucking excuse for a ship! Get a helicopter, or a boat, or something. Hell, I'll go to that island that's near us. I don't care what you do, but I want out!'

'Well, it happened. Ashlee tried to kill her,' whispered Billie in Seb's ear. 'Ashlee managed to drug two acrobats and take their place in the show. She's almost as inventive as me!'

Staring mutely at Billie, he could almost feel her infectious excitement. Her apparent lack of concern, the absence of visible anxiety, indeed the twinkle in her eyes all forced him to reassess this young woman's capability. He was beginning to think that Billie was one of the most remarkable, and strangely compelling individuals he had ever met.

Sebastian observed Janie, who had pointedly turned away from him. Brian and Sam, seated on the blue couch, had not acknowledged Sebastian either, and both appeared displeased by his presence or perhaps at the overall situation. They remained silent, tight-lipped, seemingly disinterested with involving themselves in Janie's argument for immediately leaving the ship.

'You did it then. I knew you could,' whispered Seb with a smile. 'Where is Ashlee now?'

'She got away,' said Billie. 'I think I shot her in the leg. But she fled. Ranieri eventually showed up and followed the blood trail to a kitchen where it ended. Ashlee could be anywhere by now.'

'Holy shit...' he chuckled. 'I can't believe she actually tried that.'

Billie whispered, 'I swear half the audience thought it was all part of the show. But then when I fired at Ashlee, everyone fled – like the place was on fire.'

'You can't leave,' said the captain loudly. 'You have another show, your contract...'

'Fuck the contract and fuck you!' cut in Janie. 'Unless you catch that bitch, you can forget it. She tried – to KILL me!'

Ranieri tried to interpose herself, reaching toward Janie, who swatted her hand aside. 'Don't you touch me, or I'll sue your ass. I'm getting on every social media site I can and I'm going to tell the world about this...*this* SHIT!'

'Please...' began Phillippe.

'Get out! Come back when you've organised a helicopter or something.'

'There is nowhere for one to land,' said Phillippe with exasperation.

'You need to go,' called Seb, making his presence known. The captain and Ranieri looked at Seb, and then without another word, the pair departed Janie's suite. It wasn't that Seb commanded their respect – rather they knew that Janie was teetering on the brink or perhaps had tipped over it already.

'Where were you?' asked Sam. He seemed to leap off the couch and march toward Seb, before standing close.

Seb pushed him back a little. 'Easy Sam.'

'I said...*where* were you? I pay you to look after her,' he said gesturing to Janie.

Seb looked at Brian, who averted his gaze.

'I had a job to do,' replied Seb. 'Besides, Janie is okay.'

Janie stared at Seb, but then, without a word, she stalked up to him and slapped him across the face - a stinging clap that made everyone flinch. Then she retreated to her bedroom, turned and slammed the door shut.

'You're fired,' said Sam.

Brian continued to look at his feet. Billie just gave a shrug.

'Yeah... that's fair,' agreed Seb, and walked out.

CHAPTER 31

Relieved that he no longer had to worry about Janie's safety, Seb immediately turned his mind to Hiro Yuki, the final member of the syndicate - at least that he knew of. The big meeting was scheduled for some time today. It should be easy to plant the bug as, unlike Anson, the Yakusa boss never left anyone guarding his suite. Hiro had only brought the one bodyguard, who never seemed to leave his side.

Up on the top deck, Seb found some breakfast – a salmon frittata, which he enjoyed with a black coffee. The pool was already full of swimmers, and others lazed around it, drinking juice in the morning sunlight. Billie mentioned that she had seen Hiro at this pool in the morning, usually accompanied by his bodyguard.

Enjoying the sun, he began listening in on the conversations around him, which seemed to carry easily. Everyone was discussing the attempt on Janie's life. News of the assassination attempt would soon race around the world regardless of anything Janie might post online.

He finished the plate, pushed it aside and ordered another coffee. It was then that Anson appeared on deck, accompanied by one bodyguard and his three women. Clarice wore dark sunglasses, and a floppy hat pulled low over her face. She caught his eye momentarily and looked away just as quickly. When she sat, she pulled her sunglasses off and glanced up, tilting her face just enough for Seb to see beneath the hat. The area around her right eye seemed swollen. She smiled at Seb, conveying a certain amused triumph. If she had won, and Anson had somehow lost, why was she still by his side?

Hiro Yuki appeared, and although he sat near Anson, the two didn't glance at each other. The Japanese gangster's bodyguard was a large man, though not particularly muscular. He had the build of a guy who may have started down the career path of a sumo wrestler but had given up. They tried to look like a pair of regular passengers, carrying beach towels and sunscreen.

Seb left the unfinished coffee and exited the pool area. He stepped into the lift, hit the *diamond level* deck button and felt the elevator descend.

At Yuki's rooms, he let himself in. The suite was tidy, and nothing seemed out of place. Seb cautiously entered, checking that no-one was around. Holding the bug in his hand, he thought about the best location to conceal it. The coffee table was positioned in the middle of the room and would probably do. But the light fitting seemed to be a better place. Standing on a lounge chair, Seb reached up and attached it. Satisfied, he climbed down, pulling the chair back to its original position.

'Done...that's all of them now. Harvey, you can kiss my ass. I made your deadline.'

The door behind him opened softly. 'What are you doing in here?' It was Hiro's bodyguard, and he easily filled the doorway.

Seb hesitated, '*Ahhh*...room service?'

The guy drew a slender, curved knife from behind his back. It was around nine inches long, sharp, and when he turned it, the light danced along its edge.

Seb swallowed, wondering where the knife had been hidden, wishing he had something with which to defend himself, knowing he was in real trouble. He took off his coat and wrapped it tightly around his left arm.

'If you tell me what you are doing in here, I might let you leave,' said the bodyguard as he entered, closing the door behind him.

Seb grinned. 'Hey buddy, you've got the wrong idea. Let's not do this.'

Hiro's bodyguard lost his smile, then attacked. For a big man, he hurtled forward with surprising speed, then stabbed – fast - nothing more than a flash, nicking Seb's forehead. He followed this with a slash, aiming for Seb's throat, the blade whooshing past. Seb back peddled, using his arm to block several strikes, the jacket quickly becoming slashed and tattered. Twice, the knife snicked his forearm, and Seb knew he was bleeding.

'Who sent you?'

'Put the knife down and I'll tell you.'

Seb moved around the coffee table, using it as a shield between them. The Yakusa bodyguard moved quickly but collided with the coffee table as Seb pushed it into his shins, breaking the glass top. Seb reached for a large glass shard and swept it up as the knifeman climbed slowly back to his feet.

Clearly Hiro had chosen this bodyguard more for intimidation value than true skill. Maybe he was the biggest of Hiro's henchmen – a 300-pound bullet shield. Seb recognised that the real danger was being pinned by the enormous brute, leaving him trapped beneath the mountain of flesh.

This time the Yakusa advanced cautiously. 'No guns. You fight with honour.'

'I wish I had a gun,' gasped Seb, swaying back from the blade, seeing only the glittering flash of silver near his face.

The bodyguard suddenly launched himself, somehow kicking Seb in the chest, shoving him back. Seb bounced, flipped over the lounge recliner and before he could move, his opponent was sitting across his chest, the knife descending in an arc. Seb caught the wrist, halting the blade, but he couldn't breathe – the weight pressing down already cutting off precious air.

Holding each other's knife hands, each man strained to break the other's grip. Hiro's bodyguard was strong, and positioned atop him, the killing blade inched closer to Seb's face, finally mere millimetres from Seb's eye. Seb's jagged glass shard was close to the Yakusa's ribs, pressing. They strained, sweat springing from faces reddening with colossal exertion.

Blood dripped from Seb's hand, the glass shard becoming slippery. Moments passed before Seb gave, moving his head at the same time, allowing the knife blade to skid into the floor beside his face. In this instant, the Yakusa's momentum pitched him forward, and off-balance. The knife came up again, and Seb half-shoved and kicked the bodyguard sideways, rolling out from under. Barely separated, it was Seb that was first to find his feet. He flung a lamp at the Yakusa, and it connected, the porcelain smashing across his ear. Dazed, the giant tried to steady himself as Seb kicked him in the chest, shoving him backward.

Seb dropped the glass shard, advanced, and launched an uppercut, snapping the guy's head back, teeth severing his tongue. The Yakusa's knife slipped to the floor as the bodyguard stumbled back, blood streaming from his mouth. Seb advanced, bent and scooped it up. The bodyguard backed into the kitchen and hurled a pan off the countertop. Seb ducked, allowing it to sail past, clattering harmlessly to the floor.

Hands raised, blood dribbling from his mouth, he gurgled, 'Wait.'

'For what?' Seb stepped forward, reversed the grip on the knife and plunged the blade into his foe's chest. Angry, but mostly surprised, Hiro's bodyguard slumped onto the floor, pressed against a kitchen cupboard, wide eyes on Seb until his final breath.

Seb retreated into Hiro's bedroom and slumped on the bed, feeling light-headed as the adrenaline slowed. He waited for a minute, then went into the bathroom and ran water - splashing his face, taking steadying, deep breaths. After finding calm, Seb searched through Hiro's wardrobe until he found a new jacket. It looked a lot nicer than anything he had ever owned and would cover the bloodstains on his shirt front.

His phone beeped. A message popped up from Jaz. *We heard everything - are you ok? What happened?*

Seb walked into the lounge and stood just beneath the light fitting. 'I was interrupted. Yuki's man is down. I had no choice.'

His phone beeped again. *Injured?*

'No, not much anyway. Will I leave the bug in here?'

The next text came in. *Get out now. Leave everything as is.*

CHAPTER 32

It was just after lunch as the *Estrella de Mar* neared Karabeki Island when the intercom came to life, and Captain Phillippe made the announcement.

This is your captain. We have avoided the hurricane near Hawaii, though we were forced off our course. Instead, we are cruising near Karabeki Island, which you will see from our starboard side.

On the bridge, Phillippe replaced the communication handset and turned to Hillary West. 'I've done everything you wanted, Hillary. What now?'

Hillary glared. 'I don't much like your tone, Captain. But since you ask, I want you to slow the ship and prepare for a boarding party.'

'This is most unusual,' Phillippe said, glancing at his bridge crew.

'Don't look at them – look at me. Where can they board?' demanded Hillary.

The captain glanced at the instruments, noting wind speed and direction. 'On the port side. We will open the cargo hatch on the stern.'

'Good. They will come to us. Stop the ship,' commanded Hillary.

'Here?'

'Do it,' she said.

*

Harrison called out, 'They have someone approaching from Karabeki. It's not a big ship. But big enough to appear on our radar.'

'I wish I could see it,' said Jaz.

'No satellites,' said Harrison.

'This is it. This is what we've been waiting for,' said Harvey.

Seb was already online with them. Jaz and Harvey could see him sitting before the computer in his cabin. Seb said, 'We did it folks. This is what you wanted.'

'Yeah, couldn't have done it without you Seb,' said Jaz.

'Yeah,' echoed Harvey, though without much enthusiasm.

'Thanks Harvey – that *really* means a lot,' said Seb.

'I'd give you a high five if I was there,' said Harvey.

'Great,' said Seb, sarcasm undisguised.

'They're approaching,' said Harrison. 'It's a fast vessel, whatever it is. Seb, can you get eyes on?'

'Maybe. I'll go up on deck. Is it the same ship that was shadowing us earlier?' asked Seb.

'Negative,' said Harrison. 'That ship is still out there – but at least 10 clicks away. This is a new vessel. It's approaching directly from the island.'

*

From the top deck, in the open air, Seb paused to take in Karabeki Island. It looked verdant green, with whisps of white cloud clinging to its upper ridges, close to the top of the volcano's lip. Lagoons of turquoise surrounded it, and he could make out white beaches between the lagoons and the greenery. There might have been some buildings within the trees near the beach, but it was hard to tell from so far away.

The approaching vessel was about the size of a coast guard ship, and might have been called a pleasure cruiser, except that it was much larger than he had ever seen. It came around the cruise ship, its wake long and white. Inside of a minute it nestled in against the *Estrella de Mar* on the port side. Seb left his vantage and walked aft, seeking a better view.

He pulled a phone from his pocket, and dialled Jaz.

'It's one of those pleasure super yachts. Very nice. I can't see where it is right now, but they are alongside us.'

'Try and get eyes on,' said Jaz.

'Wait.'

Seb jogged toward the aft of the ship, following the railing, dodging the occasional passenger. He arrived just as ropes were thrown from the cruise ship to the pleasure yacht. 'They're moored together now. The gang plank is sliding over. The yacht is named *Mystro*. It's hard to see what's going on – the lifeboats are in the way.'

'Who's coming aboard?' asked Jaz.

Seb looked down. The ocean was heaving a little, and the two vessels were joggling. Then the cruise ship adjusted its side thrusters and the two vessels settled together gently. Immediately people started to board. Seb couldn't clearly make them out from above.

'The angles are wrong. I can't see faces.'

Then, as the minutes went by, Seb watched as crates were carried across from the yacht. It took four guys to handle each one, two on each end. 'Seven crates just came on board.'

'Crates?'

'Yep.'

'How big?' asked Jaz.

'Took four big guys to carry each one. They looked heavy, but not full of gold heavy.'

'Crates?' repeated Jaz.

'That's what I said.'

Seb saw an Indian woman standing about 20 feet away. She had her own phone to her ear, watching the cargo come aboard. She looked up, saw Seb and smiled, before turning away. He was pretty sure she was one of the tattooed military goons he had seen earlier at the pool.

'What do you think is in them?' asked Jaz.

'I have no idea.'

'Go back to your room. I want you listening in when they have their meeting. You may still need to do something for us,' said Jaz.

'I thought I was done.'

'You're not done until I close the mission, Seb,' said Jaz.

Seb watched as the pleasure cruiser was unhooked from the cruise ship, and sped away in a wide loop, heading in the rough direction of Karabeki Island.

CHAPTER 33

At around 6 pm, Seb settled into his cabin, the laptop link with his handlers once again open. In the bathroom mirror, he observed the cut over his eye. It was shallow but looked angry. He cleaned the wound out with water and patted it dry. Then he unbound his hand where the glass shard had sliced him. This was deeper and more painful. He washed it, then rebound the wound with a fresh bandage, compliments of a small first aid kit in the bottom draw. Last, he inspected the two wounds on his forearm. These were superficial but needed some bandages too.

Billie sent a text, *are you ok?*

An hour after, she sent another. *Hellooo? Talk to me.*

Then three more within two minutes.

Seb, just answer me.

Heya, did you get it done?

Dammit, answer me. Are you fooling around with Clarice again?

Ignoring Billie's persistent messaging, Seb instead decided to monitor each of the listening devices planted, knowing that Jaz and Harvey were doing the same at their end. He cycled from Anson to Kennard, and then to Hillary West. The silence indicated that none of them were in their cabins, and annoyingly he really had no idea where any of them currently were.

Finally, he opened the link to the Hiro Yuki bug. Hiro was now in his rooms, talking rapidly in Japanese. He sounded angry, and given there was no reply to each tirade, Seb considered that he may be listening to one side of a phone call.

Someone knocked on the door. Seb stood and reflexively grabbed the curved knife he had taken off Hiro's bodyguard from the side-table. 'Who is it?'

'Room service,' came Billie's voice through the door. 'Do you ever look at your phone?'

Seb opened the door, and Billie slipped inside, immediately searching his face. Her eyes found the cut on the top of his forehead. Then she spotted the knife in his hand. 'What are you going to do with that?'

'Oh, nothing.' Seb closed the door and put the knife on the side table. 'Why are you here? Shouldn't you be with Janie?'

Billie took in Seb's bandaged hand and arm. 'I left her with Brian and Garth. Garth has the gun.'

'Shit,' said Seb.

'I know…right?'

'So, what happened?' Billie glanced again at the knife. 'That looks…deadly.'

'It's done. Anson and Hiro too. We've done it.'

'You ran into some trouble though.' Billie took his arm and turned it over, tutting. 'These could be better bandaged.'

'Hiro's bodyguard walked in on me.'

'What happened?'

'Let's just say that it was him or me.'

Billie stared hard at Seb, perhaps noting for the first time what he really was, re-evaluating what she had thought of him. Seb knew that she no longer saw him as some bumbling bodyguard. Her eyes were now properly open to him, and the situation.

'So, was she good in bed?' asked Billie. She tried to keep her tone light, but Seb detected an edge. He stared at her and then Billie continued, 'You know – Clarice?'

'It was business, that's all.'

Billie looked away, and although she wanted to say *damn you,* she said, 'I thought I could listen in on the meeting… with you. It's the least you could do for me,' said Billie.

'Sit down then, make yourself comfortable. But not in front of the computer. I don't need Jaz or Harvey seeing you here.'

Billie was texting Harry when she glanced over and saw that Seb had drifted off to sleep. She wondered how he could, knowing that they were about to discover what the cabal was going to discuss. Seb snored softly. The cut on his forehead was not deep, but it would probably end up as another scar to add to the collection on his body.

It was two hours later, the sun having descended beneath the waves, when Jaz's excited voice suddenly filled the cabin. 'They're up! Seb – are you there?'

Billie stayed hidden in the corner, remaining silent as Seb came instantly awake and positioned himself before the screen. 'Where are they meeting?'

'On deck somewhere,' said Jaz.

'Not in one of their rooms? All that bullshit and they're somewhere else.' Seb shook his head, letting out a deep sigh.

'I can hear tinkling glasses and a lot of background noise, but they seem to be in a public place,' said Harrison.

'That's odd,' said Jaz. 'Did you plant a bug on one of them?'

'No…not exactly,' said Seb. He knew that Clarice had taken the bug with her. She was with the syndicate, or close by. He smiled, relieved that she had done this thing for him when it mattered most.

'*Shush*,' said Harvey. 'They're starting.'

'What is wrong Hiro? You look upset,' said Hillary.

'He's not speaking to us,' said Anson.

'Can we get on with it?' asked Kennard.

'Yes, yes, let's get to it,' said Hillary.

'I'm glad you could all make it,' came a deep, Texan accented voice. 'I trust you've enjoyed the cruise.'

Jaz said, 'I know that voice.'

'Congressman Wyatt, I trust you know Anson Mulgrave,' said Hillary West.

'That's Lord…Anson Mulgrave,' said Anson.

'I know Mulgrave…I know them all,' said Wyatt.

'Edgar Wyatt, the Texan oil baron,' said Harvey, and gave a low whistle. 'Holy shit, what's his part in this?'

'I like your island, Edgar,' said Anson. 'It's a little out of the way though, wouldn't you say?'

'That's why I like it,' said Wyatt. 'You can do what you want out here, and nobody knows a damned thing.'

'What are you doing with it?' asked Anson.

'Wouldn't you like to know…' he laughed. 'We have a resort, a good one. We have water skiing, charter flights, the usual crap. That's what you would see if you were to fly over the place anyway.'

'Did anyone see what happened at the concert last night? Someone tried to kill Janie Reichenbach,' blurted Kyle Beacon.

'We were there, Kyle. Now please, we have important matters to discuss,' said Kennard.

'Sorry General,' said Kyle. 'My bad. I'll shut up now.'

'Perhaps you could organise some drinks for us, Kyle,' said Anson.

'Do I look like a fucking waiter, Anson?' chuckled Kyle.

'Go with him, Clarice,' said Anson.

There was a long pause. 'Alright,' said Clarice.

Chairs slid back and they heard Kyle and Clarice leave the area, chatting together. But the bug remained in place, for the conversation continued.

'Who was that asshole?' drawled Wyatt.

'He's an actor. Big in Hollywood,' said Hillary.

'Never heard of him,' said Wyatt.

'Okay, we have seven packages,' said Kennard, trying to get to the business. 'These were going to be 12 million each…'

'That's what we agreed,' cut in Anson.

'But the situation has changed,' said Hillary. 'I understand…Anson, that you have two of McTaggart's scientists.'

Anson replied, 'You have your spies I see. Yeah, I have them…all tucked up and safe.'

'So, you were thinking you would become our new chemist? You would re-commence the operation?' said Hillary.

'I was intending on sharing the technology with you all. We could all be producing the serum within a year if we each have our own subjects,' said Anson. 'McTaggart was greedy….'

'A year? That seems like a long time,' said Hiro.

'He speaks!' said Kennard.

'The truth is, I have my own scientists now,' said Wyatt. 'I also had my people get to the cliff house before the FBI made it in. We took what was left of the files, and the hard drives.'

'Sneaky bastard,' snarled Anson.

'We found McTaggart, but no signs of the skin that killed him,' said Kennard.

Seb glanced at Billie, who was listening avidly. 'It's an auction,' he said to no-one in particular.

'If you were hoping for a reduction, then you are wrong Anson. You don't get to sell the serum back to us. Indeed, we have the upper hand, because we have what you need,' said Wyatt.

'Seven skins,' reminded Hillary. 'Seven…but the price has gone up. They are each now worth 22 million. That's a very decent price I think.'

'Ohh, what's wrong Anson?' asked Wyatt. 'We don't need a chemist anymore. I've got that angle covered. But we do need money, and friends in the right places.'

'If it's all the same to you, congressman, I'd like to set my own operation up. I have everything McTaggart had, but I just need…'

'Some skins,' said Wyatt. 'Well, I thought you would say that.'

'I will buy two,' said Hiro immediately.

'That leaves five,' said Hillary.

'How many do you want Anson?' asked Wyatt.

'Can we come back to that? I want to discuss the vials first.'

*

Anson had just sent a text. It said *green light*. Darian looked at the message, then wrapped his fist on the wall. The process was repeated, and the mercenaries left their cabins at the same time, smiling as they met each other in the corridor.

Darian paused and sent back a text to Anson – *Roger – moving*. The group converged on the lift, then descended, bags slung over their backs. As they emerged on the lowest deck, they entered a narrow corridor, harshly lit by flickering fluorescent lighting that revealed grey metallic walls. They walked past cabins where the crew resided. The area was empty as most of the crew were currently cooking, cleaning, or serving drinks on the levels above. A heavy door at the end of the corridor said *Cargo Bay 2, strictly no admittance by passengers*.

Jonty went in first, followed by Clive and Robyn. Last came Wayne and Darian, who shut the door behind them. It was a bulkhead door, equipped with a lever handle designed to seal the area when engaged. Jonty swung the lever down, securing it with a *clunk*.

They emerged into a huge space that could have been a warehouse, except that shiny metal pipes ran around the ceiling, carrying water and circuitry. The silence was almost complete, except for the vague creak of the ship. There were pallets distributed throughout the area—large cubes containing food items and bottled beverages. Although the ceiling was high, the crates were stacked nearly up to it in some locations, forming a network of corridors, making it difficult to see what was around each corner.

'Gear up,' whispered Darian. The mercenaries changed into black tracksuits, with black balaclavas. They disbursed their weapons and ammo, and lastly the night vision goggles, which they wore on top of their heads, ready to use.

Darian loaded his sub-machine gun, a HK MP5. He extended

the stock and chambered the first round, then flipped it to fully automatic.

'Give me the shotgun,' said Robyn.

'Are you big enough?' asked Wayne.

'Are you? Give it here.'

Robyn loaded the double barrel pump-action shotgun, a weapon that seemed to dwarf her. She pumped in 14 shells, then slung a belt around her waist, with a row of extras.

'Let's be quick,' said Darian. 'They loaded them in the next cargo hold. There should be a door at the end of this hold. We keep moving now. Avoid killing anyone unless hostile.'

'How much is this worth?' asked Jonty.

Robyn said, 'I counted seven crates. If they are loaded with artefacts and gold…it has to be worth millions.'

'Count it when you get it,' said Darian.

'Anson is going to be so pissed off,' said Wayne.

'We have a job to do. Keep your heads in the game,' said Darian, leading them away in single file.

*

'Here are your drinks,' said Clarice. There was the sound of a tray being set down, and the clink of bottles.

'Where is Kyle?' asked Anson.

'He's with Marguerite,' said Clarice brightly.

'Here they are. The fruits of our labours,' said Wyatt. They heard a clunk and what sounded like something clicking open.

'Three vials. Those are larger than I expected,' said Anson, unable to hide the awe that had crept into his voice. 'But I'll take two.'

'I have more,' said Wyatt. 'Consider this proof that our production is underway. I could give you these, Anson, if you wanted to trade your two scientists.'

The trading continued. In the end, Anson had bought two vials of serum for around six million each, and Hiro the remaining one. Anson refused to move on the scientists that he said were his, and his alone. Their locations remained a secret from everyone except Anson.

'Do those crates have what I think they have in them?' asked Jaz.

'It does sound that way,' said Seb thoughtfully. 'They call them *skins*.'

'Jesus Christ!' blurted Harvey.

Seb glanced at Billie, who was mouthing to Seb '*What are you talking about?*'

CHAPTER 34

Ashlee dragged her leg as she entered the kitchen, leaving a trail of bloody droplets smeared over the white tiles. As a chef walked by pushing a cart, she slid under the counter and out of sight.

Amidst the clatter of pots and pans, on hands and knees, she crawled unseen, edging her way to the far end of the galley. Her leg burned where the bullet had drilled out part of the meaty flesh of her calf. Though aware of the injury, pain was, she had learned, something that could be controlled. After all, this was, she considered, nothing compared to the many injuries she had sustained when first incarcerated at the correctional facility all those years ago. And on some level Ashlee had even come to expect pain, though she hadn't formed this realisation yet.

Clear of the kitchen, she again stood, gritting her teeth, then walked fully upright into the darkened corridors beyond. None of this had played out as expected, and all she could now think of was to escape into the ship's hidden depths, to a place where she could recover and plan her next moves. With each ladder, each hatch in the floor, she descended until finally arriving in the engine compartments. Spying an engineer, who seemed to be inspecting some instruments, she held her breath, crouching in a shadowed corner and waited for him to leave the area.

She crept on and found yet another steel ladder, this one disappearing below into a corridor as shadowy as any mineshaft. At last she came to a bulkhead door - *Cargo holds* printed in red letters above it. Ashlee ducked through, and crept forward, limping now, ceiling lights in mesh cages illuminating every few steps of the passage. Voices echoed in front, though indistinct, bringing her to a halt. Scanning, she spotted a grate at just over head height. Jamming her knife into the rim, she levered it away with a screech. In moments, she was sliding inside, wriggling forward along an air-conditioning duct into darkness.

She crawled, not knowing where she was going, taking random turns, first left, then right, under fan blades that whooshed and whooped as they turned.

When the light finally appeared, dim as it was, it signalled the end to her journey. The grill at the end of the duct proved tough to move, with limited space to wriggle, let alone apply force to the covering. This time the knife was ineffective, and she was forced to punch it, over and over, leaving her fist bleeding and bruised. *More pain...* but that was okay, because after several minutes, at last the mesh gave way and fell clattering to the floor of the chamber below. When she slid out the opening, the cold air misted around her, enveloping her sweat-lathered body.

Dim orange lighting revealed a large cargo hold with metal walls. Multiple shipping containers piled three levels high created a tomb-quiet maze. The temperature within the whole area seemed low enough to keep food from spoiling. Perhaps that was the point, for there were empty wooden crates strewn everywhere. On one wall, behind a mesh screen, Ashlee found an office with a desk and a few lockers. Outside the office space, a fork-lift had been parked. Certain though she was that no-one was in the hold with her, she investigated the entire area and found there was only one entry door, which she discovered was locked. On the outside wall of the ship, she could discern the outline of a cargo hatch, wide enough for a ramp to extend when the ship docked.

Retreating to the office, she slumped in the chair and gazed up at the ceiling. Only then did the bitter rage and utter frustration well up within her, threatening to burst from her lungs in a howl. Clamping her mouth shut, her stifled cry instead escaped only as a low moan. Tears formed in the corners of her eyes but refused to flow. She rested her head on the desk, and after a while, exhaustion took her, pulling her down into restless sleep.

*

With a sudden jolt she woke to loud knocking. Shivering with cold, Ashlee called - 'Who's there?' Holding the knife stiffly at her side, she crept from the office, peering, seeking the cause of the disturbance. She stood still, holding her breath, straining her ears, and for several minutes there was complete silence. Then there arose a faint tapping. Guided by those distant sounds, she finally approached a securely locked shipping container. *Had someone become trapped in the container by accident?*

Popping the lock, she slid the bolt up and out. Instantly the door swung open on rusted hinges. Peering within, she had expected wooden crates - but these were metal. Longer than a person, and twice the depth of a coffin, she paused, gazing at the capsules. Their sleek, modern design seemed alien, and she wondered at their true purpose.

The tapping came again, causing her to flinch. Although her instinct was to back away, she instead climbed atop the object, pressing her ear to its shiny surface.

Ashlee called, 'Hello?'

'Help me.'

She sat back, bewildered. The voice was pitched low, and it had definitely come from inside. Fear mingled with curiosity, and the back of her neck rippled with gooseflesh.

The knocking started again, and she sat back. 'Who's in there?'

The knocking stopped. 'Help. I can't breathe.'

Ashlee stared at the vessel, unable to look away, confused, wondering *what the hell* was going on, and *how anyone could be in there?* She again placed her ear against the cold surface. Had the voice been in her head? Again there was silence, and yet… she could almost feel something stirring within it.

'Help.' There it was again - unmistakeable. A small voice, and now she considered that perhaps it was a child. Ashlee began running her hands over the smooth metal surface, looking for a catch or the corners of a lid.

'Help me, please!' The voice now held urgency. If anything could reach Ashlee and have a chance of finding a way into her long-buried heart, it was the plight of a child. Whether it was that, or just curiosity, she decided she needed to open it, to rescue whoever was trapped inside.

'Wait – I'll be back!' Ashlee left the container and limped back into the office. Inside the cupboard, she found a broom, a jacket, and a toolbox. From inside the toolbox, she retrieved a crowbar.

Back at the capsule, she jammed the bar beneath what seemed to be the lid and pulled hard, straining until she thought she would pop a vein.

'There's a switch,' came the voice from within.

'Just wait,' cried Ashlee. Dropping the crowbar with a clang, she felt around the edges of the capsule, and found a small depression. Feeling inside, she located a small button. For a moment, she withdrew her hand, thinking about the situation, wondering how the person inside could possibly be alive. Then slowly, cautiously, she extended her finger, felt the button, and pressed.

Click.

There issued a *hiss* as if a vacuum seal had broken, and then the outside air whooshed into the capsule. The lid slid sideways, pushed from within and a mist of cold air drifted out.

'You can come out now, whoever you are,' she whispered.

The creature that sat up had a flat, scaled face. Its dark green flesh glistened as it shifted and turned toward her. Intelligent, jet-black, slitted eyes focused on hers. They were a sharks eyes, cold, dreadful, without mercy...the eyes of death.

Its mouth gaped wide, revealing a forked purple tongue as thick as a leather strap, with rows of hooked fangs. Ashlee gaped, unable to move, incapable of turning away, her last inhalation unable to escape as if she sat snap frozen in time.

A stream of pus-yellow venom jetted from within glands behind the creature's teeth, splashing across her cheeks, into her eyes, instantly burning, and blinding. Screaming in agony, she fell, clutching her ruined face, feeling flesh melt beneath her fingers as it travelled into her skull, and beyond.

*

'What the fuck was that?' said Robyn.

They all heard the scream, long and shrill. It sounded close. Slowly they moved halfway across the hold, the way impeded by stack upon stack of pallets and crates.

'Someone is getting it on,' said Wayne.

'Someone is getting gutted,' whispered Jonty, his face turning pale. 'That sounded fucking terrible!'

They halted and listened, but the scream was not repeated.

'Which way did that come from?' asked Darian quietly.

'In front,' said Clive, gesturing.

'The way we are heading?' asked Robyn, frowning.

'Relax. Stay cool,' said Darian. 'This won't take long. We get the loot - we get the hell out. We're close now...let's not freak out.'

The mercenaries advanced, in tighter formation, with Robyn on point, the DBS shotgun aimed ahead. Within a minute they were at another door. Above it, a sign announced *Cargo Bay 3*.

'This is it,' said Wayne.

But the door remained locked, no matter how hard they pulled on the lever.

'Open it!' demanded Darian. 'Stop fooling.'

'It's bloody stuck,' said Wayne, slinging his sub-machine gun across his back and hauling down with all his strength with both arms straining.

'What's this?' asked Clive, shining a torch onto a key card panel to the left of the door. 'Looks like we need a key?'

Darian stared at the panel for a long time. 'Anson said nothing about this.'

*

Billie sipped a drink from the mini bar having barely moved from her spot in the corner of Seb's cabin. She sat there with her knees tucked under her chin. Glancing at her phone, it showed that it was 12:08 am, and she realised that technically the cruise had reached the eighth day.

A few feet away, Seb's face was lit by the glow of the laptop screen, where he sat listening as Jaz and Harvey discussed recent events. Slumped comfortably in his chair with one leg extended onto the bed, she wondered how he could be so relaxed, despite his recent altercation. The realisation that Seb had actually slept with Clarice bothered Billie more than the knowledge that Seb had killed Hiro Yuki's bodyguard, and this confused her. *Why did it matter if he'd slept with Clarice?*

'Seb, I need you to go down and see what's in those crates,' said Harvey, his voice as clear as if the FBI agent was in the room with them.

'I think I know what's in them. Opening them may not be so smart,' replied Seb. 'In fact, it could be the worst idea ever.'

'He's right,' said Jaz. 'We intercept the cargo when it comes back into port. We need to open them in a controlled environment.'

'What should I do?' asked Seb, stifling a yawn.

'Nothing. Sit tight, put your feet up,' said Jaz.

Billie liked the idea of that – *putting your feet up* sounded pretty darned good to her. It had been one hell of a cruise, and she sat thinking for a while about cocktails beside the pool, eggs benedict breakfasts, and maybe even another dance or two at a *Manson Villa* concert.

'They're moving.' Harrison's voice broke in on her musings, pulling her back to the present. 'If I were to guess, I'd say Clarice has the device in her bag or something. I think they are in the elevator.'

'Hit the button, Adam,' said Anson.

'Boss,' said Adam.

'What was Hiro on about?' asked Anson.

Adam said, 'His man was killed. Hiro found him in his cabin, a knife sticking out of his chest.'

'Shit,' said Anson, though he sounded amused more than shocked.

Billie stared at Seb, and he saw in her wide eyes something new – maybe fear, or perhaps disgust. Seb knew that look, because he'd also seen something like it in the mirror.

'He said his man followed some guy who seemed to be acting suspiciously, and never came back,' said Adam.

'That's odd, isn't it,' said Anson. 'Is there any chance that our little club has been compromised? Then a few seconds later, Anson continued, 'Check our rooms when we get there. Maybe Hillary is watching us. Make sure it's clean.'

'I did,' said Adam.

'Do it again,' said Anson. 'One of our little club members must be planning something. Let us not be caught unawares.'

It sounded like they had left the lift and were walking along the corridor. Anson said, 'Search Marguerite and Tara. Make sure they have nothing incriminating on them, or in their luggage.'

'Yes, boss,' said Adam.

'Be gentle, but make sure you do it thoroughly,' said Anson. 'And you

my dear, you had a visitor when I was away. Perhaps you should tell me who that was.'

Seb jumped from the bed and burst through the cabin door at a run.

'Where are you going?' called Jaz.

Billie tried to follow, but Seb had already disappeared around the corridor and up the stairs.

'Hey, wait!' called Billie, but she was already lagging behind.

*

Anson took Clarice by the arm and dragged her past their cabin door. Kai looked at them as they passed, his expression neutral. Adam opened the door and disappeared inside.

'You're hurting me,' said Clarice, trying to break free from his grip. But his grasp was tight, and she had no chance. She glanced back once, and saw Kai, the man-mountain stationed outside the door where he had been virtually the entire cruise. He looked at her, then turned away.

'Don't dawdle, my dear,' said Anson, marching her away. They went up a short set of stairs and emerged in a small bar area where a handful of passengers were drinking in dark, secluded booths. Not pausing, Anson dragged Clarice past the booths and through to a deserted balcony. Completely alone, Anson swung her sharply, her side colliding with the balcony rail. Clarice winced but refused to cry out.

'Who was it? Don't lie to me,' said Anson, his eyes on hers.

Clarice shook her head. 'Just a guy.' Knowing Anson's obsession with his secrecy, she added, 'A reporter, he said he was a reporter.'

Without warning he slapped her hard across the face. She tottered sideways, almost fell, feeling the sting in her cheek. From beneath the fringe dangling over her eyes Clarice glared back at him defiantly.

'If you want to cheat on me, I can live with that, but he could be dangerous. You might have created a problem for us.'

'He never gave his name,' she said quietly.

'You took him into your bed, and he never told you his name?' Anson grabbed her by the throat and pushed her against the rail. 'I could snap your neck now, and throw you overboard, and no-one would know.'

Clarice's bag fell as she tried desperately to pry his hands from her throat, unable to breathe, her feet barely touching the deck. One high heel fell from her foot. Tears formed in the corners of her eyes, before at last Anson set her back down, and released her.

Clarice's bag had spilled, and she quickly crouched to gather her belongings. Anson grabbed her wrist as she was concealing the listening device.

'What's this?' he hissed.

Taking it from her, he examined the device, turning it from side to side. 'What have you done?'

*

Seb was jogging along the corridor past cabins, once or twice dodging passengers, his phone up to his ear. 'Where are they?'

'Not in their cabin, that's all I know,' said Jaz.

'Goddam it,' he hissed.

'It's a big ship Seb… they could be anywhere. There is nothing you can do! Seb – stop! Forget it!'

Seb stopped running, slowing to a walk as he passed a porter, who glanced at him as he was entering a room with fresh linens.

Walking on, Seb could feel his frustration building. He went up a flight to the *diamond* deck and walked around the other side of the corridor from Anson's rooms. Then jogging upstairs, he emerged on another level. Finally, at the other end of the corridor appeared Clarice, and Anson. Seb heard Jaz say in his ear, 'The bug is offline. They discovered it.'

Clarice was sure to avoid making eye contact with Seb as they passed in the corridor. Anson still had his hand under her arm and was guiding her roughly. Clarice had been weeping, her eyeliner smudged.

'Hey buddy, excuse me!' Seb called, pocketing his phone.

Anson walked another couple of steps, dragging Clarice, who had lost a shoe, but he half turned.

'Hey buddy! I'm looking for the bar. Is it around here?' Seb had returned a few steps towards them. Now Clarice looked at him, and her eyes flashed a warning.

'Yes, keep going – you can't miss it,' said Anson, resuming his trek.

Seb followed, now closer to the couple. 'Hey, I know you!'

'I'm famous,' said Anson.

'Oh yeah, you're that Anson Mulgrave *asshole*.'

Anson stopped – face flushed, jaw set. Clarice looked at Seb, a small smile on her mouth.

Seb hit Anson without warning, a lightning right cross that caught him on the nose, snapping his head back. Seb stepped closer as Anson's grip loosened, and hit him a second time, a left hook that snapped Anson's head sideways, dropping him to his knees. Seb hesitated, knowing he could kill Anson right now with the right move. Instead, he drove his elbow into the side of his ear, and for Anson, the lights went out.

It was then that Billie appeared at their side, breathless. She looked down at Anson, and then at Seb. '*Mother…*'

CHAPTER 35

It was an hour after midnight when Seb and Billie took Clarice to Janie's suite. Although the singer was awake, she looked *bone tired.* Sam, Brian and Garth were waiting with Janie - Garth holding Christian's gun at his side.

'Who's this? Wait, *I know you,*' said Janie, and then looking closely at Clarice, her eyes softened, and she pulled her into the room. 'Who hit you?' She led Clarice to the lounge as Garth looked in the corridor before closing and locking the door. 'And what is this?' She sat beside Clarice, lifting back her hair and examined the bruises appearing on her throat.

'What are you doing back here?' asked Sam, staring at Seb.

'He saved me,' said Clarice quietly, finding her voice.

'She can't stay,' said Brian, realising now who Clarice was.

'Oh yes she can, and she will,' said Janie, who turned to Seb and said, 'how did you get involved in this?'

Seb shrugged, then said, 'I was walking past. He was hurting her.'

Janie shook her head. 'You hooked up with her and Anson found out.'

'What if Anson comes?' asked Brian.

'He won't,' said Billie. 'We will hide her here, until we can get off the ship.'

'Yes,' agreed Janie immediately. Then the singer looked at Seb over her shoulder. 'Can you tell me what the hell is going on?'

'I don't work for you,' replied Seb. 'I was fired.'

'Enough!' said Brian. 'I can't keep silent any longer.'

'Shut your mouth Brian,' warned Seb, 'or...'

'Or what?' asked Brian. 'We need to know what's going on. The ship is supposed to be near Hawaii, but we're in the middle of nowhere. Why?'

Seb turned his back and walked toward the balcony where he stopped and peered out at the ocean.

'Seb is no bodyguard,' said Brian, turning to Janie. 'He's working for the FBI.'

'Thanks Brian,' said Seb, turning.

Billie gave a sickly smile at Seb and shrugged. 'Too late now.'

Janie and Clarice were looking at Seb, and then Sam and Garth came and stood near him. Under intense stares, Seb shook his head. Jaz hadn't mentioned anything about being caught out like this.

'You need to tell them something Seb,' said Billie.

Seb sighed. 'I don't know why we are off course. The people I'm interested in are calling the shots.'

'What people?' demanded Janie.

'My husband – for one,' said Clarice.

'Anson? What has he done?' asked Janie.

'There's a group he's involved with. They're...' began Clarice.

But Seb cut her off. 'Clarice, it's best you say nothing. What you know could get these people killed.'

Clarice closed her mouth and slowly nodded.

'This is insane,' said Seb. 'We can't tell you anything. Just sit tight, and everything will be fine.' He went over to Garth. 'Give me that.'

Garth reluctantly handed over the Smith and Wesson automatic. Seb examined the weapon. 'And the ammo, Garth.'

'Is Billie FBI too?' asked Janie.

'No,' said Billie and Seb simultaneously.

'Brian, you knew about this, and you didn't say anything to me,' said Janie. 'Everyone is keeping secrets and telling lies.'

*

Robyn was watching the corridor of crates behind them, the DBS shotgun ready. Clive had removed the faceplate covering the security lock beside the hatch and was fiddling with some wires, his balaclava pulled up so he could see better.

'Jesus Christ! How long is this going to take?' asked Wayne.

'Have you somewhere else to be?' asked Jonty.

Darian looked at his watch. 'We're behind schedule. We should have been in there 30 minutes ago. We have to disembark by 4 am. This is going to be tight.'

'The door is locked tighter than a fish's arse,' said Clive. 'I don't know what I'm doing with this.' He dropped the wires and stood up, sweat glistening on his face.

'Fuck it,' said Darian. 'Get the c4.'

'Do we really want to do that?' asked Robyn.

'Get it ready,' commanded Darian.

'Boss,' said Jonty, unslinging his backpack. 'A small amount on the hinges should do it.'

'Thirty second fuse,' said Darian. 'Everyone find cover. We are about to earn our pay.'

*

Janie had allowed Clarice to share her bed, and the two stressed, exhausted women quickly fell into deep sleep behind her closed door.

Seb and Billie sat outside on the balcony. Despite the late hour, they could hear distant voices from balconies on levels below them. Billie was cradling a glass of whiskey, gazing at the sea. She had already sculled two, initially to dull her own anxiety, but now the buzz was feeding another feeling that was growing inside her. 'I don't know what I'm supposed to do,' admitted Seb.

'I'll stay here with them. We'll keep everything locked. You need to check in with Jaz. Tell her you have Clarice.'

'I couldn't let him have her. I think he would have killed her,' said Seb.

Billie nodded. 'Yeah, and you dragged her into this mess. Had to go and screw her too.' She leant close to him and smiled. It wasn't her usual mocking smile though. It conveyed sorrow, and something more.

'Thanks.'

'Welcome.'

'I think everyone is asleep in there,' said Seb, stretching out, his arms over his head.

Billie glimpsed his torso beneath his shirt. She had seen the scars, the full extent of them, and knew that these simply reflected the man too. He was scarred on the inside as well, from all kinds of things. It made her want to…*what*? Heal him? No – she didn't pity him. She simply wanted to know him. Her hand touched his stomach, and her fingers traced the scar along his side. It was a tender touch, and although he had not invited it, he did not stop her either. She had felt an instant connection with Seb, and she knew that what she was initiating was a natural progression for her.

'What are we doing?' he breathed as she leant close, her hair tussled, the fragrance of her body filling his senses.

'You know.' It came out like a sigh as she crawled onto him, straddling him where he sat, her legs barely touching the floor.

'Is this…?'

'*Shh*,' she whispered, placing her finger across his lips. She peeled off her t-shirt and dropped it on the balcony. Then they were kissing, frantically fumbling at the buttons of their pants, trying to stay quiet lest they wake someone.

*

The c4 charge had detonated. It made a dull *thud*.

The mercenaries came out from their cover behind the crates, still covering their ears, dust and smoke drifting around them. The hatch was hanging on a hinge, twisted sideways…and open.

'That did the job,' said Jonty, enthused at having the chance to use plastique.

They clambered through the twisted opening, into the next cargo hold, feeling cold air wash across them, their weapons up and ready. Robyn took point, but then they fanned out, looking for the security that they thought would surely be guarding their treasure.

'No-one's in here,' said Robyn.

'It's clear,' confirmed Wayne.

'Find the loot. Let's get this done,' commanded Darian.

Within 30 seconds Clive called, 'Over here! Come and see.'

'We're too late,' said Robyn, stepping in beside Clive.

'Someone beat us to the punch,' said Jonty.

Inside the shipping container, all seven glistening metal cases were open. When they looked in them, they could see that they were completely empty.

'They stink!' said Robyn, her nose wrinkling. 'So bad!'

'Was Anson wrong?' asked Wayne.

'No…' said Darian shaking his head. 'He never wanted us to open these – just flog them for him.'

'This is bullshit!' spat Clive.

They retreated from the container. Wayne looked down. 'What's this? Is this blood?'

There was a long smear along the metal floor, and it led away into the corner of the room. They crept along, following the trail. In an office, behind a mesh cage, they found a figure lying propped in a seated position against a locker. Her left lower leg was gone, ending in jagged bone and sinewy tendons.

'It's been chewed off at the knee!' said Robyn.

'What?' said Wayne.

'Look for yourself,' said Robyn.

They examined the body closely, shining their flashlights at the corpse. The side of the face was blackened, like it had been splashed with acid. One eye was gone, and the other was staring at nothing.

'What happened here?' asked Clive, coming closer.

Darian took a long breath, but he couldn't look away from the body as he said, 'I'd say she opened the case. This was the scream we heard.'

'We need to go. There's nothing here for us,' said Robyn, grabbing Darian's arm. 'Someone will have heard that c4 go off. We need to go. Come on – let's go.'

'This is bad, this is really, really bad,' said Wayne.

'Let's move,' agreed Darian. 'Whatever did this, could still be here. There's only one entrance.'

'I don't see anything,' said Jonty, peering around at the stacked crates and containers, his sub-machine gun poised.

The mercenaries exited the hold, back the way they had come. Within minutes they had again changed into their civilian clothes and stowed the guns in the carry bags. In another minute, they returned to the lift, and made their way back to their cabins, pissed off, and confused.

CHAPTER 36

Day 8

Anson was not expecting the knock on the door, nor a visitor. Perhaps, he thought, Clarice had come back, begging his forgiveness. On the way to the door, he checked the two newly purchased vials of serum were safely tucked away in his drawer, stowed safely in a lock-box.

Kai didn't know Darian, and the man-mountain stood eying the mercenary warily as Anson waved Darian inside.

'The sun's barely up,' said Anson, taking Darian by the elbow, and leading him out toward the balcony.

'Nice robe,' chuckled Darian, eyeing the multicoloured silk pattern. 'Is that yours?'

'We agreed we would have no contact,' said Anson. 'I take it that you are here because it didn't go as planned.'

'That's an understatement, Anson. We got screwed. The boxes were empty.'

'What?'

'We had to blow our way into the cargo hold because the door was locked.'

'Were you just expecting them to hand it over?'

'I was expecting some guards. There weren't any. We went in, and we found the shipping container, then we found the crates, and ... they were already open. There was nothing in them.'

Anson's eyes slid sideways, away from Darian. 'That's impossible.'

'Something happened to them,' hissed Darian. 'And our time was wasted. We held up our end of the deal. You still owe us.'

'The deal was contingent on the cargo being seized and removed. That didn't happen.'

Darian began shaking his head violently, face flushing. Before he could speak, Anson held up a hand. For a long moment, Anson stood staring out to see, clearly making mental calculations. At last he produced his phone from a pocket. 'I'll transfer the funds now.' He pressed some numbers and then turned the phone so that Darian could see the screen. 'Payment was just made. Now we're done.'

Darian nodded, satisfied. 'There's one more thing, Anson. There was a body in the cargo hold. We think that it was the person who opened the cases.'

Anson visibly stiffened, from the neck down his body became rigid. 'There was a body?'

'Yeah.'

Darian could see that Anson was thinking hard, and whatever conclusions he was quickly coming to made him very uncomfortable.

'Yes, we found a corpse...a woman. Might have been the one everyone was looking for – the woman who tried to kill Janie Reichenbach. There wasn't that much left of her. One eye was almost liquified by some kind of acid. It looked like a shark had taken chunks from her too. It wasn't pretty.'

Anson swallowed hard. 'Darian...listen...I may have a new contract for you. I'd like it if you would stay on board a bit longer than planned... delay your departure. Tell me, is your vessel still in the vicinity?'

'The Squalus is close,' he nodded. 'She's about five miles behind us.'

'Good, we may need your friends before too long.'

'What was in the cases, Anson?'

'That's hard to explain.'

'Try.'

But Anson shook his head. 'No, old boy. That's a *need to know*.'

*

In her suite, Hillary West rose from the bed, showered, and sat down to a breakfast which had been brought to her room precisely two minutes prior. She didn't expect Congressman Wyatt to visit her quite so early.

As he came in, Wyatt was on a video call using his phone. He appeared to be talking to several of his security team, who were down in the cargo hold. Wyatt's face blanched when they showed him the empty containers.

'They're gone,' said his man at the other end. 'And we found a body. A woman. It seems that she may have opened one case up.' His security team could be seen lifting her away from her position, a sucking noise carried across the call as she was peeled from her own pool of dried blood. Hillary looked over Wyatt's shoulder, morbidly curious at the state of the body they found.

'Senator, the door was blown open. We also found a duct with the covering removed. We don't know who else may have been in here.'

'What does this mean?' asked Hillary as Wyatt pressed end on the call.

'It means this ship is fucked,' said Wyatt.

'But...I just purchased it,' said Hillary, clearly alarmed. 'Can't your boys get them all back in their chests?'

Wyatt chuckled without humour. 'You have to be kidding, Hillary. Just one of these things running around on a ship is a problem. We had seven of them locked in there. Now they're nowhere to be found.

That means they've left the cargo hold area. Do you have any idea what that now means for us…for this ship?'

'Can't you just shoot them?' asked Hillary.

Wyatt's barking laugh made Hillary flinch. 'They have unbelievable regenerative properties. Why do you think we use them for the serum? They take some stopping, Hillary. No – we can't just shoot them. God no. This is bad…very, very bad.'

'Then what do we do? I can't believe this has happened. What *the hell* are we going to do now.'

Wyatt closed his eyes, rubbing and pressing gently at his temples with his index fingers. After a long moment, he looked at Hillary. 'We have to get out… cut our losses. Do you understand that the ship is now lost? We have to send the *Estrella de Mar* to the bottom of the sea, with everything and everyone on it. There can be no evidence to find.'

'This isn't acceptable,' said Hillary, shaking her head. 'We can weather any negative publicity. Blame any deaths on terrorists or something.'

'We can't afford any publicity, Hillary,' said Wyatt, moving toward her drink cabinet. 'What happens when some asshole films one of them in his cabin, and posts it online? Before long, every conspiracy blogger that ever existed will be digging through the wreckage of where this now goes.'

Hillary looked stunned as she watched Wyatt pour a double whisky. 'It's unacceptable…' she whispered.

'Hillary, look…I've seen you lose more money on a weekend of playing high-stakes poker.'

'But this is different,' said Hillary. 'I like this ship. I like how it makes me feel. It's one of the jewels in my empire.'

'You can get another one.' Wyatt swallowed half the whisky in a single gulp.

She pouted, then stalked to the couch, sat, and fell into sullen silence.

'*Grow up* Hillary. We've been put in a *no-win* situation.'

Hillary stared straight ahead, arms crossed over her chest. Wyatt knew she was processing the emerging situation and needed a minute to think. But they didn't have time to think. They only had time to act.

'Hillary...look at me. Think – there's only one way this can possibly play out.'

Abruptly she stood and began pacing around the room, a hand caressing her forehead like she had a sudden headache. At last, deflated, she halted before Wyatt, and met his eyes. 'Alright, alright... *Goddamit*... but what about Anson Mulgrave?'

Wyatt smiled. He was always amazed at how quickly Hillary could leap ahead to the next issue. Faced with losing her precious ship, she had already started thinking about how she could gain some kind of advantage from the situation.

'Anson is no longer needed,' agreed Wyatt, explicitly saying what Hillary seemed reluctant to admit. 'He tried to hide the scientists from us. I don't appreciate that at all.'

Nodding, Hillary said, 'Was he the one who had Hiro Yuki's man killed? It had to be him.'

'I know it wasn't me. And I know it wasn't you. That leaves Kennard and Mulgrave,' said Wyatt.

'Kennard was with me at the time,' said Hillary thoughtfully.

'Then we agree? Anson has to go,' said Wyatt.

'Agreed. Let him take his chances here.' She giggled with nervous energy. 'Imagine his face when he realises we've left him all alone.'

The congressman took Hillary's hand, pulling her over to the couch where they sat.

Wyatt asked, 'Can you make the necessary arrangements? The ship needs to disappear, firstly off the radar, and then it needs to sink, before any chance of a rescue.' He said this matter-of-factly, like he was discussing whether to have poached or fried eggs for breakfast.

'The first part I think is easy enough,' said Hillary thoughtfully. 'I can arrange that myself. But the second – you will have to handle that yourself.'

Wyatt nodded. 'I'll make arrangements. A large hole or two in the right place on the hull should do it. It will look like a terrorist attack.' He opened his phone and called someone.

'This is a mess. What a waste of resources,' said Hillary absently.

His call was answered - 'Yes, we need to make something happen. I need you to come and get me...yes, as soon as you can. That's a good man. And another thing, bring some explosives.' He paused, then 'Big ones - yes, enough to send a ship to the bottom of the ocean. Well... it's a long story. No...no – I'm not kidding around.'

CHAPTER 37

It was raining outside. From his window seat, Harrison saw that San Francisco harbour was covered in sea mist.

When he played back the discussion in Hillary's room, he ripped off his headset and shouted, 'Jaz, Harvey, we have a problem!'

Jaz had slept on a couch in the room next door. Harvey had not slept at all and came into the comms room cradling a mug of steaming coffee.

'What?' asked Jaz sleepily.

'Listen.' Harrison played back the last few minutes of conversation between Hillary and Wyatt.

'When was this recorded?' asked Harvey.

'I only just got to it now,' said Harrison.

'When?'

'An hour ago. I'm sorry, I'm really sorry.'

Jaz opened her phone, and dialled Seb. It rang, then beeped. The call had not gone through. 'Try the video link.'

They gathered around the computer and tried to contact Seb via his terminal on the laptop. 'Nothing,' said Harrison.

'Were they serious?' asked Harvey. 'That's madness.'

Jaz began pacing, 'Yeah, I think they meant what they said.' She stopped pacing. 'Keep trying, Harrison.'

'I am...I am.'

*

Seb and Billie were sitting on the balcony in Janie's suite, eating a breakfast of bacon and eggs. The sun was warm, and it felt pleasant upon their skin. Seb realised that for the first time he actually felt like he could relax since they had boarded.

'About last night...' began Billie.

'It was .... I mean, for me it was...'

'I was going to say...that I was a little drunk. And I'm sorry if I came on too...'

'No,' he interrupted, 'We were blowing off steam, and well – I think we were *in a place*. It was no mistake. Let's just leave it at that,' he said smiling. Then, feeling slightly awkward, Seb changed the subject. 'Where do you think she is?'

Billie knew who he was referring to. 'Ashlee is hiding somewhere below in the cargo hold. I was thinking it's the only place she could be.'

They ate for while in silence. Then Billie said, 'Why do they call them *skins*? It's a strange name.'

Seb thought, then said, 'I only ever glimpsed one once, with my own eyes. It was *kinda* blending with the background. I was in a living room, in an old house with really fancy wallpaper. It was patterned - you know...anyway it blended right into the background - just barely visible to me.'

She gazed at him, puzzled. 'Like a chameleon.'

He nodded slowly. 'But that wasn't the worst of it.'

Billie didn't want to know more, but she heard herself ask anyway. 'No? What was?'

'It spoke...these things are intelligent.'

Billie suppressed a shiver.

'Relax, if they're on-board, they're all locked up – in the crates.'

She nodded. 'What do you think they are?'

'If I was to guess, I'd say some kind of mutated person. You know – a blend of human DNA and a lizard or a snake. Scientists mess around with these things. I'd say they are some kind of science experiment.' He gave a nervous laugh, then said, 'It sounds nuts.'

Billie couldn't disagree. 'You've been thinking about it? The creature you saw – the *skin*.'

'Not every single day...but nearly every other day since I left the *cliff house*,' he admitted. 'How do you *not* think about something like that?' He didn't want to admit he also dreamt about them – that sometimes he woke in the middle of the night with his heart pounding, convinced that one of those damned things was in his room.

Billie said nothing. Until she saw it for herself, she wasn't sure she could believe they existed – not truly. It wasn't that she didn't trust Seb anymore, and the evidence from the conversations she'd *eves-dropped* were compelling. It was simply that to accept the existence of a humanoid hybrid species would turn her relatively stable world upside down. It was the same concept, she mused, as actually seeing an ET. It was just too much to process.

An hour had passed before Ranieri came to Janie's room. Clarice remained hidden as the security guard positioned herself in the middle of the lounge. When Janie, Sam and Billie had gathered, she announced, 'Ashlee Donovan is dead. She has been killed.'

Janie sat down, her face a mask of relief mixed with sadness. Ranieri had that look people get when they haven't slept long enough – black beneath the eyes, skin dull, and a slight slouch in her posture. Hearing the news, Seb strolled in from the balcony. He noted that there was something still bothering Ranieri, something in her eyes that hinted at a tension that she was still under.

Despite the sombre mood within the room, Sam couldn't hide his elation. and said, 'Thank God that's over with. Let's have a drink, shall we.'

Ranieri glanced at Sam with irritation, then strode toward the exit, Seb following close behind. With a light hand to her shoulder, he stopped the security guard in the corridor.

'What is it you aren't saying?'

Ranieri faced him, and looking up, said 'I just saw her body. It was brought into the infirmary a short time ago.' She swallowed, and licked her lips, before she could continue. 'I was shocked.'

'What do you mean?'

She hesitated, then said, '*Something* killed her, and something then fed on her.'

'Okay.'

'Do you have any idea what that could mean?' Ranieri met Seb's eyes, searching his face.

'I wish I did,' he lied.

'Because I'm a little freaked right now. The doc examined the body, and she doesn't know what's going on either.' Ranieri leaned on the wall of the corridor and ran a trembling hand through her hair.

'You should get some rest. At least have a stiff drink.'

'Rest? I don't know how I can right now. If you saw Ashlee's body, you might understand.' She pushed off the wall, then retreated along the corridor. Before she disappeared from his view, she called back – 'Keep your gun close, Seb. I have a terrible feeling that you might need it.'

Seb stared after Ranieri for a moment, then turned and retreated back to the rooms where he could hear Sam and Billie chatting to Janie about the news. Entering the room, Janie and the others ceased their animated discussion.

'What's wrong now?' asked Janie. 'You look disappointed somehow. Isn't this good news? I mean, I didn't want her dead, but at least now the danger's passed.'

'Nothing,' replied Seb, shaking his head, putting on a fake smile.

'Let's have a drink then – I know it's early, but…' began Sam.

'I need to go,' cut in Seb, striding toward the exit. 'There's something I need to do.'

As the door closed behind Seb, they stared after him, then Janie said, 'I think I will have that drink now, Sam.'

CHAPTER 38

The link was down. His phone was not working either. 'Not this again,' raged Seb. He needed to talk to Jaz. It sounded very much like at least one of those creatures was loose on the ship. They needed to be informed, and he needed to know what they thought he should do next.

'What?' asked Billie.

'We have no reception. None.'

'Yeah…that's strange I guess,' she said absently.

'Not strange at all. Deliberate.'

'Huh? You think someone has done this?' she said smiling.

'Let's find out if everyone onboard is effected,' he said, exiting the cabin with the handgun tucked in his belt, concealed beneath his jacket.

Up on the top deck, Seb and Billie had intended to talk to one of the stewards, but found a group of passengers already around her, everyone firing questions about when the Wi-Fi would be reinstated.

'That answers that,' said Billie. 'Doesn't mean it was deliberate though.'

Seb walked out onto the promenade deck and leant on the rail. 'I don't think this is good.'

'What's wrong? Everything is fine,' she said. Billie flashed him her best smile, and Seb wondered how she could be so upbeat after everything that had happened.

'We haven't moved in a day,' he said, staring out at Karabeki Island. 'Shouldn't we be sailing for Hawaii?' As they watched, they saw the pleasure cruiser approaching. 'That's Wyatt's ship - *Mystro*,' said Seb. 'It's returning.'

Seb and Billie hustled along the deck, trying to maintain their view of the approaching vessel. They followed the cruiser as it came alongside, gliding up to the same hatch that it used before. Eventually it settled against the cruise ship's hull. A hatch just above the waterline opened, then a gangplank was laid across the gap. Billie and Seb watched as three men they didn't recognise boarded the cruise-ship, carrying large canvas bags, slung over their shoulders.

Ten or twenty minutes passed, maybe longer, before they saw Wyatt, Yuki, West and Kennard, and all their entourages traipse aboard *Mystro*. The last to leave were the three men who had arrived carrying the bags.

'No bags this time. Did you see that? What do you think they were carrying aboard?' mused Seb.

Billie shrugged. 'Where are they going now?'

'Leaving us,' mumbled Seb. 'Meeting's over now I guess.'

'Notice that Anson wasn't with them? He was left out of whatever they are doing,' observed Billie.

Seb and Billie watched the super yacht as it powered away, until all they could see was its small white wake. It was clear that they were going back to Karabeki Island.

As Billie and Seb came back into the atrium, they could feel the ship beginning to move. Then the ship's announcement system came to life.

This is your captain. I have an announcement. Please note that the ship's communications are experiencing technical problems. I hope that these will be rectified in our next port. We apologise for the inconvenience. Thank you for your patience.

There was brief hiss of static before the captain came back on.

We are again underway – now sailing for Hawaii. Our next destination is Honolulu. The weather is clear. I look forward to a quiet, star-filled night, and calm conditions.

Seb threw a sharp, sideways glance at Billie as they took seats at a bar. They leant forward over polished timber, the gleam reflecting coloured lights from the myriad spirit bottles sitting in neat rows on glass shelves. Seb swivelled in the stool and focused his attention on the island in the distance.

'See, nothing to worry about,' said Billie. 'Hey buddy! Two margaritas!' she called, snapping her fingers to get the attention of the barman.

But Seb's jawline remained tight, his mouth set in a hard line. His flat gaze lingered on the island they were slowly departing, as if dissatisfied with what he'd seen.

'Relax!' said Billie, glancing sideways at him, then playfully clapping him on the shoulder. 'It's over. You're done. Have a drink and chill out.'

'Ashlee Donovan let them out, Billie. They're loose…and now most of the people I was sent to watch have departed. This isn't looking good.'

'So…' she said, glancing around 'you think the *boogie men* are running around on the ship?'

Seb finally looked at Billie, who was doing her darndest to hold in a smile, her sparkling eyes regarding him with ill-concealed mischief. 'You think this is funny? You don't really believe they exist, do you?' He turned away, only to meet her eyes in the mirror behind the bar.

They sat for a while in silence, lost in the murmur of soft conversations, the clink of glasses, and salt air. The drinks arrived, though Seb seemed to hardly notice.

Billie pulled the little slice of lime from her glass, then flicked it onto the bar. She hoisted the margarita between them, gazing over its rim, then said 'Cheers!'

Seb barely glanced at Billie as she took a big swallow, letting out a long sigh of contentment.

*

On the bridge, Captain Phillippe replaced the intercom phone and turned to his first mate. 'Hopefully people will stop asking now. Can you repair it?'

'No – look at it.' The officer was crouched beside a cabinet, examining the circuit boards. 'I can't tell what is wrong with it.'

Phillippe raised his binoculars, and staring through them, he said, 'It *is* strange. There is no reason why it should stop working.'

'Perhaps one of the engineers can examine it. But without spare parts, I cannot see this being repaired until we get to a port.'

'That will be soon enough,' said Phillippe.

'We can't even radio anyone,' said the officer with disgust. 'What happens if we have a real emergency?'

Phillippe sat in his pilot chair and looked at the bank of monitors arrayed around him, each showing a different camera angle, looking aft, to port and starboard. 'At least Hillary is leaving us. She has made this whole cruise difficult.'

'You could have ignored her requests,' suggested the officer.

'Not if I wanted to stay captain of the Estrella de Mar.'

*

Anson Mulgrave was encamped at the Endeavour Bar, sipping whiskey. Dark sunglasses disguised two black eyes and the tape across the bridge of his nose.

The whisky was good, but it was doing little to remove the dark mood that had suffused him. His humiliation at having been soundly thrashed, and the realisation that Clarice was now unlikely to come crawling back as expected left him teetering on the edge of a complete melt-down.

But it was his other friends that he was most urgently interested in. He had sent Kai to find Kennard. Not finding him, he had then sent him to locate Hillary. It was now after lunch, and he had not seen or heard from any of his associates for hours. Their cabins were locked, and no-one was answering.

Beacon joined him, a cheesy smile plastered to his moustached face. 'Hey Anson, you seen the general? He was supposed to meet me for a drink.'

'No Kyle.'

Beacons girlfriend sidled up to Marguerite and Tara, and the three women found their own table where they sat talking, casting glances at Anson, perhaps wondering what had happened to his face.

'They had better not be meeting somewhere without me,' said Anson.

'I did see Wyatt leave,' commented Beacon, sipping a drink.

'What?'

'Yeah, his cruiser, *Mystro* - came and went. Maybe they all went with him,' suggested Beacon. 'Might be just you and me buddy.' Beacon clinked his glass on Anson's.

Anson stared at Beacon, trying to think what it could all mean. *So - the syndicate had left the ship. Did they also know that the skins had escaped captivity? Did Wyatt and the others really think they'd left him stranded here?*

'We may need to leave the ship too, sooner than you think Kyle.'

'What's the problem? Captain said it was plain sailing back to Honolulu.'

'I have an exit strategy, when the time comes. We'll be safe enough until then.'

'What are you talking about?' asked Beacon. 'What's going on?'

Anson was considering his reply when Kai returned, drawing stares from everyone around. The bodyguard was a huge man, and people had trouble ignoring his size.

'Boss.'

'Yes, Kai,' sighed Anson.

'I've found someone.'

'Well, who did you find?' asked Anson, feeling petulant.

'The guy who broke your nose.'

'What? You did hey,' said Anson, rising off his seat. 'Where is he?'

'Over there.' Kai pointed to the other end of the deck. 'He's at another bar – the one near the outside pool.'

CHAPTER 39

Seb and Billie left the bar, headed for Seb's cabin, with the intention of trying to establish a link back to Jaz. Billie whispered as they walked along a corridor heading for the lift, 'We seem to have some friends tailing us.'

Seb glanced back. 'Anson's goons - okay, you go one way, and I will go another.'

They parted then, Seb taking the stairs, with Kai and Adam following him, but ignoring Billie. Seb only went a short distance down another corridor before he took a lift down, the doors closing just as Adam and Kai stepped inside. They were huge guys. There was another couple in the lift, and with everyone inside it – the space was jammed. They stared at Seb, waiting for the couple to get out on the next floor. Would they ask where Clarice was? Seb knew he could take some hits, maybe cop a bit of roughing up. It seemed inevitable.

'What do you want?' asked Seb as the door closed, and Adam put a large hand on Seb's shoulder, turning him around. It was at that moment that Kai slammed a fist into Seb's gut, dropping him to his knees.

'Wait!' Seb gasped.

The gunshot in the confines of the lift was slightly muffled.

Seb dropped hard, clutching his chest, eyes glazing over. He could already feel air rushing from a lung. The lift doors opened and then closed. He tried to get up, but his legs scissored and then wouldn't move at all. He couldn't even roll onto his back. Face pressed hard against the carpet, his breathing quickened as his heart laboured, now in a fight to stay alive. Darkness crept across his vision as a pool of blood formed around him.

*

On the observation deck - Janie, and the whole of *Manson Villa* had gathered in a piano bar at the stern, sipping drinks, watching as the sun began to set. Janie's fans were hanging around, and she had already signed her autograph several times.

'Where is he?' asked Janie.

Billie shrugged, 'We got separated. He'll be okay. He can handle himself.' But she *was* worried. Anson's goons were big, tough looking *sons of bitches*.

Janie posed for a photo with a couple of guys, her smile practiced, but somehow fake, thought Billie.

'That's enough, guys, give her some room,' said Billie, helping Janie disentangle from her admirers, and pulling her closer to the band. 'Is Clarice still in your room?'

'Yeah, I told her to stay put until we get to port,' said Janie.

Garth showed that he could also play the piano, and he struck up a tune, which made everyone stop talking. The sun was just starting to slide beneath the waves. It all seemed very serene as Janie started singing, her voice easily falling in with Garth's playing. Billie didn't know the song, though it sounded familiar. She looked around, wondering if Seb would soon join her, or if he had run into real trouble.

An hour passed, with Billie waiting tensely for Seb's return. Then Ranieri strode up, looking serious, pushing through the crowd that had formed around Janie. Billie turned, instantly recognising that something was wrong. Stopping before Billie, Ranieri leant close and whispered, 'Your friend, Sebastian, has been shot. Come with me.'

Billie trailed after Ranieri - numb, hollow, barely registering the power of Janie's voice as it lifted, filling the room, swelling into the night.

CHAPTER 40

Billie strode into the infirmary where Seb lay deathly pale, hooked to life support through a series of tubes. As she neared, a young female surgeon turned to face her. Billie noted the name badge – *Dr Shepherd.*

'Are you the next of kin?'

Billie hesitated – 'Yeah…yes I am.'

Small rivulets of perspiration had gathered across the surgeon's brow. Absently patting dry her face, Shepherd said, 'We've stabilised him, but he needs an operation.'

'Oh God…'

'I don't know how long he's got,' admitted Shepherd, frowning. 'There's a bullet inside him. There was no exit wound, and a lung has collapsed.'

Billie swallowed, staring first at Seb, then back at the doctor.

'So, you are his next of kin?'

'No…he…no…he has a sister…but she's not here.'

'I brought you here to say goodbye,' said Shepherd quietly.

'What?'

'We can't wait to operate. Look around – I'm no trauma surgeon, and we have a small blood supply, which he's already used.'

'I don't get it, I don't understand why…'

'He's been resuscitated twice already. I'm telling you – I don't' know how long he's got. I'm so sorry.'

'Can we get a helicopter?'

Shepherd shook her head slowly. 'It would take too long, and he wouldn't make it.'

Billie collapsed on a chair, suddenly feeling woozy with the realisation that Seb was going to die. Her riddle wrapped in a confounding mystery was going to die before she could unravel his strange existence, before she could finally make sense of him. So much of what he'd told her seemed utterly unbelievable, and yet – some part of her knew that he had not been lying. As a PI, deception was her stock and trade, and she knew what it looked and smelled like. Seb had none of it. He was a novice at pretence, no matter what he thought of himself.

Whether she had stumbled into his world, or he had deliberately drawn her into it, she now had the overwhelming feeling that it had been for a purpose. She hadn't believed in fate until this moment. But if there really was a power from above or beyond, had it brought her here, to this moment, to sit and idly watch Seb Straeker die? If fate did exist – wouldn't it deliver her with a plan, a super-power to heal him, to give him another chance at life?

Staring at him, tears formed and rolled down her cheeks. It was not that she loved him, or perhaps she felt that she didn't know him well enough to say she loved him. Her grief was born of the understanding that life was unfair, that good people died, and evil sometimes prevailed.

Today, the evil was Anson Mulgrave, who had sent killers to find Seb. Anson, the wife beater, the guy who didn't age, who used a serum that Seb had said was like a *force of nature*.

Billie had not heard Ranieri approach until the security guard asked, 'Does this have anything to do with Ashlee Donovan?'

'No.'

'Do you know who shot Seb?' asked Ranieri. Jackson, her partner, stood nearby, hand resting on his holster, looking tense.

Billie finally looked up and met Ranieri's eyes. 'Yeah, I saw him.'

'Who was it?'

'Anson Mulgrave,' lied Billie. 'You should ask where his wife is too.'

CHAPTER 41

'You stay here. I will have some questions for you later,' said Ranieri. Billie watched Ranieri and Jackson walk out of the infirmary. She thought she knew where they were going. Anson would at least have to answer some uncomfortable questions.

'Where are his things?' asked Billie, rising and going to Seb's bedside.

Dr Shepherd frowned, then pointed to the nurses' station outside. 'Top draw, left side.'

Billie slid the drawer open, revealing Seb's wallet, and the programmed room key that would let anyone enter nearly any room on the ship. But the gun was not there. Ranieri may have taken it, or maybe it was Anson's goons. She snatched up the *magic key* as Seb had called it and slipped it into her pocket.

Staring over her shoulder, towards Seb motionless form, she hesitated, resisting the urge to stay, to take his hand one last time. But this was not how life was supposed to go. *No way*...not on her watch... and if death was Seb's fate after all, then she'd be damned if she just stood by and watched like some pathetic, lovestruck fool.

'Look after him,' she called to Shepherd, before turning into the corridor and striding for the elevator.

Stepping out of the lift on the *diamond* deck, Billie immediately heard raised voices, one of which belonged to Ranieri. Outside, through the salt-crusted windows, she barely noticed the bright orange moon riding low, just above the silvered waves. Taking a deep breath, she thought *You can do this Billie* and started purposefully toward Anson's room.

*

The stairs led up into darkness, and his feet creaked on the treads.

'You've finally come to join me,' said Krystal. He looked up at a face that was pale, bright arterial blood trailing wet down from a large wound on top of her head.

'I'm not dead yet.'

'Oh Seb, you will be soon,' Krystal's voice floated to him through a frozen smile. 'Take my hand,' she said, reaching out.

'No.'

Dr Shepherd and the nurse were standing close to Seb's bed, watching his vitals. 'Look at his brain activity.'

'He's dreaming,' replied the nurse. 'I wonder what he's thinking about.'

'To stay or go?' mused Shepherd.

*

The party in the piano bar had not been planned, but Janie had attracted a large gathering, with guests all standing around drinking and dancing. The singer was now atop the grand piano, shimmying and belting out tune after tune. An hour earlier *Manson Villa,* realising the party was just getting started, had brought in some amps and hooked Janie up with a mic.

Brian stood off to the side, a smile creasing his face. He recognised that the real Janie was back, that this performance was her way of letting the ghosts of the past finally rest.

From the corner of his eye, Brian saw the elevator from the deck above begin to descend. It was encased entirely in glass, and he suspected that the view from their vantage of the party below, as it descended, would have been epic.

Janie's voice hit a high note, the crowd rising to applaud her. Inside the lift, Brian saw frenzied movement, a sudden spray of blood, and then a steady stream fountain across the glass. It was hard to see exactly what had happened.

Screams erupted as the crowds in the bar pointed and shouted at the slowly descending lift - for standing in it, it's face pressed to the glass was a creature of nightmare. Human remains were slumped on the floor at its feet in a jumble. Its body, roughly humanoid in shape, shimmered and glistened, giving the impression of fish scales. The black eyes regarded the humans with intelligence. Brian ran, with everyone else, fleeing the area, as the hairless, earless head suddenly opened its mouth, hissing, displaying long yellow fangs.

The elevator doors opened, and it slowly walked out, head swinging from side to side as it surveyed the area. A woman, swaying in high heels, filmed the thing with her phone, holding a cocktail in the other hand.

It sprang, and the cocktail glass spun from her hand, as the *skin* bore her down to the floor, sinking claws into her back. Pinned, it sprayed her with putrid, steaming venom, unleashed from glands behind it's teeth. Where it splashed, her flesh smoked as it began eating into her.

Elsewhere on the ship, more screams erupted, from close and far. Brian roughly grabbed Janie's arm as they fled, bouncing off passengers, jostling aside anyone too slow to move. Neither could find voice, instead running as a primal fear closed their throats, and injected their bodies with adrenaline.

*

Ranieri and Jackson commanded just enough respect to have Anson appear at his door. The celebrity stood obscured behind Kai and Adam, listening as Ranieri laid out Billie's accusation.

'Don't be stupid,' said Anson, pulling his robes close.

'Come back inside Anson,' called Marguerite from the rooms beyond.

'Just fucking wait, okay?' called Anson over his shoulder.

'Where's Clarice?' demanded Ranieri.

This question took the smile off his face. 'Oh, she can't come to the door.'

'I didn't ask her to,' said Ranieri. 'I already suspect that she's not in your rooms. Where is she?'

Anson tried to shut the door, but Ranieri shoved her foot into the opening. 'Move it or lose it, bitch.'

Kai pulled Ranieri back, and she stumbled as the door slammed shut. Jackson pulled his pistol and so did Kai. Adam was also reaching for his piece when Ranieri said, 'Everyone just cool it!'

Into that uncomfortable standoff Ranieri's radio suddenly crackled to life. 'Ranieri...come in!' It was the executive officer, stationed on the bridge.

She slowly reached for the radio – 'Just chill, I have to get this okay,' and took it from her belt. Holding the button down, she said, 'What is it? I'm in the middle of something.'

'Get up here, now. We have a situation!'

'What is it?'

Over the radio, the terrified voice barked - 'Jesus Christ! Get your asses up here.'

*

Billie had been listening intently to the conversation from just around a corner. And she'd heard the voice over the radio demanding that the security guards return to the bridge. Retreating, she heard Ranieri and Jackson's footsteps as they hurried back along the corridor toward her. Billie let herself into the nearest room using Seb's special key, hoping that the guests were no longer there. Finding the room vacant, she closed the door to a crack as Ranieri and Jackson swept past, heading for the lift, Ranieri firing questions into her radio.

She waited as the security officer's elevator departed, was about to step back out of the room when she saw a moon-cast shadow moving quietly along the corridor. Instinctively she held her position, holding her breath, because whatever was moving outside the door was incredibly, inhumanly quiet. Her throat suddenly dry, she strained her ears, listening for the footsteps, but only hearing distant screams. Backing away from the cracked door, Billie edged toward the nearby bathroom and slipped around the corner. Crouching in the blacked-out room, holding her breath, Seb's tales of terrifying boogeymen filled her mind, fuelled by those distant screams of terror.

The door to the cabin squeaked open. She could sense that someone was standing beyond, just around the corner. Placing a hand over her nose and mouth, desperate for her breathing to not reach the ears of whatever was out there, she waited.

'Hello? Anyone here?' The voice seemed hollow, like an imitation of a voice that a child might use. It was neither male nor female. Billie's flesh prickled, an instant chill crawling across the back of her neck.

After a minute, Billie realised whatever was outside had moved on because she heard it knocking softly on the next door along the corridor. The creature then went to the next door and the one after, knocking, knocking, knocking. Billie knew that nearly everyone was on the top-decks, because it was dinner time. She stood slowly, though slightly unsteady, taking some much-needed deep breaths before edging back toward the corridor.

At the cabin's entrance, Billie chanced a quick look around the corner, into the corridor. Nothing moved. She swallowed, then crept out quietly, wishing she had a gun or something. Then she heard shots, several, rapid fire, just ahead, shattering the night. Billie backed up to the room she had just been hiding in and closed the door. Anson's room was under attack. Fighting back rising panic, Billie waited several minutes as more shots broke the silence, only to be replaced by screams - first of terror, then of agony.

The silence that eventually followed was almost as dreadful as the preceding mayhem. No longer able to determine what was going on, or where anyone was, she imagined the *skin* creeping back toward her hiding place. But time was against her, or rather against Seb, who she now pictured lying in his deathbed, waiting for the inevitable. It was that image that forced her to stand, to walk, and finally leave her concealment.

Billie edged along the corridor, back pressed to the wall, placing her feet as carefully as if she were on a precipice, and the drop a thousand feet.

Rounding the corner, she found Anson's bodyguards lying in the corridor, throats ripped open. The ceiling light had dimmed, splashed by an arterial spray from either Kai or Adam. Billie bent and took a large pistol from Kai, and then rifling his pockets, found a spare magazine. She ejected the spent magazine and slid the new one in, her hand trembling. As she was about to go into Anson's room, Kai's eyes flicked to hers, and his mouth worked, his dying words meant for her ears, 'Be careful.'

Billie pulled her arm away, and Kai's flopped down, eyes now fixed elsewhere. 'No shit,' she hissed, jumping to her feet and barging into Anson's room, the Colt .45 held in a two-hand grip.

Beyond the living room, she found Anson and his mistresses lying sprawled across a king-sized bed, the nearly naked trio most assuredly dead. The *skin* was gone, she realised, walking slowly forward, allowing the handgun to drop to her side. Examining Anson, she saw he had come in for special attention, as though the *skin* had somehow known him. Billie pulled her eyes from them and sidled toward the cabinet. Opening the bedside draws, she searched through them.

She turned, keeping the Colt ready, trying to steady her breathing. 'Where is it?'

In the bathroom she found a number of bottles, and a few medications. 'God-dam-it – *nothing*.'

Back in the reception room, she went to the main console. There was drink bottles arrayed across it, a small stereo, and below – several more draws. In the second draw she found a metallic case. She brought it out and placed it on the floor. It had no discernible lock. She turned it over and then again. There was a small pad, on top of it, where a biometric reader had been installed.

She walked it over to the bed and took Anson's index finger, then pressed it to the pad. The case clicked open, and Billie looked inside. Two large vials of blue liquid sat safely within padding. They looked like they held around 400ml each. Carefully, she removed them, then looking at them closely, she saw specs floating or swimming in the liquid. Almost microscopic, they seemed to glow with a sickly luminescence.

'What *is* this shit?'

She pocketed each vial in her jacket where they sat bulging. So far, everything Seb had told her had played out as true.

'Adios,' said Billie, glancing at Anson, moving quickly now for the door, the Colt .45 ready.

CHAPTER 42

Seb was standing on the edge of a frozen mountain road, snow dusting his feet. The car was on its roof, and despite the cold, it was smouldering. Two forlorn, ragged figures stood near the wreckage rather than in it. They were holding hands, and as Seb came close, they turned and looked at him, their charred faces almost unrecognisable.

'Mum...Dad?'

'Seb, is that you?' said his mother.

'Oh Mom, I've missed you so much.'

'Are you coming now?' asked his Dad.

Seb didn't know. He stood facing them, wondering. Then his mother held out her hand, and Seb stared at it.

Billie hurried to the lift and hit the *call* button. She waited as it descended, standing to the side, the pistol aimed at the doors. When they creaked open, she peered inside, and gasped. A couple were lying in a pool of blood. Billie averted her eyes, not wanting the image to imprint on her mind. Stepping in, she closed the doors and descended to the lower level, where she knew Seb was either still clinging to life or had already died.

In the infirmary, Dr Shepherd lay dead, slumped face down beside Seb's bed. The nurse had clearly fled. Billie edged forward, around the bed, seeing that Seb seemed to be holding on. The tubes down his throat pumped air. He also had tubes in his arms, one hooked to a drip. His heartbeat seemed fast, and reading the monitors, his blood pressure looked dangerously low.

'Here goes Seb,' she said, opening her coat pocket and laying a blue vial on the side of the bed, while she looked around for a syringe.

Seb pulled back from his mother's outstretched hand. Instead of being angry as he feared, she smiled, and in it he felt a deep love, radiating out, and enfolding him. Then she nodded, and slowly they faded.

Something was stirring inside, something that coruscated across his body, tingling like walking into sunshine after being down a black hole. The feeling grew, and warmth flooded across his whole body, tasting like nectar, humming and vibrating through him, the feeling of building velocity… of flying.

Billie had lain her head across Seb's chest as the blue liquid made a slow trail down the intravenous line and into his arm.

Then after a minute Seb came awake with a jolt, his eyes terrified. He grabbed the tube from his throat, both hands needed as he pulled it slowly out, gasping and disgorging resinous liquid.

'Where the fuck am I?' he finally croaked.

Billie stood back, her eyes going wide. 'Holy shit!'

Seb stared at Billie, and Billie stared back, her mouth moving, but words refusing to form.

'How did…' he began, his heart beating so hard that he could feel blood pounding in his ears.

'You were shot.'

'Was I? Oh yeah.' Seb was recalling what had happened, his chest heaving.

'*Jesus* Seb, that stuff is…' began Billie.

'What stuff?' Then he looked at the intravenous line and saw a smoky blue colour in it.

'You were dying…the doctor said so. I couldn't just sit by.'

Seb stared down beside the bed, his eyes widening as he saw Dr Shepherd's body. Her throat was torn open, and blood had spurted from the wound, across her face and onto the wall and ceiling.

'What's happened?' he asked.

'The *skins*...they are everywhere,' she hissed. 'We need to get off the ship.'

Then Seb was taking deep, rapid breaths. 'How much did you give me?'

Billie placed the emptied vial on the bed. In a small voice she said, 'All of it.'

Seb was smiling one second, and the next his spine arched stiffly, forming a plank. Eyes rolling back into his head, he collapsed back onto the bed and began convulsing uncontrollably. Billie grabbed feebly onto his arms as he jerked and spasmed. 'Seb, what's wrong!'

CHAPTER 43

The bridge was locked down. Designed to withstand a terrorist attack, the command centre of the ship was perhaps the safest place to be. The *bridge crew* could see out through a small, reinforced window, and if they kept the door locked, nothing could get in.

Captain Phillippe was holding the intercom phone and calling out the positions of the creatures when they were seen on the ship's CCTV camera system. Ranieri and Jackson were pacing, pistols drawn, watching the only door into the area.

'What are they?' asked Ranieri.

But no-one answered because no-one knew. The crew was standing around in muted, shock-induced silence.

Phillippe called down to the engine room. 'Pick up engineer. Pick up.' He wanted more power, to make for Honolulu with all the speed the ship could muster.

'They're not there,' said Jackson. 'Or if they are, they're hiding.'

'Hillary West and her friends leave, then we discover the *ship to shore systems* are broken,' said Ranieri. 'Then these *things* appear.' She shook her head. 'I need to go and help.'

'Are you mad?' asked Phillippe.

Ranieri was watching a bank of monitors showing different

areas all around the ship. She could see people crouched, trapped behind bars, others trying to hide in corners behind anything they could find. Rarely did she see any of the creatures, for they seemed to blend, like chameleons. They stalked along, heads bent slightly forward, as if sniffing. 'I can't stay in here. It's not right.'

*

Darian had tried to call Anson. The guy was a chump, and so he figured he was ignoring his calls. Robyn and Jonty had earlier joined Darian in his cabin, turning up the music, now engaged in a loud card game.

Clive and Wayne burst in, Clive going to the radio and switching it off.

'Hey!' protested Robyn.

'*Shush*.' Clive had his finger to his lips. They all knew to shut up, and when they did, distant screams could be heard, emanating from the decks above.

'Party?' asked Darian.

Clive shook his head. 'Something bad is happening. I heard the captain on the intercom making some announcements – but they made no sense.'

Darian said, 'Jonty – get the *Squalus* on the radio. Tell them to stand by for a pickup. It's time to get of this tub.'

'Yes major.'

'Robyn and Wayne. Go see what's going on,' said Darian.

Robyn nodded, and Wayne turned to leave. Before they could go, Darian said, 'Take a side-arm. But don't scare anyone, okay?'

*

The room was blacked out. But the moon was full, the ocean calm as the ship slipped through the waves. Silvered light shone in from the balcony, diffused by the billowing curtain, revealing the silhouettes of the band members. They were seated around the edge of the room, shocked into silence, trying, but failing to process what they had just witnessed.

Janie and Clarice were seated on the blue velvet couch, with Brian and Sam nearby. Everyone was cradling a drink in stiff fingers. They reasoned that if they stayed quiet, kept the lights off, and the door locked, they could ride out whatever was going on outside.

'Where's Seb and Billie when you need them?' whispered Sam.

Janie raised a finger to her lips, though Sam could barely see her.

Something tapped on the door. It was a light touch, but the room was so quiet that they all heard it. Then it came again. *Tap, tap, tap.* Then louder *knock, knock, knock.* 'Hello?'

Brian was about to get up, but Janie grappled his arm. He pulled away from her and walked toward the door. 'Someone needs our help,' he hissed back at the group.

Thump…thump…thump. The door shook with each blow. Brian stopped and stared at the door. Then it started again – *THUMP… THUMP…THUMP.*

CHAPTER 44

The seizures that had taken Seb slowly abated. When he settled, his body was bathed in so much sweat that the sheets were also damp. But he had passed out, and though Billie gently shook him, he would not wake. She could see his heart rate was elevated, for a pulse was jumping in his throat. The serum had dragged him back from the brink, had stabilised him, and more – it had healed him in a way that she knew should not be possible. Even as she watched, his wounds seemed to be healing, colour came back into his face, and death now seemed just a memory.

Billie considered what had just happened. The initial attack on the ship's human population seemed to have stalled, or perhaps the *skins* were now enjoying stalking everyone, taking people that were isolated, one by one. Billie did not know if this was true or not, but the screaming had died down, and the ship seemed to be cruising in silence. She waited at Seb's side, willing him to come awake. She resisted the desperate urge to leave him, to find somewhere else to be, some dark hiding place where they would not find her.

Instead, she crouched in the corner, no more than a few feet from Shepherd's body, pistol in hand. Then she heard footsteps approaching, and her breathing became hurried.

'Who's there? Is anyone there?'

Billie rose over the edge of Seb's bed, pointing the pistol past the nurses' station where the intruder would have to approach. When Ranieri stepped into view, the two women were pointing their pistols at each other.

'Ranieri? Oh thank God.'

The security officer lowered her gun and walked in. She glanced down at Seb. 'He's alive?' Ranieri came close and whispered, 'You need to come with me. I can take you to the bridge.'

'No. He's alive, and he will wake again.'

'He woke?' asked Ranieri, her eyes again on Seb. Then she noticed that the tubes had been removed from his throat, and the intravenous lines were no longer attached. 'That's…'

'A miracle,' said Billie.

Ranieri came closer still, and both women watched the corridor carefully. Ranieri whispered, 'Do you know what these things are?'

Billie shook her head and then glanced at Seb. 'He knows more.'

Ranieri glanced at Seb, then said, 'What do you know?'

'I know there are seven of them, and that they came aboard in crates. I know that Ashlee Donovan let one or more out, and she was killed by them. But that's it, that's all I have.'

'I seriously doubt that,' said Ranieri.

'I also know we need to get off the ship, or we're all *dead meat*.'

*

Thump, thump, thump.

Although the hinges somehow held throughout the beating, the door was splintered right through in several places.

Shots rang out, and they heard a scream of rage, which was not human. Then more shots, and they heard voices just outside the door.

'Did you kill it?' asked Wayne.

'I hit it, but…where is it?' spat Robyn.

'Did you see it? What an ugly bastard.'

'Look – you hit it alright. There's blood.'

Janie opened the door and found Robyn and Wayne's pistols pointing at her face.

'We came to see what was happening,' said Wayne, wiping a hand through his hair subconsciously as he stared at Janie.

Janie abruptly closed the door.

'Rude bitch,' said Robyn. 'No – 'thankyou' or anything.'

Janie turned to the others, and Sam said, 'Find out who they are.'

Wayne and Robyn were still there when Janie opened the door again. It was Robyn who hurried into the room, pushing past Janie.

'Come in… why don't you,' said Janie.

'Did you see that thing?' asked Wayne, eyes darting.

'They appeared on the top decks first, and started attacking everyone,' said Sam.

Wayne and Robyn just looked at each other. Then Wayne said, 'The cases - we never saw what was inside. Imagine…'

'What cases?' asked Sam.

'Who cares!' said Janie, coming and standing in front of Wayne. 'You have guns – can you kill them?'

BOOM…the detonation rolled across them, rocked the ship, jolting everyone. Clarice screamed, finally giving voice to the terror that had been building in her. Her voice was joined by many others all over the ship.

In the aftermath, they all stood staring at each other in silence, listening for a few moments, and then there came a second explosion, a low resounding *thud* which seemed further away, deeper in the ship's belly.

Brian rushed out to the balcony, with Sam and Garth close behind. They looked down and around at the side of the ship. There was no smoke, nothing visible, although the ship seemed to be slowing.

'This is very fucking bad,' stated Sam.

'What was it?' asked Garth.

Sam leant out over the rail.'Oh, *I don't know* Garth, maybe it was fireworks. What the fuck do you think just happened!'

'It was a bomb,' said Robyn, appearing beside them. 'Maybe a limpet mine. Whatever those were – they were big.'

But there was no announcement from the captain, no alarm either. The ship slowed, and listed slightly, then they knew that the *Estrella de Mar* was taking on water.

'Oh my God,' breathed Sam.

Robyn retreated – then paused at the door with Wayne. 'There are seven of them. Those things can't be everywhere. You should try to get to a lifeboat and...'

Janie grabbed Robyn's arm. 'Wait! Can't you help us? You could escort us to the boats.'

'Please!' said Sam.

'I'm sorry,' said Robyn, turning away, pulling her arm free.

Sam and Janie watched as Robyn and Wayne disappeared at a run along the corridor. Sam closed the door as Janie turned to her entourage, 'It's just us.'

Brian said, 'Where is Billie and Sebastian? Should we wait for them?'

The intercom crackled to life. *This is your captain. Make your way to the lifeboats. Good luck and God speed.* The evacuation signal started, a *whoop - whoop* sound, which seemed to make it all worse.

CHAPTER 45

Ranieri and Billie had felt the explosions. What lights were left in the infirmary dimmed and then switched over to the backup systems. Seb didn't even stir in his bed.

'Is it just me…?' asked Billie.

'I feel it,' said Ranieri. 'The ship has tilted. That was a big bomb.'

'You should leave - go back to the bridge. I will be okay,' said Billie.

Ranieri was about to depart, then turned, gripped Billie's hand, and smiled. 'Would he do this for you?'

Billie nodded. 'He would…I think.'

"Then good luck Billie.' Ranieri ran, and Billie heard the lift doors open and close. The silence of the ship gathered around her. She knew that she had a little time before the ship sank.

She turned to Seb and shook him. 'Wake up!' But Seb seemed comatose. She took the remaining bottle of serum from her coat and placed it on the bed, then thoughtfully glanced down at Seb.

*

Wayne and Robyn decided against the elevators, preferring to take the stairs as they made their way back toward Darian and the rest of their crew.

They didn't see the figure detach from the wall, until it landed on Wayne, ripping its talons into his neck. He slammed into the stairs and pitched downward with a cry. Robyn screamed and brought up her pistol, trying to aim as Wayne flopped over and over. The lights flickered and dimmed. When Robyn had caught up, Wayne was lying twisted, his throat torn out. The creature was gone.

She turned, rage and fear making her face what had somehow slipped behind her. Firing, screaming, she unloaded the weapon. The first couple of shots tore into its chest but did not stop it. The *skin* slammed into her, suddenly more visible, knocking aside the pistol, and biting her on the face.

Robyn backed away, firing wildly, emptying what was left of the magazine. She allowed the spent magazine to clatter to the stairs and fumbled for another.

'The venom works fast.'

'I shot you.'

'Not in the right place.' It gave a wheezy laugh.

Her vision swam, and she could not see it anymore, then within a heartbeat she could not see anything. She slumped down, allowing herself to collapse near her friend's body. She had heard it speak, and that surprised her, because it sounded human. Then the venom began eating into her face, and pain engulfed her. Her screams lasted a minute before she fell silent.

*

On the bridge, Phillippe had gone pale. He was watching the bank of monitors over the shoulder of his executive officer. 'Let's see the engine room. Bring it up.'

'Captain, we have no power,' responded the executive officer.

'I know that!' barked Phillippe. 'Just do it. I won't leave until we know for certain.'

The executive officer nodded and then concentrated on hooking into the closed-circuit camera in the engine room.

The screen was now showing the main engine room, where the turbines and salt-water filters were overseen by twenty engineers. There was a pall in the air, of smoke and debris, still wafting about. They could see bodies lying on the floor. But two engineers were running around the room, desperately adjusting instruments.

'Engine room, engine room come in,' said Phillippe into a telephone. But the engineers, if they could hear him, kept working.

'Show me the holds. We must have cameras down there somewhere.'

The monitor showed a hold. It was dark. They couldn't see anything. 'Bring up the second hold.'

The monitor flickered and bay 2 was shown. It was filling with water.

Phillippe put down the phone and sat heavily on the chair behind him. 'No power, and we have a large hole somewhere, maybe more than one. Let's get to the lifeboats. We have to save whoever we can.'

CHAPTER 46

Ranieri and Jackson were creeping, taking it slow and steady, doing a methodical sweep of the lower passenger decks. The hallways were dimly lit with low, flickering light as the backup systems struggled to find the power needed. An unnatural silence weighed down on them, broken only by their quickened breaths and the thumping blood in their ears.

'No-one will be here still. They'd be crazy,' said Jackson. The big security guard glistened within a membrane of fear sweat. As Ranieri faced him, a thin rivulet ran down the side of his nose.

'Try to chill,' hissed Ranieri, though she held her Glock in a white-knuckle, two-hand grip. Her stomach was doing somersaults despite having emptied it.

They approached a door, and Ranieri pushed, suspecting it was already unlocked. It creaked inward, exposing the barest outlines of the furniture within the darkness. Glancing once at each-other, they darted in fast, guns trained forward. Ranieri swung her torch around, seeking danger. The balcony door was open, and a phantom breeze swayed the curtain. Jackson flinched, bringing up his pistol.

'Easy,' she said, moving deeper into the room.

'What's this?' Jackson had picked up a piece of paper from the bed. He shone a torch onto it. 'It's a suicide note. Oh man...this is a fucking nightmare.'

They glanced toward the open balcony door, Ranieri holding back tears. Then she said, 'Let's go. We have more work to do.' Jackson folded the paper and slipped it into his pocket. 'Someone, somewhere deserves to be given this note.'

Further along the corridor they stopped at another door. Although they didn't hear anything inside, Ranieri knocked lightly.

'Go away,' came a muffled voice.

'No, we can't do that. You need to come with us!' said Jackson.

'Keep your voice down,' said Ranieri. She looked at him and shook her head, her eyes conveying her fear. In reply, Jackson slowly nodded understanding, his face dripping sweat.

'Come out folks, we have to get to the lifeboats,' said Ranieri, pitching her voice low.

Then she pushed on the door, and it swung inward. Darkness hid whatever was inside. Ranieri and Jackson listened, and carefully peered within, straining to see anything in the beams of the torchlight. The hair on their necks stood up, as primal instinct anchored them to the spot.

'Hello?' called Jackson softly, peering further inside.

'Come in...come closer,' came a small voice, that of young child. Moments before, the voice they had heard was that of an adult male.

Jackson stepped forward, but Ranieri grabbed his wrist. 'Wait.'

Ranieri lifted her gun, extending her arm. Jackson followed her, gun tucked behind the torch. Slowly they crept forward, Ranieri leading the way. In the middle of the floor, they could now see the outline of a dark shape, low to the ground. The shadow seemed to blend into the carpet. It was bent over something, and when they listened, they could hear a crunching, and slurping. As it turned to face them, they could just make out the dim outline of its dread eyes.

Then Ranieri and Jackson started shooting, and through the muzzle flashes, they could see the creature bucking as it was struck.

Cordite hung in the air, thick within the confined space. The skin had fallen back, but now it was twitching, and beginning to sit up. Ranieri was already slapping in another magazine. But the creature darted through the balcony door, even as Ranieri fired again, trailing it by a heartbeat.

Jackson, feeling bold, stuck his head out into the night, and watched as the creature leapt from balcony to balcony, fleeing along the outside of the ship. Perhaps ten balconies along, he saw it duck inside another room.

'It's gone. I can't do this…that's it…we need to leave.'

On the floor, under torchlight, they saw a man lying face up. His legs had both been chewed off just below the knees. 'Goddam it,' said Ranieri again, perhaps for the twentieth time that night.

Then his eyes opened, and he croaked, 'Kill me.'

'He's alive,' said Jackson.

'Hold on sir, just hang in there,' said Ranieri, taking the victim's hand.

But it was clear that the man had little time remaining. His face was deathly pale, and they could feel the large pool of blood beneath their hands where they knelt on the carpet. In his tortured eyes, Ranieri could see that he knew his time was close. 'Don't let them have me,' he whispered.

'Wait outside, Jackson,' said Ranieri quietly. 'We have more rooms to check.'

When Jackson had retreated to the corridor, Ranieri took a pillow and put it against the victim's head, pressed the Glock in close. After a moment, she pulled the trigger, and the muffled shot sent feathers flying everywhere. As she retreated from the room, they drifted back toward the floor.

At the next door, Ranieri stopped and bent over double. But she had already thrown up twice and had nothing left in her stomach. 'Open the door,' she gasped to Jackson, wiping moisture from her eyes.

He kicked the door open, and they waited, guns poised. But

nothing emerged, and no-one spoke. They waited, listening for a full minute, before Jackson hurriedly pulled the door closed again.

'We need to get out - look after ourselves now,' said Jackson. 'It's time to go. Come on, we're nearly out of ammo.'

'Just a few more doors, Jackson...okay?'

He looked at her, and she could see the strain in his face. She wondered if she looked like Jackson and knew that she probably did. At last, he nodded, tight lipped and pale.

At the next door, as they approached, it opened before they could knock. A woman and her two daughters were huddled there. The mother said, 'Is it safe to come out yet? We don't know the way to the boats.'

Ranieri grabbed her arm and said, 'Mam, I don't know how safe it is, but if you stay in there, you and your beautiful daughters will surely die. Come with us.'

*

'Wake up...wake up...wake up,' Billie said over and over, each time giving Seb's arm a pull. But he was in a deep sleep, his breathing now regular and calm.

She sensed rather than heard the movement at the end of the corridor. She had filled a large syringe, using all the serum that Anson had purchased. *Could she give Seb the other bottle? Would it be an overdose that would kill him?*

She waited, holding the syringe, barely breathing. Seb's face had not changed. She began tapping his cheek, then she pinched it lightly, then harder still. He refused to stir.

Then she heard the footsteps, slow and light. They were creeping steps, from something that knew how to stalk prey. Billie brought up the pistol and held her breath. Ranieri had not come back. And if it was human, she would hear shoes on the hard floor. No – it was a *skin*.

It was close now. Just past the nurses station it paused. She saw it in the reflection of a mirror on the far wall. It was standing just around the corner, barely an outline, taking on the colour of beige paint. The creature stood rock still, it's face tilted up at a slight angle as if sampling the air.

'Fuck it!' she said and stabbed the syringe into Seb's leg.

If she had meant to give him only a little, before she knew it, she had fully depressed it, and Seb was given the whole lot. He now had two large doses of the serum within an hour.

He surged awake, looking around wildly. The *skin* appeared, its dire black eyes falling on them.

Billie unleashed a hail of bullets, and at close range she struck it in the upper torso, centre mass. It didn't die, though it pitched back, seeming to absorb the impact of every bullet.

Seb surged out of bed, his muscles swollen, tendons standing out like ropes, a wild exaltation coursing through him. It gathered momentum, and as the serum travelled, he roared, a beastly sound that had Billie ducking away from him. Fire and ice sluiced through his veins, and he wondered if he would survive the tumult. It felt like he had been struck by lightning, and his heart laboured under the strain.

The *skin* stood and came back at them, black blood seeping from bullet holes.

Seb stepped into its path as it flung itself at Billie. He caught it by the neck and swung it around, flinging it into the wall. Its head broke through the plaster and for a moment it was stuck there.

'Go!' growled Seb, shoving Billie away. She skidded along the shiny floor on her backside, out into the corridor.

The *skin* backed out and flung itself on Seb, opening its gaping mouth, spraying him with venom. Thick liquid splashed across his face, and arms. It smoked, but he didn't seem to care. The skin clung to him, and he tried to strangle it. The two - locked together, fought for control. The skin tried to bite him, and Seb moved his face, inhumanly fast, avoiding its probing fangs.

Face to face, he could smell its reeking breath, could see rubbery bile-coloured gums where the razor-sharp teeth sprouted in nests, some straight, others hooked. The skin glistened with an oily residue which shifted and swirled under the light, perhaps playing a part in the beast's chameleon ability to almost hide in plain sight. All this Seb absorbed in what was only a few heartbeats but imprinted forever in his mind.

Billie stood and ran, instinct to flee, to survive. She slid to a stop beside a fire reel box and flung it open. The hose was there, but so was an axe.

Seb punched the skin in its torso, feeling his fist meet dense flesh, perhaps cartilage. It seemed to absorb the blow, and the next, before raking a talon across his chest that was meant for his throat. Seb felt pain, but it seemed distant. The venom was burning, and his chest bled from five long inch-deep gashes.

Then he backhanded it, a lightning-fast blow, and the *skin* skidded sideways. Then for the first time it warily looked at Seb, wondering why he hadn't yet succumbed.

'Hey!' Billie flung the axe. It slid across the tiled floor and ended up at Seb's feet.

Grinning, Seb bent and picked it up. The *skin's* tongue flickered out, forked and purple, and something in that look conveyed deep unease.

'Get it Seb!' shouted Billie. 'Kill the *mother*.'

He stepped forward and swung. The axe felt lighter than a baseball bat and he carved into the side of its belly, the momentum lifting it off its feet. The *skin* shrieked, a high-pitched wail that shredded the night. It fell to the floor, clutching its open torso. Then it unsteadily managed to crouch, holding up a taloned hand as Seb flipped the axe with a flick of his wrist, testing its balance.

'No,' it moaned.

The axe flashed, the *skin's* head bounced away, and it toppled sideways, disgorging a black torrent from its open neck.

'See, they can be killed,' growled Seb, gazing down at the corpse, trying to understand what it was. There was some human aspect to it, though everything about its skin and face was reptilian.

Billie tentatively came to his side, reached out slowly, placing a hand to his shoulder, as if to steady him. Feverish sweat had sprung across his body, drenching him in thin rivulets. A vein visibly pulsed in the side of his throat.

'I gave you all of it,' she said quietly.

He could feel the serum, seeping through every pore, crawling along each artery, to his every extremity. 'I can feel it. It's…' His eyes bored into hers, and she could see his predatory hunger. Billie withdrew her hand and backed away, putting space between them.

Seb continued, 'It's like I could fly, but I feel so…*angry*. I'm only just in control,' he warned.

Staring at him, she noted the acid burns on his face and chest were no more than charcoal smudges, and the deep punctures across his torso, inflicted by the creature's long talons were no longer seeping blood.

'I'm sorry.'

Shaking his head slowly, he said, 'Why are you sorry? You saved me, Billie.' He tried to offer a reassuring smile, but she could see the darkness lurking behind his eyes. The Seb she knew was somewhere back there, but she had the sense that he was sharing his body with another version of himself, one she hoped would not turn psychotic.

Billie felt a shift beneath her feet. Almost imperceptibly, the floor began to tilt. Now at around 20 degrees past horizontal, the *Estrella de Mar* was turning slowly onto its side, preparing to slip away into the depths.

'Seb, we need to get the hell off this ship right now!'

They started toward the elevator, Seb still clutching the fire-axe. Billie trailed close behind, holding the pistol ready.

CHAPTER 47

On the top deck, the night sky was bright with stars, the moon an orange eye that gazed unblinking upon them. Phillippe personally engaged the switch that lowered the lifeboats, dropping them into position on their mechanical arms. Hundreds of the passengers and crew had gathered on deck, clumping in groups of fifty or more in case the *boogey-men* came back. There was a hum of quiet, worried voices, and some pushing and shoving as people of all ages tried to get to the front of the pack where the lifeboats would soon be opened.

Phillippe strode around the deck, barking orders at his officers, sometimes in English, sometimes in his native French when he forgot himself.

Darian, Clive, and Jonty didn't know where Robyn and Wayne had gone, but they knew when they didn't return that they were likely dead. They stood, guns ready, watching the shadows, trying to at least provide some meagre protection as the boats were readied. No-one knew where the three soldiers came from, nor did they care. Guns were all that stood between them and certain death.

As the ship tipped to over 30 degrees, the final lifeboat reached its departure position. Ranieri and Jackson had arrived, escorting several passengers. They too were watching, trying to prevent people climbing into the boats before they were in a safe position to board. Equipped with lifejackets, these vessels, shaped like rigid capsules, were designed to protect those within from the sun and rain as much as the ocean itself.

'I think we are going to make it.' Sam watched eagerly as their lifeboat was made ready, silently willing the crew to hurry.

A strange, subdued quiet settled across the passengers who could now see the way was almost clear to escape, to survive the terror they'd endured.

'Is this everyone,' asked Janie, glancing around at Sam and the rest of her entourage as they gathered close to the railing.

'I don't know what happened to Bille and Seb,' said Brian. 'Maybe they are at another lifeboat station.'

Ranieri came by with her gun drawn, eyes darting. She halted near them, face pale and drawn. 'Have you seen Billie?'

Janie could only shake her head, refusing to give voice to the possibility that Billie and Seb were gone.

Ranieri said, 'Stay close to everyone. I haven't seen one of *them* for a while. They seem to be staying clear of us for now. I don't know why.'

'It's time!' bellowed Phillippe into a loud hailer.

The crew began shepherding passengers onto the boats, and within moments the first was lowered on pullies into the water. The hooks holding it disengaged, and the boat's motor coughed to life. It steered away from the sinking liner, slowly propelled into the calm waters. More boats dropped onto the silky surface, and within minutes nearly all of them were in the water, and slowly departing, their hatches shut. Faces peered from within the portholes, some still showing fear, others merely stared out in shock.

There were two boats left. Janie and *Manson Villa* entered the second to last, Clarice with them. Clarice turned, her eyes scanning for Seb or Billie, before stepping inside. Their boat lowered and within seconds they were safely away.

Captain Phillippe raised his arm and fired a flare into the night-sky. As it burst, hundreds of feet above, a bright, sizzling light hung in the air, painting everyone remaining on deck in a luminous red glow.

'Come in *Squalus*,' said Darian into his radio. 'Come in Ariki. Mate, are you there?'

Got you major. Ariki sounded relieved.

'Ariki, we need an immediate evac, as in right now,' replied Darian.

Look aft, major.

Darian and Jonty looked toward the stern, and saw the *Squalus* approach, its lights dim. No larger than a tug, or trawler, the small vessel powered through the calm waters, closing the gap with every second. Darian clapped Jonty on the shoulder. Now less than a quarter of a mile distant and coming fast, they could see Ariki's silhouette standing in the wheelhouse.

'That's my ride, captain,' said Darian, as Phillippe came nearer, squinting at the approaching vessel.

'I don't know what part you played in this devilry,' said Phillippe.

'We had nothing to do with it, captain. But I know who did,' responded Darian. The two men looked at each other for a long moment, and then Phillippe stiffly nodded before turning away.

A deep reverberating moan echoed into the night as the ship listed closer to the waterline. Phillippe gazed about – despair and disbelief etched in his face. After a moment of contemplation, tilting his cap down, he walked toward the final lifeboat, joined by a few remaining crew. Jackson and Ranieri fell in beside their captain as he entered, with Ranieri closing the hatch behind them. They operated the pully from within the lifeboat, and soon they too were bobbing away from the hull.

The motor had just started, the lifeboat heading out to meet with the others when its top hatch opened suddenly and Ranieri scrambled out, shouting obscenities. She stood atop it, balancing with her feet planted wide, pistol drawn, peering back inside. Darian and his men watched on helplessly, as screams of terror burst from within the lifeboat.

'Jesus...' breathed Darian, staring down.

Ranieri gripped the pistol in both hands, fired a shot down through the opening, then another. Slamming the hatch shut, she turned, and without further hesitation dove into the sea. Her lifeboat motored away, unpiloted, away from the rest.

*

Twice they had been delayed as *skins* appeared in the darkness ahead, but with Seb's improved eyesight able to see them clearly, they had backtracked. He was no longer terrified of them, but Seb knew that should they come against more than one, he would be hard pressed.

And they'd now discovered that the elevators were no longer operating. In near darkness, they could only guess that the corridor was several levels below the top deck. With water already up to their knees, they pushed ahead, searching for stairs.

'Everyone's gone,' whispered Billie.

'I wonder why,' replied Seb.

'Why are there no lights?' asked Billie.

'Seawater in the generator compartment will do that,' quipped Seb.

'Will they wait for us do you think?'

Stalking ahead, the fire axe balanced on his shoulder, Seb mumbled, 'Let's hope so.'

'We're going to drown. I don't want to drown. And if I have to die – I'd rather it wasn't in the dark.'

Seb abruptly turned - 'I think we have one behind us, pretty close.' That feverish gleam in his eyes told her that he wanted to confront it.

'Are you listening?' she hissed, grabbing and yanking his arm.

He turned, raised a hand as if he was about to strike her, but then slowly dropped it.

'Get a hold of yourself,' she said, staring him down.

Taking deep breaths, he fought for control. Within moments his eyes somehow changed, and she could see the old Seb in there once more. 'Let's go,' he said through gritted teeth, and pushed forward, the water now at their thighs.

*

'We're nearly there,' said Billie, recognising the chandeliers hanging from the ceiling were a fixture of the main dining hall. No longer lit from below by coloured neon globes, the curved stairs ascended out of the water.

'Not much further,' he agreed, pulling her by the hand. Around the bend in the stairs, they could now see the glitter of stars above. From below they heard splashing, and Seb pushed Billie behind him, lifted the axe and waited to confront the creature.

'Oh my God,' said Kyle, coming up the stairs, his white suitcoat stained and soaked. 'I thought I was the only person alive.'

'Kyle Beacon?' said Billie, shaking her head.

'You know me?' he replied. Despite everything, an idiot grin split his face.

'I don't believe it!' said Billie, turning away.

'Come on,' urged Seb, striding upward. Shudders and moans vibrated through the ship's superstructure. The sea was hungrily pulling the ship down, sucking her under with each passing moment.

Emerging on the top deck they found the ship deserted. As they hurried to the rail, barely ten feet from the waves, they could see the lifeboat flotilla perhaps a half a mile away, their cabin lights dancing in the darkness.

'We've gotta swim it,' said Seb. 'You should take your clothes off. They'll weigh you down.'

'You'd like that, wouldn't you,' said Billie, but she was already peeling out of her shirt, the buttons flying.

Beacon was hopping up and down as he pulled thousand-dollar loafers from his feet, all the while swearing under his breath.

A figure suddenly slammed into them, knocking the movie-star cartwheeling into the waves below. Billie crashed against the rail, air exploding from her lungs. But Seb had absorbed the blow, and he turned as the *skin* leapt onto him, trying to pull the axe from his grasp.

'Seb!' she screamed, her voice shattering the night. A second creature appeared from the other end of the deck, drawn by the commotion. 'Oh God!' Billie yelled, turning, extending her arm, and taking aim down the barrel of the .45. Squeezing off each shot, Billie watched in horror as the bullets struck their mark, punching flesh, but seeming to have little impact as the creature slowly advanced.

From his position on the *Squalus* - Clive looked up as the shots rang out. Bobbing slightly in the black waves, around 400 yards from the sinking ship, hovering there, they had been waiting to see if anyone else would make it out alive. Her captain, Ariki was at the wheel. Beside him, Darian stood tensely staring through night vision binoculars.

'There was shooting. I heard a woman scream something,' said Clive, sticking his head into the cabin.

'Get us closer, Ariki,' commanded Darian.

Ariki turned to starboard and cruised slowly toward the sinking ship. 'I don't want any of those things climbing on-board us Darian.'

'There! Look!' Darian pointed at Billie and Seb. 'They're in trouble.'

Ranieri stood on the front of the converted trawler, a towel wrapped around her shoulders, dread filling her, but unable to look away. 'We have to do something!' She turned, and screamed at Jonty, 'Do something!'

Billie backed away as the skin approached, pulling the trigger until the magazine emptied. Seb had wrenched the axe away from the skin and was trying desperately to strike it, but this one seemed faster, and every time he swung, it dodged aside.

The skin edged slower toward Billie, then bared its fangs. Billie screamed again, backing away along the rail, looking desperately for a way out.

Seb managed to plant the axe in the creature's side, but it became lodged. Then it struck him, a blow that tore into the flesh of his shoulder. He howled, yanking the axe free, and the two separated - the beast warily eyeing him. Tilting its head back, a jet of venom sprayed out, aimed at his eyes. Seb ducked, swung the axe as it leapt toward him, sheering off its arm at the shoulder. The *skin* slowed, shrieking piteously. Seb dropped the axe, grabbing it by the throat and began squeezing, bringing all his strength to bare. Clawing desperately at his arm with its remaining limb, Seb refused to let go.

Billie stumbled backward, trembling, unable to take her eyes from the *skin* that was now close enough to almost touch. It's forked tongue licked out, and she could see its muscles bunch as it prepared to leap. Instantly its head exploded as the high velocity round punched a hole the size of a fist through it. The thing's legs collapsed, and it toppled sideways, twitching, then slid toward the railing, an arm preventing it from sliding into the sea. Billie froze, a spray of black blood across her face. She turned in time to see Seb drop the strangled creature to the deck. Looking up at the moon, he lifted his face and gave a long, triumphant cry.

'Man, did you see that?' said Jonty. 'Ship bobbing around, and I still made the shot.' He pulled the sniper rifle's bipod back against the stock and stood.

Clive grinned. 'You were lucky.'

'Get in close! Pick them up,' instructed Darian, but Ariki was already closing on the last survivors to leave the *Estrella de Mar* as it sank, twisting and groaning in its final throes, the rail of the promenade deck now level with the ocean.

Wordlessly, Seb walked over to Billie and gently took her hand. She looked up at him, their eyes locking.

'Are you okay?' he asked.

She nodded, took his hand, and together they leapt into the sea, before they smoothly swam out to where Kyle was flailing about, attempting to tread water.

FIRST EPILOGUE

Fifteen days later...

San Francisco by night was beautiful to Seb, and he loved the China Town district the most. He had just exited his favourite bar, an intimate place off Columbus Avenue when the FBI goon squad pulled up in a black SUV. This time, when the door opened, Jaz was sitting in the backseat, her legs tucked up neat and smooth in high heels. Dressed in black evening wear, she smiled and patted the seat beside her.

Seb slid in and said, 'I thought our arrangement was at an end, Jaz. I mean, I got the money. Whether it was worth it, I don't really know.'

The SUV drove back through the city. Before they arrived, Seb knew where they were headed. As they stopped, he said, 'Here again? I thought we were going dancing or something.'

'We just have a few things to discuss, okay?' Jaz climbed out, and then with a deep sigh, Seb followed, walking past the two suits on either side of the door, then on into the warehouse.

They took the elevator up. Walking into the office, Seb saw that the operation had been wound down. The big screen TVs and banks of monitors were all gone, though Seb could still see tell-tale cords sticking out of wall sockets.

The one thing that remained unchanged was the original oak desk. Harvey sat there behind it, and when they entered, he swivelled in his seat and stood up, offering Seb his outstretched hand. 'You did it. I'm the first to admit when I am wrong, and Seb – I was wrong about you.'

'Yeah...' Seb reluctantly shook his hand and sat on a chair. 'Why am I back here?'

'Nothing bad Seb,' said Jaz. 'I just wanted to personally thank you for your service. There *are* some details I would like to go over with you. We lost connection with the ship right when it all went *south*.'

'Yeah...well, those things got out...and a lot of folks saw them... right before they were killed. Then the bombs that Kennard, Wyatt or whoever left as a little surprise went off. You guys had already sent the coast guard from Honolulu. That's the whole *shebang*.'

Harvey nodded, then said, 'You saw them up close?'

'Yeah, you could say that.'

'What are they? I mean – if you had to take a guess.'

Seb hesitated and looked at Harvey first, then Jaz. He gave a slight shake of his head, then said, 'They look like a hybrid of a human and snake. Hell, they could be ETs for all I know. And they're smart...' Seb sat back and crossed his arms as the memories returned, stark, and real. 'They can mimic our voices...very well in fact.'

'Anything else?' asked Jaz, sensing he had more to say.

Seb hesitated, then said, 'They hate us...a lot. Hunting us... stalking us, was like a game for them. Guns have a mixed effect. Low calibres at close range had little impact on them. They seem to absorb the bullets or maybe they have organs in different places to us.'

Jaz and Harvey scribbled some notes. Then Harvey looked up again. 'When was the last time you saw Wyatt, Kennard and West?'

'They were getting on a super-yacht called the *Mystro*.'

'You know where they were headed,' said Harvey. It was a statement rather than a question.

'I could guess,' nodded Seb.

'Well, forget you ever heard of the place,' said Harvey.

'Karabeki Island you mean?' asked Seb.

Harvey nodded. 'Forget you ever heard of it.' There was note of warning in his voice. 'Karabeki is ours, okay? Don't go anywhere near the place. We will move on it when we are set.'

Seb stared at Harvey, and after a minute, he nodded.

Harvey picked up a square briefcase that was sitting in a shadowy corner. He clicked it open and removed some papers. When he returned, he said, 'When did you last see Clarice Mulgrave?'

'I never did…I mean, after we abandoned ship, we were separated. Why?'

Harvey glanced at Jaz momentarily before placing a newspaper on the table between them. Harvey opened a British publication to the third page and folded it to show an article.

Seb slumped when he read the print. *Clarice Mulgrave, socialite, and local philanthropist, wife of the late Lord Anson Mulgrave, was found unresponsive in her country estate this morning. Her cause of death is at this time unknown. Toxicology…* Seb stopped reading. He didn't need any more information.

'They killed her.' Seb looked at his hands. 'This is on me.'

Harvey abruptly stood and smoothed down his suit. 'I'm late for a dinner.' He leant over the table and held out his hand, but Seb was in no mood to take it. Then Harvey nodded and left the room.

Seb heard the elevator descending. He looked at Jaz and said, 'What an asshole.'

Jaz smiled. 'He's not so bad when you work with him.' She looked away momentarily, and when she returned her gaze, it was direct. 'Seb, can you keep your mouth shut about all this?'

'I can, but a lot of people on that ship saw what I saw.'

'No one will believe any of it,' said Jaz. 'Hell, they could take photos, and no one will believe it. Some folks reported seeing a crocodile, while others said it was an ape. I suppose anyone that got close enough to get a proper look never survived to tell anyone exactly what they saw.'

'The truth has a way of getting out…eventually,' replied Seb.

Jaz nodded, and Seb could tell she was thinking about something else that was bothering her. She said, 'Where did the serum go? The vials that we think Anson purchased.'

Seb shrugged and looked away. Jaz noted the micro expression. She knew that Seb was feigning ignorance, but she let it go.

He abruptly stood, the chair scraping back. 'Is that it?'

'That's it…for now.'

He grinned, though the expression was not genuine. 'Next time I might not be so easy to find, Jaz.' He walked to the door.

'Hey Seb.'

He glanced back. 'Yeah?'

'*Have* you forgotten where Karabeki Island is?'

'Hell no.' He turned and walked out.

Travelling down in the lift, Seb's phone began ringing. He stared at the screen. *Unknown number*.

'Hello?'

The lift bumped to a stop and the doors jolted opened with a squeal. Seb glanced around before walking toward the exit along the darkened warehouse corridor, his phone pressed to his ear.

'Is this *Seb Bonney*?' The voice was male, mid-thirties, with a slight English accent.

Seb stopped. 'How did you get this number? Who am I speaking to?'

'You gave it to me, after we plucked you out of the water when the ship sank. You and that girl with the smart mouth.'

'Hard to forget.'

'You're telling me.'

'Darian?'

'Yes – you remember, that's good. I have a proposal for you. Something we should meet to discuss.'

'I'm listening.'

'Better in-person I think,' said Darian.

SECOND EPILOGUE

Twenty-one days later…

The *Squalus*, an Orca-class fishing boat, timed her run to enter the waters three miles off Karabeki Island, arriving just after sunset. Ariki cut her engines, allowing the boat to glide to a stop. The dark water around their vessel swirled and heaved, causing them to bob up and down with the swell. Careful to douse all the lights within the cabin, they wanted to ensure that if anyone ashore happened to look out to sea, they might only make out a dark smudge against the ocean.

Darian, Jonty, and Clive were taking a last look at the map under the light of a torch in the aft cabin. Seb, having already studied the map, stood on the deck outside, scanning the shoreline through night-vision binoculars. Dressed from head to toe in a black wet suit, he waited impatiently for the others to prepare.

'The resort is located here.' Darian's finger stabbed at an area near a lagoon. 'We will come ashore here. Ariki will stand by for an hour before moving further offshore. The tide will be high when we go in and the reef should pose no threat to us. But when the tide goes out, the reef around the island is no place for the *Squalus*.'

Ariki held up a thumb, indicating he had heard Darian from his seat at the wheel.

Seb came from the stern, then sat on the back of the boat, inches above the waterline, cradling an M4 carbine equipped with a suppressor.

'Are we ready?' called Seb.

'Mr Straeker wants to know if we're ready,' said Darian.

Clive only grunted, an indication that he still wasn't sure about Seb's involvement, about whether he could be trusted at all. He had raised concerns about the mission, if one could actually call it that. And perhaps Clive was right. They had done little in the way of planning. There were several unknowns – such as the number of guards they were likely to discover. Was the island inhabited by civilians? What would they do if the *Squalus* was discovered before they could return? All these questions made Seb consider going it alone, because one man could slip through defences where a group might attract attention. He'd even suggested this idea, but Darian and his mercenaries refused to be left out. Until they avenged the deaths of their friends, they had unfinished business. Darian had called it *a matter of honour*, though Seb only thought of it as *pay back*. Either way, they were bound together by a shared, urgent desire for retribution.

For Seb, he needed to make them pay for Clarice's death, which he was sure they must have somehow orchestrated. And the sinking of the *Estrella de Mar*, the fear they had wrought, and the lives lost - all demanded a response. Someone had to pay, and someone would. Finally the mercenaries emerged from the cabin and sat in a group around Seb.

'What if we can't locate them?' asked Clive.

'Then we come back again,' said Darian. 'And again if we have to.'

'What if there are too many? We're no army,' said Clive.

'We'll make that call when we locate them. If we think there are too many, then we back off,' said Darian. 'Do you want to do this or not?'

'As long as we keep our options open,' muttered Clive. 'We don't know what we will find over there.'

'Agreed,' replied Seb. 'But there's only one way to find out. We will treat this as a reconnaissance. If we find the defences are weak, then we take advantage. If they appear too strong, then we regroup and come up with a real plan.' Seb faced them. 'And…I don't care what else might be on the island. I'm here for the syndicate only.'

'What else do you think is over there?' asked Darian.

'Maybe more of the… *skins* - *those* creatures…' muttered Seb.

'I have no doubt,' agreed Darian. 'I was thinking the same thing… but I have no intention of ever seeing one of them again. Not in this life.'

After Billie and Seb had been plucked from the waters beside the sinking *Estrella de Mar,* they'd exchanged stories with the mercenaries. Seb discussed his part in spying on the syndicate, though he was elusive about who he was doing it for, and he left out everything he knew about the serum, about how he'd been given two massive doses that had brought him back from the edge of death.

Darian had then admitted his mercenaries had always planned to relieve Anson of his treasure, and of their utter dismay at finding that the cargo they'd intended to take was something else entirely. After that, it was only a matter of time before the two men had decided they could trust each other – at least for as long as it took for some payback.

Darian looked down at the map. 'I'd say the facility you are talking about is on the opposite side of the island. They have a port over there surrounded by barbwire, electric fences – all that kind of shit. If I was a *betting man* – I'd say that the *boogey-men* are kept in labs far from where they have their resort.'

'*Boogey-men,*' chuckled Seb. 'Yeah that's as good a name as any for them,' agreed Seb, smearing black paint onto his face, and adding a single dark green stripe. He checked the M4 one last time, snapped in a large magazine, and slung it across his back.

Darian pulled a black balaclava over his face, then fitted night vision goggles, though he did not engage the lenses. Jonty and Clive picked up their guns and made final checks, each man shouldering a light pack. Lastly, they each fitted a throat mic and headset, allowing hands-free communication.

Darian signalled, and the *Squalus* coughed to life. In less than an hour, Ariki piloted her closer to the island. As they neared, he slowed and cut her engine, allowing the craft to drift just beyond the reef where he dropped anchor. Now they could see the extinct volcano clearly, a massive shadow rising into the night sky, blotting out the stars. In the distance, beyond the beach, through a lattice of palm trees, dim lights shone, beckoning them.

'How many will there be do you think?' asked Jonty. He carried a silenced sniper rifle. Seb recognised it as a Russian special forces weapon called a VSS. It was a sub-sonic weapon - very quiet and accurate.

'We'll soon find out,' said Darian.

They left the *Squalus* in total darkness, steering a small dirigible, its impellor a soft whir beneath the water's surface. Crossing the reef, Seb estimated that they were in around ten feet of water, then, as clouds shifted, under sudden moonlight, they realised they were crossing the shallows of a sandy lagoon. Clive cut the motor, and they drifted forward into the knee-deep water, before jumping out and hauling the inflatable craft up onto the beach.

Advancing in a small wedge formation, they crept through a thin layer of palm trees, manicured lawns, and into an area of pools with underwater lighting. Stone paths snaked amongst bougainvillea and *birds of paradise* shrubbery. Advancing between small villas with lights that shone from living rooms, and restaurant bars, they began to realise that the whole place was deserted. There were no bar patrons, no staff, and no sign that anyone had ever lived there.

Seb crept around the edge of a neat little hut, peered in a window, and found that there wasn't even furniture inside. Over the radio, he said, 'This place is completely empty.'

Clive responded, 'Same over here.'

They paused, listening. There was no quiet talk emanating from restaurants, or music - no hum of air-conditioning units, indeed - nothing at all except the wind rustling palm fronds, and the distant sound of the sea where it met the reef.

'What's the point of this place?' asked Seb.

'It's a front. Just something that you can see from the air if you fly over it and take pictures,' said Darian.

'Seems a bit over the top,' said Seb. 'Most of these buildings have been outfitted with kitchens and beds.'

'Well, maybe they intend on opening soon – how should I know,' said Darian.

Then Jonty spoke, his voice clear in their ears. 'Up the hill, 500 metres, there is a big house. I can see lights.'

The mansion sat in the valley between two ridges coming down off the mountain. To one side, a waterfall spattered from the heights above, where rockpools shone dimly in the moonlight.

Seb followed the right-hand ridge, picking his way carefully around the boles of palm trees up a steep incline. On the opposite ridge, Clive, Darian, and Jonty crept along, coming to a spot where they could easily overlook the mansion, almost level with the second floor. Through open balcony doors, and oversized windows, all designed to capture tropical breezes, they observed movement in nearly every room.

They could hear a television, children's laughter, music, a woman singing along, her voice raised like she didn't have a care in the world.

'Would you look at her?' breathed Jonty. On the second floor, through the VSS's scope he watched a lithe young woman in skintight gym pants enthusiastically leaping and swaying her arms.

Seb watched as she executed a decent pirouette, hair flying. 'That's Kennard's girlfriend. He's here.'

'Guards are in each tower,' confirmed Darian quietly. 'They're well-armed… could be more inside too.'

'What now?' asked Clive. 'We know now where they are, but do we come back better equipped?'

'I'm going in,' replied Seb, who had already begun trotting down the slope toward the mansion, slinging his M4 over his back, and pulling a silenced Beretta pistol. 'But hold your fire until I'm set. Wait for me to get into position.'

'So – its decided then – we're doing this?' asked Clive.

'I didn't come all this way for nothing,' grunted Seb as he reached the house.

*

Congressman Wyatt sat at the table with General Kennard, smoking cigars and sipping whiskey on a second-floor balcony. Their view, toward the resort and the moon dappled ocean beyond seemed perfect.

Wyatt's mansion, in a hacienda style, included high stone walls with four towers. There was an inner courtyard, and bougainvillea grew in white and red clumps around the facade. The entrance to the villa was via an internal courtyard wide enough for a vehicle to drive through, and where a car might stop, a couple of wide stone stairs led past a circular fountain and into the living area. From the bedrooms and balconies on the rear of the house, guests were afforded a grand view of dense jungle, rockpools and beyond, the looming ancient mountain that had once been a volcano.

A side door into the kitchen, that Wyatt had called a *tradesman's entrance*, was the only other way into the mansion. Seven chefs were still cooking meals, and the aroma drifting across the mansion hinted at lamb cooked over a rotisserie.

The mansion had 27 bedrooms, presently occupied by some of the congressman's closest friends and relatives. In a room down the hall from Kennard, his girlfriend was doing cocaine while enjoying an interpretive dance to *Invisible* by *Duran Duran*.

Wyatt puffed on his cigar, and into the smoke he said, 'I'm expecting a call to come through any time now. West has confirmed that non-disclosure deals have been reached with nearly all parties. It's costing her a lot, and she will want a higher cut from our venture over the next year or more.'

'Seems reasonable,' said Kennard. 'Anyone opting out?'

'So far - only a few. The rock group – *Manson Villa* – all but one of them accepted a deal. Some guy called Garth, a hippie type...said he wouldn't be silenced.'

'Any others?' asked Kennard.

'A few. The ship's Executive Officer was reluctant, but in the end, he accepted a very, very good retirement plan. Most folks are pragmatic when it comes right down to it.'

'Most folks are greedy,' said Kennard.

'Everyone has their price,' said Wyatt. 'It's just finding out what that price is – sometimes it's what they want, and other times it's what they can't bear to lose.'

They lapsed into silence, both men considering how close they'd come to the whole operation being blown wide open.

'This place is unique,' said Kennard, gazing out at the night, and noting the armed presence in each tower. At that moment, he realised that he felt better than he had in years. Not only was he a rich man, with connected friends, but soon he would start using the serum, and the drug would vastly extend his life.

'Cost me next to nothing,' said Wyatt proudly. 'There were some good carpenters and masons amongst those refugees.' He puffed out a long white cloud, then continued, 'The nine-hole golf course is almost ready too. Had to remove a lot of rainforest to make that a reality. The third hole is a doozy. You'll need to see that for yourself.'

Kennard chuckled. 'You'll need to ramp up the production to pay for all this my friend.'

'I know.'

'Edgar, have you considered that maybe Anson wasn't the one

spying on us? I mean, we don't really know that it was him that killed Hiro's man.' Kennard sipped his bourbon.

'Who else could it be? If anyone knew about us, we'd know,' said Wyatt.

Kennard heard something in the senator's voice that hinted at uncertainty. And neither man wanted to consider the possibility that the operation was under surveillance, that an outside agency could be monitoring their activities.

Wyatt stood, arching his back, stretching his arms, a relaxed groan easing from his lips. It was then that the bullets ripped through his chest. Like the hissing spit of a cobra, he jolted, dropping the glass to the courtyard below where it shattered on the paving stones.

Kennard toppled off the back of his chair, his feet suddenly over his head. Crawling back into the house through French doors, more rounds hissed and spat around him, cracking off the handrail and breaking earthenware pots. Safely inside, he drew his pistol and ran down the corridor and into his bedroom.

'Don't move general.' Seb waited, pointing a silenced pistol at the head of Kennard's girlfriend. Held tight against his side, the woman squirmed and kicked. 'I hope she's good in bed, because she can't sing for shit.'

'How did you get in here,' gasped Kennard, pointing the pistol at Seb.

'People never lock their windows,' chuckled Seb, pulling the struggling woman even tighter, until she settled. 'I thought you'd run in here like a little bitch if they missed you on the balcony.'

Gunfire continued amongst shouts and screams.

'Make me an offer, Kennard.'

Kennard nodded. Here was a man he could understand. It was always about the money in the end. 'I pay you and what? You go away?'

'You brought cash to your gathering on the ship. Where is it?' asked Seb.

Kennard's frightened eyes betrayed surprise but quickly narrowed. 'Very well - behind the painting there is a safe.' He pointed to the wall. 'You will find ten million in cash.'

Seb's eyes widened. 'Okay - get it.'

Halfway to the wall-safe Seb noticed Kennard hesitate. The general stopped and raised the pistol toward Seb, obviously concluding that his girlfriend was not worth ten million bucks. Seb shot Kennard, expending four hissing rounds, two into his chest, two into his back as he fell crashing over a drinks cart.

Pushing the girl away, Seb walked over to Kennard, who was feebly crawling across the carpet, aimed the pistol and fired point blanc. Instead of running, the woman just stood in the middle of the room, hands over her face, and began screaming.

At the window, Seb paused and said, 'Kennard's dead. I'm leaving now.'

Darian responded – 'Roger that. Any sign of Hillary West?'

'I don't think she's here.'

Jonty cut in – 'I can see three vehicles approaching. They're a click away at least. But they're heading our way fast.'

Seb climbed out the window and leapt the twenty feet to the ground, where he landed and rolled easily. While the serum was still in his system, he knew he could get away with such careless feats as jumping out second story windows.

A guard emerged from the shadows, but Seb fired before he could lift his weapon. Readying the M4 carbine, he began jogging back toward the beach. Reaching the deserted resort, beyond the gentle rustle of palm fronds in the night breeze, he could just hear shouting voices at the villa.

FINAL EPILOGUE

The office, her home away from home, seemed too quiet to Billie. Outside she could see waves crashing on the beach under a full moon. She left the blinds open and retreated to her desk where her latest case file waited for her on the monitor. But feeling restless, she turned on the radio, tuning it to the local station - hoping to banish the silence that was gathering around her.

On her desk, an old newspaper lay folded, showing a bold headline - *Cruise ship sinks! Terrorism blamed.* The article displayed a photo of Janie Reichenbach, her hand raised against the flash photography that caught her in mid stride into her Manhattan apartment. Janie had so far refused to comment on her experience. And what would Billie say if asked to comment? Not that anyone would. Perhaps, if she was being honest, she too would *clam up*. She didn't need people to think she was *losing her marbles*.

Billie wanted to throw the paper in the bin, to forget that it happened, and move on with her life. But it *had* happened, and she *had* survived. Knowing that there were those creatures in the world, that they were still out there was one thing. But knowing that no-one knew the truth was what bothered her the most.

Glancing at her phone, she saw that Harry had left four messages for her. She unlocked the mobile and read them.

Hey kid, come around for dinner tomorrow night. It's my treat.

Then the next...*Can you bring the wine though? It's only fair.*

Hey kid, its tomorrow and you never got back to me. You need to work less, ok?

The last message was only an hour before. *Billie? I know you don't want to talk about what happened but at least come and see your friends.*

Billie dropped the phone on the desk, went to the bar fridge, bent, and took out the bottle of red. She unscrewed it and poured a glass. Taking a sip, she stared out the window again, watching as cars coasted along the busy avenue. The feeling of emptiness was like a weight on her chest, and where her work had always been a place to retreat, to gather herself, and find purpose, it now seemed banal. She turned back and nearly had a heart attack, the wine sloshing over the rim, some of it going up her nose.

'Miss me?' Seb had slipped in quietly and sat down in the visitor chair. Leaning back, his feet up on her desk, crossed at the ankles, he looked way too pleased that she had not heard him, for a slight, crooked smile teased her. 'You know you should lock your door.'

Billie grinned, her face lighting up, for the first time in...well... since she had last seen him.

CREDITS

Cover Designer

Stephanie Talevski of Coven Press
Cover elements from pexels.com and unsplash.com

Internal Typeset & Design

Alana Lambert of Coven Press
Body: Adobe Jenson Pro/12pt/16pt leading
Heading: Corbel/18pt

www.ingramcontent.com/pod-product-compliance
Lightning Source LLC
Chambersburg PA
CBHW030622310726
48979CB00003B/832

* 9 7 8 1 7 6 4 1 4 7 6 5 1 *